THE TA

AND OT

Viktoria Tokareva is one of Russia's most popular living woman writers. Born in 1937 in Leningrad, she published her first story in 1964 while still a student at the Moscow Institute of Cinematography. This story brought her instant acclaim, and she has since gone on to publish her work in Russia's leading literary journals. As well as the several collections of short stories and novellas which have been translated into many languages, she is also the author of thirteen film scripts, three of which have won international awards. Viktoria Tokareva lives in Moscow.

VIKTORIA TOKAREVA

THE TALISMAN
AND OTHER TALES

TRANSLATED FROM THE RUSSIAN
BY
ROSAMUND BARTLETT

PICADOR

A Picador Original

First published 1993 by Pan Books Limited

This edition published 1994 by Picador
a division of Pan Macmillan Publishers Limited
Cavaye Place London SW10 9PG
and Basingstoke

Associated companies throughout the world

ISBN 0 330 32337 7

1 3 5 7 9 8 6 4 2

A CIP catalogue record for this book is available from
the British Library

Typeset by Cambridge Composing (UK) Limited, Cambridge
Printed and bound in Great Britain by
Cox & Wyman Ltd, Reading, Berkshire

PIRATES ON THE HIGH SEAS

. . . For a technical project, each piece of equipment is counted separately according to its name and *tiporazmer* . . .

I was just wondering how to translate *tiporazmer* into English when my doorbell rang.

I opened the door to find my neighbour Tamara from the ninth floor standing there. Tamara told me that she had to be at the hospital tomorrow at nine sharp and was insisting that I take her.

I wanted to ask: 'Why me?' I live on the same staircase as Tamara, but we hardly ever run into each other, only about once a month by our letter boxes. My flat is number 89 and Tamara's is 98, so the postman often puts my letters into Tamara's letter box. And vice versa. That is the only thing which brings us together, so I really could not understand why I was the one who had to take Tamara to the hospital rather than her husband.

'Why me?' I asked.

Tamara thought for a moment in response to my question, then looked at me.

'So you won't take me, then?' she said.

I felt rather uncomfortable. I realized that if I said no, Tamara would turn round and walk away and then I would start feeling bad about it and not be able to work. I'm a complete neurotic, you see. I would start going over her requests, thinking up answers to them in my head, which would mean I'd waste the time when I am normally nodding off and then not be able to catch up on my sleep later. I would just lie there sighing loudly, thinking things over. But none of that thinking would be any use for what I was going to do tomorrow, for example, because it would all be retrospective. I would go over everything I had said and everything I had done a hundred times, and it would take up the whole night, all of the next day (which meant I would get no work done), and half a kilometre of my nerves. But to take Tamara to the hospital and back would take up only two hours. Two hours plus a feeling of moral ease.

'Sure,' I said. 'I'll take you.'

'Meet you at half-past eight downstairs, then,' said Tamara as she turned to leave.

I am incapable of saying no to people when they ask me to do things for them, you see. In medicine this condition is known as 'hypertrophy of the response mechanism'. It means that whenever I'm with someone, I put myself totally in their position and forget all about my interests. Perhaps way back in time one of my ancestors was a real lout, and so my delicacy in these situations is a kind of compensation to nature, which demands that things be balanced out ultimately. So it's sort of as if it's fallen to me to pay back my ancestor's loan to nature.

I went to bed and soon fell asleep feeling morally at ease with myself. While Tamara's husband must have gone to sleep next to the the rotund and beautiful Tamara with a feeling of supreme moral discomfort and human inadequacy.

The hospital, when we eventually found it, was in the middle of nowhere.

I stopped the car near the entrance.

'Come in with me!' Tamara ordered.

'I think it would be better if I waited here,' I said. 'I'm scared.'

'I see. So you're scared and I'm not.'

'Why have you got to come here anyway?' I asked.

'I need to make sure I haven't got it,' answered Tamara gloomily.

'Can't you do that anywhere else?'

'The consultants are better here.'

Tamara got out of the car and walked up to the wide stone steps. I locked the car and plodded off after her like Orpheus following Eurydice.

We went into the reception. Tamara was given some sort of card at the desk and was made to sit in some sort of queue. She made me sit next to her. I wanted to ask whether we would have to wait for a long time, but was too embarrassed to ask such a mundane question in what was fundamentally a tragic situation.

'Why didn't your husband come with you?' I asked.

'I didn't want him to. I haven't told him about it.'

'Why on earth not?'

'Because a husband wants his wife to be healthy, and a brother wants his sister to be prosperous. That's the way things are . . .'

'Only if the husband and the brother are complete wretches,' I said firmly.

'What do you mean? They're like everyone else. It's normal.'

'Well, if that's what you call normal, I think it's absolutely terrible.'

Tamara fell silent.

An old man was sitting against the opposite wall from me. He was telling jokes and laughing at his own punchlines. No one shared his sense of mirth, though. These people had all been thrown into a state of despair, as if they had been tossed into the ocean. They were trying to stay afloat, but they kept swallowing water, and could not see land. The old man was trying to show his strength of spirit, but no one believed in it. They looked solemnly and critically at him.

3

I took Tamara's hand in mine, and she put her head on my shoulder.

'I'm an idiot,' she said.

'What do you mean?'

'"The Galvano-Magnetic Effect in Germanium Crystals" – that was what my dissertation was called, you know. It was nothing but a heap of meaningless scribbles. Katka is doing badly at school, Lev is being unfaithful to me, and I've ended up here. That's what the effect is . . .'

'But you have to strive for something.'

'It's all right for you. You live properly. You aren't trying to achieve anything. And you're healthy.'

'What do you mean, I'm not trying to achieve anything?' I said, rather offended. 'I'm a professional translator.'

Tamara coughed. She looked at things the following way: technical translators translate information from one language to another, while the amount of knowledge stays the same. But she was creating a new field of knowledge, so therefore her life was worth more, objectively speaking, than mine. However, there was nothing to threaten my useless life, and so on and so forth.

'But you're healthy too,' I said. 'Go and look at yourself in the mirror. You'll find out that you really haven't got it, and then we'll just go home. We could even go for a drink.'

'The problem is, Dima, that science just gets in the way of everything. You can never really think about anything else. You can't see anything but science. In the morning you jump out of bed, you grab some breakfast, whatever there is, and you run off to work. And then in the evening you come tearing back, you have a bite to eat again so you won't die of hunger and then it's back at the typewriter. You eat just to give yourself the energy to keep going. You might go for walks to have a change of scene. But nevertheless, all your thoughts are channelled

4

in one direction. It's like in Lermontov's "Mtsyri". Remember how it goes? "I knew the power of one thought, a single raging fire. It lived within me like a worm, gnawing at my soul . . ."'

'But that's the only way to do something properly,' I said. 'That's what happiness is as far as I'm concerned.'

'Maybe. But look at the way we prevent ourselves from enjoying life. To think that I could be getting up in the morning and greeting the day with a smile instead. Hello, day! I could spend my time cooking borscht with cabbage that crunches – real bortsch is a work of art, you know. And my husband would come home in the evenings and I'd be able to greet him with a smile too. "Hello, dear!" Well . . . whatever. We work ourselves into the ground chasing false goals, you see, and then . . .'

Tamara closed her eyes and leant her head back against the wall.

The old man who had been cracking jokes got up and went into the consulting room. We were next.

A pair of elderly lovebirds were sitting in the opposite corner. They were like Pushkin's Eugene Onegin and Tatyana Larina fifty years on, except that for this couple everything had worked out. When this particular Tatyana had written Eugene her famous letter, he had decided to propose to her after reading it instead of turning up to rebuke her. It can happen like that. But now he had fallen ill and she was sitting beside him, actually happy at the thought of being able to provide some comfort to him even in these troubled times. As for him, he was feeling a little bit guilty about having so much attention focused on himself, and he felt bad that he was making his loved one worry. But Eugene had remained true to himself even at seventy, as he was wearing a rather flamboyant striped cravat round his neck. The couple sat close together, their hands entwined. Everything will turn out all right for them, I thought. Joy will come through suffering.

'Where have you come from?' asked a young woman with six layers of lipstick on who was sitting near Tamara.

Tamara did not answer because she did not want to talk. This other woman wanted to talk very much, but there was no one to talk to.

'I'm from Donetsk. This institute is the best in the country, you know, perhaps even in the world. It's awfully difficult to make an appointment. How did you do it? Did you pull some strings or something?'

'No,' I said. 'The usual channels. How did you get it?'

Tamara did not like my being sociable, but I find it impossible not to answer when I'm asked something and people are looking at me.

'I got it from contamination at work,' the woman said.

'You'd better leave your job then,' I advised.

'Whatever for?' asked the woman in genuine surprise. 'Other people work there. Am I any better than them?'

'But if you've got ill . . .'

'So what? They're all ill too,' she said, casting her eyes over the people in the waiting room. 'Am I any better than them?'

This philosophy of wanting to be like everyone else depressed me. I looked closely at the woman. Just then it became Tamara's turn to go in.

'Come in with me!' she said, grabbing hold of me with her cold hand and marching me off to the consulting room. Inside, an earnest young doctor was writing up someone's medical history, while a young nurse was busy clinking instruments together.

The doctor lifted his eyes to us as we came in.

'She's got a tumour in her nose,' I said.

'Well, we'll have that checked out in just a minute,' promised the doctor.

'Thank goodness! At least we have got one patient who is in a good mood!' the nurse rejoiced. 'Everyone else walks around looking like this . . .' she said, pulling a face to show how people walked around.

The nurse was fed up with the patients' low spirits, which she had to immerse herself in every day.

Tamara sat down on a chair.

I left the consulting room and returned to where I was previously sitting.

'I'm not going to lose heart, though,' said the woman from Donetsk. 'I'm going to follow my mum's example. Do you know what sort of a mother I've got?'

I gazed at her as I listened to her tell me.

'She used to give bread to the people working for the Resistance during the war, so the Germans burned her house down together with her two small children. Then right at the end of the war she stepped on a mine which blew her leg off. But despite all that she got married in forty-six without her leg and had me. And now she has come up to Moscow because of all this stuff happening to me, to give me a bit of moral support. I'm going off to the Tretyakov Gallery when I'm done with here. Goodness knows when I'll get the chance to come to Moscow again . . .'

The nurse came out of the consulting room and starting looking around for someone. She espied the old man who had been making jokes and walked over to where he was sitting.

'You're going to need a bit more treatment, I'm afraid,' she said, going up to him.

The old man got up to talk to her. His eyes had now become strained, and his face completely lost its previous merry look. Weightlifters have that same strained and blank expression when they are holding some huge weight above their heads. I did not know that fear looked like that too.

I went over to the consulting room and poked my head round the door.

'Who referred you?' the doctor was asking Tamara.

'My local clinic.'

'They obviously haven't got anything better to do with their time, then! It's not as if we're short of patients. It's appalling, really . . .'

Tamara was looking at the doctor fondly, and the angrier he became, the more she felt she liked him.

But the doctor was evidently genuinely annoyed with Tamara and her trivial complaint, together with her breasts and stomach that were like three big pillows.

She gave the doctor a smacking kiss on the cheek, which he was not expecting at all, and skipped out into the corridor. Grabbing me by the arm, we set off together down to the cloakroom to collect our coats. The woman from Donetsk followed us with her eyes. I smiled at her guiltily. I felt guilty because I was going, and she had to stay.

We put our coats on and went out on to the street. Tamara produced two oranges, one for me and the other for her. I started peeling the skin off with my teeth and my mouth was filled with a fragrant bitterness.

The day was overcast, but the colour of the sky together with the snow on the rooftops made a very beautiful combination.

'Hello, day!' I shouted, remembering what Tamara had said earlier.

'What are you yelling for?' asked Tamara in amazement. 'Just look at you, standing there and screaming like that. Really! Come on, let's go.'

We got into the car.

'Next stop the black market!' ordered Tamara. 'To the lady I deal with – she lives on Vavilov Street.'

She had acquired health; now she wanted beauty. So I

drove Tamara to Vavilov Street, but she did not take me with her this time.

She was gone for about an hour, or maybe even an hour and a half, and when she finally reappeared she was wearing some sort of contraption on her feet which was rather reminiscent of the foot clamps prisoners wore during the Time of Troubles. All she needed now were some clanking chains.

Tamara got into the car and inspected her purchase.

'What are they?' I asked.

'Platform shoes. You know, like cows have hoofs,' said Tamara.

'Are they comfortable?'

'Come off it . . .'

'Why did you buy them, then?'

'Oh, I don't know. They're fashionable . . .'

'How much were they?' I asked.

'I can't tell you that, it would be too embarrassing. I'm ashamed to say it out loud.'

'Why do you have to provide financial support for the unworthy elements in our society? It's immoral.'

'I hope you're joking.'

'No, I'm not joking.'

'But you don't have the slightest idea of what it's like. She treats me as if I was the one dealing on the black market, and she was the learned physicist. I've always been afraid of those sharpsters.'

I drove the car out of the street and on to the main road.

A gypsy with a baby gypsy in her arms was walking along the pavement, her skirt flapping around her legs. She was wearing felt boots and the remnants of a velvet jacket were draped round her shoulders. But her gaze was directed somewhere beyond the people around her and seemed to be inspired by proud and noble thoughts.

'I wanted to roam around like that once,' said Tamara

9

dreamily. 'Just think; you'd never have to depend on anything, on having a place to live or other people.'

'Why don't you become a hippy?' I suggested. 'Hippies are sort of intellectual gypsies.'

'Well, that's hardly possible at my age, is it?' said Tamara, disagreeing with me. 'You can only really be a hippy between the ages of fifteen and twenty-five.'

'And how old are you?' I asked.

'How old do you think I am?'

'Sixteen?'

'Correct!' Tamara said. 'I will always be sixteen. Sixteen plus old age. Sixteen plus death. Now we have to go the the library.'

'Why?'

'I need to pick up some materials.'

'I thought you were planning to cook an artistic bortsch.'

'They'll wolf down the bortsch without even saying thank you. But my thoughts will live on. In about a hundred years' time some scruffy student will go to the library and look for my little book. He'll go off and study it and say "Thank you Tamara!" Then he'll save mankind.'

'Why only in a hundred years' time?'

'Well, maybe in a year's time. In that case he'll turn up and the book won't be there. Let's go!'

. . . For a technical project, each item of equipment is counted separately according to its name and *tiporazmer* . . .

I started trying to think how I could translate into English the word *tiporazmer*. Just then the phone rang. A man's voice informed me that he was getting divorced from his wife, and needed some help carrying books.

'Who is this speaking?' I asked.

'Volodya,' the voice said.

I did not know any Volodyas, so I asked, 'Which Volodya?'

The voice said that he was my cousin. I do actually have a cousin called Volodya, but we only talk on the phone about once every seven years, so I tend to forget what his voice sounds like. They shortened his name when he was a kid to 'Lodya' rather than 'Vova', and I can't get used to imagining him with any other name.

'You mean Lodya?' I asked.

'Well, yes,' replied Lodya reluctantly. He cannot bear that nickname.

A long time ago, in that same distant childhood, my dad had given him a cup with the inscription: 'To dear little Lodya from Uncle Yury'. Lodya immediately hurled the cup on to the floor, for which he was soundly smacked by his parents. It did not hurt all that much, but it was humiliating for him.

'You couldn't come and pick me up, could you?' asked Lodya.

'I'm working at the moment actually,' I said.

I really was working. I am contracted to turn into the publishers twenty-four printer's sheets, which amounts to about half a year's work. If I sit at it from morning till night without eating or sleeping, I can do it in one and a half months. But for that I must not be disturbed. However, I am not married, and I don't have any responsibilities. Plus I work from home, so other people get to organize my time however they like.

'I'm getting divorced, you see,' said Lodya. 'I need some help.'

Lodya had held a wedding at some point, but he hadn't asked me to it. It hadn't even occurred to him since I was only a distant relation, and there were enough people coming already as it was.

'Look, I'm really busy,' I said.

'You could spare half an hour, couldn't you?'

When we were small we used to meet every Christmas. But now we are grown up, we hardly ever see each other, except on occasions such as when someone has died. Whenever that happens, everyone gets together to learn all the latest news from each other. They talk in hushed voices, quietly and animatedly swapping remarks like school children during a test, while the relatives of the deceased turn round and look on disapprovingly, their eyes lowered.

I could have said no to Lodya, of course. But it would have been a betrayal of our childhood and our common roots to refuse him. After all, I hadn't been born all by myself. Before me came my father, who was the cousin of Lodya's father. And before him there was my grandfather, the brother of Lodya's grandfather. And then there was our common great-grandfather. Essentially we came from the same family. But spiritual and business ties bring people closer together these days than blood ties do. And people live as if they came into this world all by themselves rather than into the bosom of a family. Eventually that way of living is avenged by loneliness.

'Oh, all right,' I said. 'I'll come over.'

'It's the building with the yellow balconies,' Lodya said, reminding me. 'I'll be waiting outside for you.'

I came up from Lomonosovsky Prospect and stopped the car outside the building with yellow balconies.

Lodya was nowhere to be seen. So I turned off the engine, got out my folder from the back seat, and started to work, resting the folder on my lap.

Tiporazmer could either be translated as two words – 'type' and 'size' – or I could find a third whose meaning would signify *tiporazmer*. I started trying to come up with some synonyms.

I had translated all kinds of books while I had been

working at the publishers, on everything from the transportation of red whortleberries (which we export to Italy) to the rearing of large-horned cattle.

I am pretty well read up on a lot of subjects to do with industry and agriculture thanks to my translation work, so I can be an interesting person to talk to. The problem is, though, that no one ever wants to talk to me about red whortleberries or the quantity of items of equipment. Everyone wants to talk about the vagaries of love, and on that topic I am as unoriginal and banal as Chekhov's character Ippolitich in his story 'The Russian Teacher', who steadfastly maintains that the Volga flows into the Caspian Sea, and that it is better to sleep at night, rather than in the daytime.

My translations go abroad, so I have never met any of my readers. If only some under-developed capitalist were to come over to this country, ring me up at home, and say, 'Is that Mr Mazaev?'

'Speaking,' I would say.

'Thank you, Mr Mazaev,' he'd say.

'Don't mention it,' I would say.

And that is all I ever dream of.

Lodya, however, was evidently not going to turn up, even though we had agreed that he would meet me outside with either one box or several, depending on how they divided up their belongings.

Finally I got fed up with waiting, so I went up to the fourth floor and rang on their door bell.

My cousin's wife answered the door. She was pale, dishevelled, and consumed with negative passion.

'You tell him!' she barked into my face without saying hello. 'Tell him he can't take the dacha away from me! When am I going to be able to earn enough to buy another one? I am a woman! We have a kid!'

I went into the flat. Lodya was standing by the window with his back to me, his hands thrust into his pockets. He was fat. He had been fat when he was a boy too, with a pudgy mouth.

'Go on, why don't you give her the dacha?' I said. 'You're not going to live there after all.'

'No, you're dead right I'm not! I'm not even going to show my face there! I hate that dacha! But I'd rather burn it to the ground before I had to give it to her! Seriously, I'd burn it down!'

Lodya took one hand from his pocket and shook his fist above his head.

I had never seen him like this before. Lodya was a phlegmatic sort of person, and I had always thought that his average body temperature was about 34 degrees Fahrenheit, like that of a bear in hibernation.

'Why?' I asked.

'Because she's a tart, that's why.'

I went along down to the kitchen, trying to think of a synonym for *tiporazmer* along the way. My cousin's wife was standing in the middle of the kitchen, awaiting the outcome of the discussions.

'He won't hand it over, because he says you are a tart.'

My cousin's wife looked at me with eyes glistening with tears. Her face was very beautiful when it was full of anger.

'Mitya,' she said quietly. 'Listen, I'll tell you what happened. We were getting ready to go out one time and he told me, "Don't put any lipstick on, it doesn't suit you." But I went ahead and put some on anyway because that's what is fashionable at the moment.'

'But if it doesn't suit you . . .'

'But if that's the fashion . . .'

I went back to my cousin.

'OK, so she put some lipstick on; what's so bad about that?' I asked.

'I'm not bothered about whether she put lipstick on or not. What bothers me is that she is totally preoccupied with herself and her own pleasures! I can just go to hell as far as she is concerned! Even if I fell under a bus tomorrow, she'd still go the cinema in the evening. She'd tell our friends that she was feeling distraught and needed a distraction to take her mind off things. She's really dreadful, Mitya! You don't know her! She's a heartless egoist!'

I stood there for a while, then went back to the kitchen. It was an old flat, which had been built before the war, and the hall was very long. I was getting tired going back and forth.

'He says you are a heartless egoist,' I said to my cousin's wife.

'That's only because he has got bored with me and he needs something to find fault with,' she said, her eyes still shining with tears. 'I gave up everything for him. He's destroyed my life.'

I gave a sigh and set off back to my cousin.

'She says that she gave up everything for you. That doesn't sound very good, you know.'

'And what did she have that she regretted losing? I was the one who had to abandon my sick parents! I curse the day I met her! Jesus!' Lodya placed his hand on his heart and raised his eyes to the ceiling like St Sebastian. 'If only I could wake up and discover that none of this had ever happened. That it was all a dream. If I could only go back in time, to five years ago, I would run a mile to avoid the place where I met her.'

'Right!' I said. 'I'm off!'

'Where to?' asked Lodya distractedly, no longer looking like St Sebastian any more. 'What do you mean, you're off?'

'You quite plainly love each other still. And I'm just going back and forth between you like an idiot.'

I realized that they were locked in a power struggle. Lodya wanted his wife to submit, but she was standing up for her rights. She wanted to preserve her own individuality.

'But there's the books . . .' said Lodya, coming after me.

'You're bound to make up soon and then I'll just have to help you bring your books back again. It'll be just the same. Back and forth, back and forth. I haven't got the time.'

My cousin's wife darted out of the kitchen and grabbed me by the arm. Her fingers were thin, but very strong.

'Wait!' she shouted.

'Let him go!' shouted Lodya, grabbing me by the other arm and pulling me towards the door.

I made two steps to the right, then two steps to the left, as Lodya and his wife both tried to pull me in different directions. His wife was stronger, and I started to worry that I might injure my shoulder.

'Ouch, that hurts . . .' I said.

'Let him stay and have a bite to eat! He sat down there waiting for two whole hours, for Heaven's sake,' pleaded Lodya's wife.

That was all quite reasonable, but Lodya also quite reasonably feared that if I stayed, their wobbly relationship would tip over again, and then he would end up with no wife and she would end up with no dacha.

'I don't want your dacha anyway,' his wife said.

'Take it. You can have it,' said Lodya, giving in finally.

'What use will it be to me? I'm hardly going to go and stay there by myself like a hermit.'

'You won't be by yourself. You've got lots of friends, haven't you?'

'Maybe I do have lots of friends, but there's only one of you.'

Lodya's wife looked at him. Her lips were all swollen

from crying, like young spring buds. But there was a gleam of sunlight in her eyes.

'I'm sorry. Forgive me,' she said. 'I won't put lipstick on any more.'

'I can't forgive you. I swore by the health of our child. If I forgive you, God will punish me . . .'

'But God's got so many other things to do. Like changing the seasons, for example. Maintaining the balance of nature. Do you think he's got time to listen to your stupid curses?'

Lodya's wife took him by the hand and they walked down the hall together. Then they went into the living room and shut the door behind them.

I wanted to leave, but I did not know how the lock on the door worked. I squinted through the peephole and saw the stairs and the lift in miniature.

Then I went into the kitchen and sat down on a stool. I really was hungry. There was a newspaper lying on the fridge. I opened it and read, 'The production firm "Kzyl-Tu" is now manufacturing a brand new thermos flask for transporting and keeping warm three different dishes . . .'

I went back to the front door and started grappling energetically with the lock. At some fortunate point the door opened and the stairs and the lift now appeared in real-life size.

How about 'standard'? Then you would get: 'counted separately by name and standard'. No, that would not do. Perhaps 'individuality' would work. But the word 'individuality' can only be applied to an animate object, and cannot be used for an item of equipment. For example, my individuality consists of a complete absence of individuality. Kira's individuality consists in the fact that she is a woman. The most important thing about her is the aura of femininity emanating from her, which has the power to overcome not only people, but also animals and even inanimate objects. When she holds a spoon in her hand, for example, that spoon is no longer just a spoon, but a spoon plus something else; something weird and suggestive.

All the people I know have a job somewhere where they do something or other. They invest in reason, goodness, and in things that will last, and they walk around in the same coat for ten years. Kira invests in nothing, and she is always dressed according to tomorrow's fashion. She has a habit of always being at least an hour late for everything too. But even if she were to completely forget about a date we had, I would still wait for her; for a whole day, two days, or even an entire week. I would wait for her until she happened to leave her house to go and get some bread or something, and came across my car by accident.

Two people happened to be walking past my car: a woman and a little girl who looked about four years old. The woman's eyes were full of tears, and the little girl's lips were firmly pursed.

'It's slovenly, that's what it is, just slovenly!' said the woman in a pained voice.

'So?' replied the girl.

I watched them as they walked past. How I wished that was my family, with Kira as my wife instead of that woman. That slovenly little girl could definitely stay as my daughter, though.

Kira came out through the doorway. Seeing her made me feel like a little boy who has been taken to the circus.

She got into the car, and asked, 'Want an apple?'

'No, thanks,' I answered. Then I remembered how fragrant and crunchy Antonov apples are and I said, 'Well, actually I wouldn't mind one . . .'

Kira got two apples out of her bag; one for her, and another, smaller one, for me. In spite of all her lack of interest in living, she takes good care of her health and does not forget about her daily vitamins.

I rested my glasses on the top of my head and began eating, while she watched me out of the corner of her eye. I could see that she disliked everything about me.

'Maybe I should get an office job,' Kira said reflectively.

'No way!' I exclaimed in alarm, being utterly incapable of associating those two concepts together: Kira and a nine to five job. Then I began to think that if she had to go to work every day it might discipline her a bit.

'Well, maybe it would be a good idea, actually . . .' I said.

'Have you ever played badminton by yourself?'

'I beg your pardon?' I asked, not understanding.

'Well, first you hit the shuttlecock. It goes whizzing up into the air then falls back down on to the grass. You go and pick it up, and then you return to where you were standing before. You hit it again with your racket. The shuttlecock flies up into the air again and then falls on to the grass. You walk over again, pick it up . . .'

'I don't get it. Why are you telling me all this?'

'Because having a conversation is like playing a game of badminton really, isn't it? You know, return and serve. But I'm the only one doing any talking here, it seems.'

'What do you mean?'

'I ask you, "Do you want an apple?" You say no. Then immediately afterwards you say yes. I ask you, "Shall I go and get a job?" You say no, then you immediately say yes. What's wrong with you? Are you mentally subnormal or something?'

I was scared I would say no, then immediately say yes.

'I don't know,' I said. 'I mean, I always did well at school . . .'

'God almighty . . .' said Kira, sighing.

I felt a bit hurt by this, but I didn't show it. Otherwise, she would have said, 'Never suffer in a woman's presence.

Wait till you get home. Then you can do as much suffering as you want.'

She was feeling cross and so she was venting all her frustrations on me because I'm not the man she needs. She needs a completely different sort of man, and instead she has to put up with me. She does not like being with me, but she finds it is worse without me. Without me she would have no one to display her anger to and no one to take it out on.

We went for a drive out of town; we call it 'visiting the vegetable patches'. There is a tarmac road leading off the main road which no one ever drives along or walks down. Where does it go to? Where does it come from?

'You ought to have a baby,' I advised Kira.

'Who with?'

'Me.'

'I don't want to have a baby with you. You aren't good looking.'

'I was very pretty when I was a little boy. Do you want to see a photo?'

We turned off the tarmac road and drove off on to a bumpy track, past little cottages with chicken and geese outside. A tall man in a grey cap followed us with his eyes. He saw that we were having fun, and would have liked to come along with us.

At this point I handed over the steering-wheel to Kira and gave her a driving lesson. I'd been teaching her for two months now, and she was showing clear signs of ability.

Kira is not planning to drive a car ever, so my lessons won't have any practical benefits. It's just that she has come to me from her life in confusion and disarray, and I am helping to put her back on her feet again. So I placed the steering-wheel in her hands, turned her attention to the traffic, the speedometer, and to the right and left turns, and she soon began to forget about everything else. When she gripped the steering-wheel tightly, with her eyes glinting, she looked just like a little girl playing a game. Never mind her ineptitude and lack of refinement; it is in moments like these that I truly love her. I feel like taking her to the deep blue sea and teaching her water-skiing. I feel like bringing her back to life like a frozen bird, so that the inertia which comes from sheer desperation will gradually be replaced by the conviction of someone who is sure of what they are going to be doing the next day.

'Marry me,' I said.

'But I don't love you.'

I knew what the problem was: she loved someone else. That was not something new to me, but I still felt as if someone had put a block of ice inside my chest.

Kira looked at me and felt sorry for me.

'You see, I love the fact that you care for me, but things between us are just not right.'

'Well, yes, I understand that . . . So why don't you get married to him?'

'Because he's a mess. He has no desire for any sort of order. He prefers things to be total chaos.'

'Why do you love someone who is a mess?'

'Well, the thing is he can be a real pig sometimes, but then at other times he is utterly divine. I've never known anyone like him. I've experienced moments with him when he's been sublime, you see. He's a sublime sort of person, really. Next to him you are like a mouth-organ compared to the real thing.'

I locked up the car and we set off into the wood.

We are enjoying a beautiful autumn at the moment; it's both cool and crisp. We walked past delicate silver birches and majestic fir trees, but I was so lost in thought that I did not notice their beauty. It reached me through my eyes and my ears anyway though, filling me with calmness and humility.

Kira stopped and looked straight at me.

'Do you want me to marry you?'

I did not answer, expecting this to be a trick question.

'If you do, you should go and kill him,' Kira said seriously.

I could see that she was not joking.

'I can't do that,' I said, also seriously. 'What would be the point of doing that anyway?'

'Don't you love me?'

'Yes, I do.'

'Do it for love, then.'

'You think that's enough of a reason.'

'A hundred years ago it was enough of a reason.'

'But he's done nothing to me.'

'He has destroyed my soul. That's a crime.'

'Why don't you ask someone else to do it?' I suggested.

'I don't have anyone else who could do it. Only you.'

Such devotion touched me. I wavered.

'Where am I going to get a gun from?'

'From a policeman, from a huntsman, from a rifle range, I don't know; there are thousands of places.'

I thought for a while, staring at the trunks of the birch trees.

'I'll get sent to prison . . .' I argued.

'I'll come with you to Siberia.'

'You? Come to Siberia?' I was doubtful.

'Why not? There aren't many people there and there's lots of fresh air.'

I imagined myself and Kira in tall boots, walking through the snowdrifts and getting stuck every step, and laughing at ourselves.

'Well?'

Kira bored right into my pupils, as if her 'well' could bring an end to my vacillation.

'Oh, all right,' I agreed feebly, since I am incapable of saying no when people ask me things.

This was my 'hypertrophy of the response mechanism' at work. Although if you think about it, the same thing happens when you fall in love, because you start placing the interests of someone else above your own then too..

My friend Garik says that I am like the open-air swimming pool on Kropotkin Street, heating the world. Actually Garik has also got enough energy to heat the whole world, but he would only do it for money or for something in exchange. His philosophy of life could be formulated as: 'If I do something for you, you do something for me.' It is all quite reasonable and fair really.

Garik is a genius at getting hold of things. He can get you anything you want, from Yugoslavian kitchen units to East German sewing machines, a Moscow residency permit, chocolate éclairs, running water . . . And if Ruslan needed Ludmila, like in Pushkin's poem, he would not have to fly off through the skies for her, risking his life and clutching on to Chernomor's beard. Garik would bring Ludmila round in a taxi, to the right address, and at the appointed time. For cash or something in exchange.

I asked Garik to get me a gun. Garik said a gun would make too much noise, so he got me some potassium cyanide instead by pulling a lot of strings.

We went into the kitchen. Garik sprinkled half a teaspoonful into an empty Vaseline jar that had been rinsed out. The potassium cyanide looked like finely ground coal, and the sharp crystals glittered with a brown light.

'That's not manganese, is it?' I asked dubiously.

'Don't know. Never tried it.'

'How can you be sure?'

'You can't.'

In actual fact, I thought, who would want to make sure? Even a fifty per cent risk was still a hell of a risk.

'How much did they charge you?'

I was trying to work out the cost. Manganese costs 11 kopecks, you see. They could, of course, multiply that figure by ten, taking into account its scarcity, but even then it would only come out at a rouble ten.

'Nothing,' said Garik. 'It was a favour in return for another favour.'

'What was the favour?'

'Theatre tickets.'

'But that's not at all equal.'

'How can you tell?' Garik objected. 'You've got a theatre show on the one hand, and . . .'

'What do I owe you?'

'Nothing. You can translate my letters.'

'Who are writing to?' I said in alarm.

'A private detective. In England.'

'But that's hardly any bother . . .' I objected.

'Well, you're my friend,' said Garik, reminding me.

Friendship also went into the reckoning.

Garik closed the jar and told me on no account to think of opening it and sniffing inside. He also said that potassium cyanide was a very scarce substance, and that if I had any left, I was to return it.

I put the jar in my pocket and decided to ring up the 'dishonourable man' straight away, so as not to delay matters.

For a long time there was no answer. Deep down I was hoping that no one would be at home. But he was at home.

'Hello,' said the rather hoarse voice of a heavy smoker.

'Good afternoon,' I said.

'Good afternoon.' He was polite, but I nevertheless sensed that he was an impatient sort of person, who was not disposed to having long conversations with people he did not know.

'I need to come and see you. There's something I want to talk to you about.'

'Oh, what's that?'

'It won't take long,' I promised, 'I won't need to bother you for more than . . .'

'Two seconds,' prompted Garik, thinking of the effectiveness of potassium cyanide.

'Two seconds,' I repeated.

'All right,' he said. 'Come round, then.'

I was expecting a sinister-looking but handsome man to open the front door: a man in control of his life, a pirate from the high seas, who preferred total chaos to boring old order. But the door was actually opened by a short, balding, slightly pock-marked man. His large head and thin legs reminded me somehow of a grasshopper, but one with a velvet jacket and a sad expression. I thought that maybe I had got the wrong person.

'Was it you who rang?' asked the Grasshopper.

'Yes.'

'Come on in.'

I walked through into the hall. I really did not want to kill him. On the contrary, all I felt was a desire to do something for him, make him a cup of coffee, perhaps, or fry up some potatoes. I just could not imagine how I was going to get out of this situation that I had created.

'I have to apologize to you,' said the Grasshopper, 'because I've been called away urgently to attend a meeting. So I've got to run, I'm afraid. Perhaps you could talk about it on my way out, and be brief, if you wouldn't mind.'

He looked straight at me, gently and at the same time firmly.

'I have to kill you,' I said, also gently and firmly, looking at him in a calm and friendly way. So that he would not think I was a lunatic.

He stood there staring at the floor, thinking for a

while. Then he went into one of the rooms in his flat and came out again with a cigarette lighter in a suede cover, which he put into the pocket of his raincoat. He still did not say anything, which put me into a difficult position.

'Why aren't you saying anything?' I asked.

'What am I supposed to say? "Go ahead" or "Oh, please don't"? What are you expecting me to do?'

'I don't know. I feel really awkward,' I admitted.

He put his foot on to a small stool and started doing up the laces on his shoes, while I stood next to him watching him. First he made a loop with one lace, then he made another loop with the other. Finally he tied them both into a bow.

'You lace up your shoes in a funny way,' I said in amazement.

'I was taught to do it that way when I was a kid.'

I had read somewhere that there were beings from other planets who come out of flying saucers, and that they were called humanoids. They come in three sorts: small, medium, and twelve foot tall. Maybe this man was a humanoid? Maybe he had got out of a flying saucer one day and stayed here? And now he was homesick for his planet. How else could one explain his sad look?

'I don't have anything against you personally,' I said. 'Maybe you could . . .'

'What?' he said, straightening up.

'Kill yourself,' I said straight out.

'But I don't want to kill myself,' he said bluntly.

'For Kira's sake . . .'

'Oh, I get it now.'

'She cries a lot,' I said sadly.

'She's always going to cry. That's what she's like.'

'Maybe. But it's one thing to cry by yourself. It's quite different if you can cry on a man's shoulder.'

'But I can't give her my shoulder to cry on,' he started to complain suddenly. 'If I start doing that, I won't be able to do anything else. I'm a busy man. And I'm sick and tired of . . .'

'But she's suffering.'

'That's because she hasn't anything else to do. She's a layabout.'

'Yes, she is a layabout. But she is *your* layabout.'

The phone rang.

'Pick up the phone, will you?' asked the Grasshopper as he went into his study.

'Hello,' I said.

'Who's that?' asked Kira's voice.

'It's me.'

'I'll ring you back in ten minutes,' said Kira, putting the phone down.

I also put the phone down. It started ringing again immediately.

'Hello.'

'Is that you again? What's going on? I was ringing someone completely different and I dialled your number instead.'

'No, you dialled the right number,' I said. 'I'm at his place.'

'Ha, ha, very funny, you idiot,' said Kira. 'You and your stupid jokes.'

She put the phone down. I waited for her to ring again and said, 'Hello . . .'

Kira said nothing for a while, then asked, 'What are you doing there?'

'You know, We agreed . . .'

'What did we agree?'

'That you would come out to Siberia.'

'Siberia? What on earth for?'

'Do you mean you've forgotten?'

'About what?'

And to think I was on the verge of . . .

I put the phone down and ran all over the flat looking

for the Grasshopper. He was standing in his study, hurriedly leafing through some papers.

'I don't have to kill you!' I informed him.

'I'm very glad for you,' the Grasshopper congratulated me as he continued to rummage through his papers.

The phone rang.

'I'm not here!' shouted the Grasshopper.

I picked up the receiver and heard Kira's voice again.

'He's not here,' I told her. 'And stop ringing up every damn minute.'

The Grasshopper had still not found what he was looking for and was starting to get anxious.

'Don't worry,' I said. 'I've got a car. I'll take you.'

'Really? That would be great. In that case . . .' he said, looking at his watch, 'we've got eleven more minutes.'

The Grasshopper took me into the kitchen and got out a bottle of gin from the fridge that was all clouded over with ice.

'Not for me,' I said.

'I shouldn't either. But this is just to make a toast.' He poured the gin out into glasses.

We raised our glasses and looked at each other. His face was thin and sad, as if he knew something immeasurably greater than all the rest of us.

'Truth is, I'm not worth killing,' he said sombrely. 'Why go all the bother anyway? I'm far too old for passion . . .'

'Even more reason to hurry up and make someone happy.'

'Haven't got time. I've got a thousand things to do that no one else will do for me.'

'But that is also something you have to do. Maybe the most important thing.'

'What is?' He frowned as he tried to work out what I was saying.

'Make someone happy.'

He looked at me carefully then put his glass down.

'If I understand things correctly, we are rivals, is that right?'

'No,' I said, 'I'm not a rival. She never wanted to kill me.'

We drove in silence. The Grasshopper sat next to me in the front, but I felt as if he was not there at all. I realized that he had unplugged himself from reality and was busy thinking about his affairs.

'Where do you work?' the Grasshopper asked suddenly, coming back into the car.

'I'm a technical translator. You probably thought I was a complete lunatic, I expect,' I hazarded.

'No. I was thinking that we were the ones who were mad,' he said, nodding at the pavement where a river of pedestrians was streaming past, 'and that you were perfectly normal in fact.'

I stopped the car in front of a large, impressive building.

The Grasshopper got out of the car and walked off, his large head slightly bowed.

I sighed, reached over to the back seat to pick up my file, and settled it on my knee.

The Grasshopper glanced round and then came back to the car.

'What are you waiting for?' he asked.

'For you.'

'So you can kill me?'

'No. To take you home.'

I do so much waiting that it has become a reflex action.

'There's no need for you to do that,' said the Grasshopper in surprise. 'I'll get home by myself. Thanks a lot, though.'

He lifted his face slightly to smile at me, his eyelashes flickering. Then he turned and walked away. Lonely, inscrutable, and celestial. A person from another planet. He gets on with his work and does not get embroiled in other people's affairs. That is why Kira has chosen him and not me. Although, objectively speaking, I am better looking and more positive, and I prefer order to total chaos too.

A month later the inevitable happened. I was given the sack.

My boss Lebedyev said that he had no alternative, because if he did not sack me, his boss would sack him. And he was not morally prepared for that.

'I'm sorry to have been such a nuisance to you,' I said.

I was hoping that my submissiveness would embarrass him into making him change his mind. But he just shrugged his shoulders and said, 'People are always going to be a nuisance to each other. It's called life.'

I could tell from the fact that he was talking to me so politely and rather distantly that he already struck me off the records. He already had another translator in mind, to whom he had promised my job. Quite possibly the new person was sitting in the cloakroom right now, waiting for me to leave.

I left Lebedyev's office. His secretary Rosa was sitting at a desk in front of his door. Last summer I had driven her and her family out to their cottage in the country.

'I've been fired,' I said to Rosa.

I was hoping that Rosa might abandon her work and get all the employees out on to the street. Get them to march up and down outside the publishers with placards and signs.

'Why?' asked Rosa.

'Because I haven't done anything . . .'

'Ah . . .'

So Rosa was evidently not planning to organize a strike. She was staying put at her desk.

'What are you going to live on?' she asked.

'I'll think of something . . .'

Rosa became lost in thought, and her face took on a dreamy expression. She was evidently trying to work out in her head what she would live on if they ever gave her the sack.

Tamara was standing by the stove and getting supper ready: she was frying up some eggs and sausages.

Her ten-year-old daughter Katya walked into the kitchen.

'I feel ever so sad!' she exclaimed, her small voice piercing the air shrilly, like a bird squawking.

'It's normal to feel sad,' Tamara explained. 'No one can be happy the whole time. If they're not completely stupid, of course.'

Katya stood there for a while, then went out again.

'Tamara,' I said. 'Lend me some money, will you?'

'But you were there when I bought those platform shoes. My whole advance went on them. I was wondering myself where I could get hold of some money. Honestly!'

Tamara turned her genuinely wide open eyes on to me.

'I believe you,' I said. 'I'm sorry I asked.'

Tamara's husband Lyovka appeared in the kitchen. He looked bleary-eyed, and was dressed like some political refugee. He liked sleeping in the middle of the day.

'Why don't you take your coat off?' Lyovka asked.

'Because I'm not stopping long.'

'Why did you take her to the hospital?' Lyovka asked, looking at me with a mixture of curiosity and revulsion.

'She asked me to.'

'Lyovka! I told you that I needed to make absolutely sure I didn't have it!' interrupted Tamara.

'She's just neurotic. Next time she'll drag you off to the morgue. Will you take her there too?'

'I expect so,' I said, shrugging my shoulders.

'But at least I'm not worried any more now,' said Tamara.

'Yes, but you didn't need to go to such lengths to find out you could stop worrying.'

'It's only you who manages to get things for free,' said Tamara. 'But I always end up paying three times more for everything; for shoes and for my peace for mind.'

'You pay for things when there is no need to. Why? Because your brain has a low problem-solving capacity.'

Tamara looked at her husband carefully, trying to work out what this complicated formulation meant.

'You're a fool,' said Lyovka, interpreting it for her.

'If I was a fool, I wouldn't have got my doctorate at thirty-five.'

'Well, so you're a clever fool then.'

Lyovka picked up an opened bottle of vodka.

'Sit down with us,' he suggested.

'Thanks, but I won't actually,' I said, turning down the invitation, since I eat sausage and eggs every day.

'Well, how about a drink, then?'

'No, sorry, I can't. I'm not allowed to.'

'Do you always only do the things you are allowed to do?'

'I've got gall stones.'

'They won't notice.'

Lyovka poured out the vodka into teacups. He raised his cup and waited.

'Well?'

When I feel someone's will directed at me, I am incapable of resisting. I drank the vodka down and then shook my head violently from side to side.

'Maybe you could stay after all?' suggested Tamara.

'No, really,' I said. 'I must be off.'

Once, when I was a student, I brought back from Odessa an old ship's wheel and fixed it to my balcony, on the outside. I imagined that my flat was a ship going out to sea and that I was a pirate with a patch over one eye. I would jump from my ship on to another, and run clattering up the wooden deck to thieve and plunder. If people refused to hand things over, I would kill them. I would slip their valuables into my pocket, kiss beautiful aristocrats, and wear a bandage over my right eye. I had paid for a turbulent lifestyle with my eye, but perhaps I had actually put the bandage over my good eye just for show.

By now my wheel had become all dark from the rain and the dried dirt encrusted on it. Next to it stood some empty mineral-water bottles and a tall tin of drying oil.

I sat down by the telephone without taking off my coat, and dialled Lodya's number.

'Everything is fine here, thanks,' said Lodya. He thought that I had been worrying about his relationship with his wife, and was thanking me for my concern.

'Can you lend me some money?' I asked.

'How much?'

'However much you've got.'

'For how long?'

'For however long you can.'

This vagueness caused Lodya to think for a bit.

'I can give you ten roubles for a week,' Lodya proposed.

'That's no good.'

'It's all I've got.'

I said nothing. Lodya interpreted my silence as a sign that I did not believe him.

'Well, actually I have got more,' admitted Lodya. 'But

it's in a deposit account. If I take it out, then I won't get any interest.'

I said nothing, but carried on listening.

'But ask me for anything else you need. I can get you a good flat if you want to swap, or a car without you having to go on a waiting list. But I don't lend money. I'm tight with money.'

'Thank you,' I said, meaning the car without the waiting list.

'Well, give us a ring some time!' Lodya was anxious to end a conversation that he found unpleasant.

I turned on the television and started watching. The cold vodka was roaming around my insides and making me feel all shivery.

Before when I watched television, I would be unable to forget my work sitting there for me to do, and it would gnaw at my conscience. My conscience made all the programmes I watched exceptionally interesting, and I would watch whatever was on, from beginning to end.

Today I could sit in front of the TV with a clear conscience.

There was a programme on about how sailors are chosen to be captains for long voyages. They all have to take a test, and the answers are fed into a machine, which tells you whether the person will be a good captain or not.

The phone rang. I picked it up.

'Who is that?' asked a clear voice, belonging to either a child or a woman.

'Who do you want to speak to?'

'Who is that speaking?' insisted the voice.

'Dmitry Mazaev.'

'You're an idiot!' shouted the voice agitatedly. Its owner hung up abruptly, so that I would be unable to reply. So that whoever it was had the last word.

But it really was true, I realized. I was an idiot. Idiots, like every biological creature, come in different shapes and sizes. There are clever idiots, like Tamara, and then there are prize idiots. But I was just a stupid idiot. At least those other sorts of fools have some points to them. I had none whatsoever.

A seed thrown on to the earth will only start growing in the spring, when the soil is ploughed and ready for the seed. I'm like some dim-witted ploughman, who scatters his seeds into snowdrifts or on to asphalt. My seeds will perish and will never bring forth grain. The books I translate go to different countries. The woman I love goes off into her life every day. I really am like the open-air swimming pool on Kropotkin Street, heating the entire universe. But even if they suddenly decided to close it down and drain out all the water, the world would not notice. Its climate would not be affected.

It is impossible to heat the universe and there is no need to anyway. I ought to be heating just one person; someone who needs the warmth. But I do not have someone like that in my life.

Fate equals character. And my character is impossible to change, because that is my *tiporazmer*.

What options did I have?

I could, of course, tackle the problem by taking up sport. I could do morning exercises, for example, then transfer to the swimming pool, go for long walks before going to bed, do yoga and starve myself one day a week. But to live like that you have to really love yourself. I'd find it boring.

It was then that I remembered the potassium cyanide. I had not returned it to Garik yet, and it was still sitting in the bottom drawer of my desk.

I poured out a few crystals on to my palm, and was about to toss them into my mouth, but my whole being was saying no. Then I went into the kitchen, cut myself a slice of bread, spread some jam on it, sprinkled the potassium cyanide on top, and began eating. I ate standing up, both listening to what was going on inside my body, and mechanically trying to think of a synonym for the word *tiporazmer*. I hit upon 'model'. Now I could die in peace.

The doorbell rang. I finished my sandwich, shook the crumbs from my hands, and listened again to the workings of my body. Everything was the same as before. Maybe that potassium cyanide had sat around too long in the warehouse. It was past its sell-by date and had lost the powers it was supposed to have.

I went into the hall and opened the door. Garik was standing there.

'Have you come for the potassium cyanide?' I asked. 'Because I haven't got it.'

'What have you done with it?' asked Garik with curiosity.

'I've eaten it.'

'Oh, that doesn't matter. That you don't have it any more, I mean. Look, I've brought you a letter. Can you translate it for me?'

We went into the living room. Garik saw the ship's wheel behind the window.

'Where's that come from? A spinning wheel or something?'

I did not even attempt to explain. Something was going on inside me that felt like lots of champagne bubbles fizzing. I became rather alarmed and opened up the letter to distract myself.

The private detective from England was advising Garik only to take on jobs which corresponded with his moral principles, so that what he actually did would not contradict what he believed.

'What's all this for?' I asked. 'Are you planning to do something for someone?'

'If I don't change my mind,' said Garik.

'You won't change your mind.'

'Why not?' said Garik, taken aback.

'Because you like material things. You like having everything.'

'But having everything and having nothing is one and the same thing,' said Garik with conviction.

'Perhaps,' I agreed. 'But it is better to declare that when you already have everything. Otherwise it looks like the platform of someone who has failed.'

'Having everything is only a prerequisite to rejecting it all and entering a new plane of existence.'

'And what is there on this new plane of existence? How do people live there?'

'Like you . . .'

'You mean . . .'

'With love. In the broadest sense of the word. Give everything to your neighbour and ask for nothing in return. People like that are few and far between. But there always have been people like that, and they still exist.'

'All right. Suppose I am on this new plane of human consciousness. What do I get from it? What are the benefits?'

'You will live a long time. Nature keeps people like you on the earth for a long time.'

I closed my eyes. The sensation of effervescence was growing stronger in me with every minute, and I felt as if I was being brought up to the surface from the briny deep.

'Who can tell,' I said quietly. 'If I were to be put through a computer, maybe it would turn out that my vocation was to be a pirate on the high seas. Maybe my natural element is stealing things from people, and killing them if they won't give them up.'

'But a pirate can be killed too.'

'Yes, that's true, but at least when he is living he is really alive.'

'How can you possibly tell what pirates think about?'

Garik went over to the telephone and dialled a number.

37

'Tell my wife that I am at your place,' he whispered hurriedly, handing me the receiver. I had to get up from the armchair to take it.

'I can't get up,' I said.

Garik did not bother to ask 'Why not?' Instead he stretched the phone as far as the cord would go, and put it down on the floor next to me.

'Garik's at my place,' I said without saying hello.

'Tell her I'll be back soon,' whispered Garik.

'He'll be back soon,' I repeated.

Garik's wife listened as if she was determining the percentage of truth in my voice. Garik took the receiver from me and repeated the same things to his wife. The habit of lying and getting himself out of situations had become something of a reflex with him. The same as with me waiting for people all the time. Even when Garik told the truth he was still lying really. He put the phone down and sighed with relief, as if he had just managed to steer clear of some terrible danger.

'Well, I'd better be going,' he said pensively, and then he actually did go.

I made it with difficulty over to my bed and lay down still in my coat. The pain inside me was increasing and gathering strength. It was threatening to become intolerable.

I tried to lie in a position that would ease the pain. Then I lay down on the floor and started rocking back and forth.

I cannot remember how much time passed. But at some point I started to become indifferent to everything. I realized that I was dying. But even that did not bother me.

Human beings are unable to resign themselves to the prospect of dying, so wise old nature bestows indifference on us. As a means of self-defence.

I had read in books that people go back mentally through their whole lives before they die. But I had forgotten all about my life. I felt as if as I was floating on the ocean on a narrow wooden raft. My raft was swaying gently on the waves, and was being carried further and further away from the shore.

I opened my eyes and saw Kira in the middle of the room. I wasn't at all interested in how she had got into my flat. I did not care. But I did not want to let her see me dying. Dogs, incidentally, also prefer to die without witnesses.

I finally managed to focus my mind through an immense effort of will.

'How did you get in?' I asked, sort of rising up from my raft.

'The door wasn't locked,' answered Kira. 'Why are you on the floor?'

'I'm dying,' I said dispassionately, as if I was talking about someone else.

'Well, I'm going to get married,' Kira informed me, as she sat down next me on the floor. 'Are you glad?'

'Yes.'

'But not really?'

I had become incredibly tired, and wanted to sink back down on to my raft. But I concentrated hard and said, 'I'm very happy for you. Congratulations.'

'You're the one who should be congratulated. You raised me to the status of a queen and made me start looking at myself differently. People relate to a person the way they relate to themselves, isn't that right?'

I closed my eyes, and my raft started to drop down from the waves as if it was falling off a mountain. It was going up and down, up and down . . . But something had gripped me, as if by my hair. It was Kira's question. She had asked me something. I could not fall out of time until I had answered her question.

'That is why I don't work,' uttered Kira from some-where far away. 'After all, queens don't work.'

'Don't work,' I said, mechanically repeating the last words I heard.

'Or do they actually do something?' doubted Kira.

'Do something,' I repeated.

Kira could have got cross and said that she was having a conversation with herself again, but I did not care.

'What's the matter with you?' she asked.

'I'm dying . . .'

'That's very likely, I must say . . .'

'Will you go and run me a bath?' I asked, in order to get her to leave me.

She ran into the bathroom and started singing. I heard the water splashing and the sound of her voice.

Then she came back.

'Would you rather I went away or stayed?' she asked.

I wanted her to go away, but it would have been impolite to say so.

'Whatever you prefer . . .'

'I'll go, then.'

Kira slammed the door shut and skipped down the stairs. I lay for a while listening to her footsteps. A pale shadow of regret fluttered inside me, pulling me away from indifference.

I closed my eyes. Once more I was pulled down towards the bottom of the ocean, but I could not stay down there. Something was preventing me again. The telephone. It was ringing incessantly, as if something had gone wrong with the line.

I stretched out my hand, fumbled for the phone, and picked up the receiver. When I lifted it to my ear I heard Tamara's voice. We live in the same apartment block, but even so, Tamara's voice sounded as loud as if she was standing right by me and bellowing in my ear. She was shouting that I had to take her the next day to all the foreign shops: Wanda, Vlasta, Leipzig, and Yadran.

A salty wave covered me from the head to toe. I

swallowed the water and said: 'But Leipzig and Vlasta are just across the road.'

'Uh-huh . . .' yelled Tamara, as if I had just thrown dry sticks into her bonfire. 'Wanda is in the centre of town, though. And Yadran is on the road out of Moscow. It's half-way to Leningrad.'

Tamara fell silent. She was waiting. I had to say something in reply.

'All right,' I said. 'If I don't die in the mean time . . .'

I put the phone down and rested a while. The pain began to ease. It now felt like a recollection of pain.

Maybe potassium cyanide produces a neutral compound when combined with jam? Most likely Garik had just been swindled. The system of 'I do something for you, and you do something for me' had proved unstable.

I closed my eyes and drifted into a normal sleep. I was still being tossed on the waves, but my raft was going towards the shore.

I knew now that I would not die. Otherwise, who would be able to take Tamara shopping?

BAD MOOD

Viktor Petrovich, the local paediatrician (a young man who looked rather like a nineteenth-century intellectual from the lower classes), was sitting with his back hunched over, listening to his next patient. First he moved his stethoscope over her bare little back, saying, 'Breathe in . . . hold your breath . . .' Then he fell silent and just sat there gazing into the distance.

The child's mother was also present in the consulting room. She stood there clutching her child's clothes and looking anxiously at the doctor, trying to work out from the expression on his face what was going to happen to her daughter. But it was impossible to tell anything from it. Viktor Petrovich's face bore the sort of expression it might have had if his wife had rung up ten minutes earlier and told him never to come home again. Or if the head physician at the paediatric clinic had summoned him to his office and demanded his resignation.

The girl breathed in and held her breath obediently, looking out of the corner of her eye delightedly at her mother. She was a vain child and she liked being at the centre of attention.

Viktor Petrovich finally pulled the ends of his stethoscope out of his ears. 'Write out a prescription, please,' he said to the nurse.

The nurse was sitting on the other side of his desk in a white coat and a red fluffy hat. It did not seem that she was at work somehow, but as if she had just dropped in to sit down for a minute. She had been passing by and had just called in to pay a visit.

'What's your name?' the nurse asked.

'Whose? Mine?' the mother replied. 'It's Larisa.'

'No, not you!' said the nurse crossly.

'Masha Prokhorov,' said the little girl, intervening.

'All right, get dressed,' ordered the nurse.

Larisa hurriedly started pulling Masha's dress over her head, but it would not go, because her hair had got caught on a button. She was trying to get a move on, but Masha had started whining. Viktor Petrovich sat waiting politely, but his annoyance was only thinly disguised.

'Next!' summoned the nurse.

Next to come in were a grandmother with her grandson. They were both dressed up very smartly and had beaming faces, as if they had just arrived at a party and knew their hosts would be extremely pleased to see them.

'Get undressed, please!' said Viktor Petrovich, looking despondently out of the window.

Larisa and Masha finally managed to sort out the problem with the dress. They took their prescription and left the consulting room.

Three-year-old Dasha had been sitting on a chair outside, waiting patiently. When she saw her mother and sister, she slid off the chair and slipped her hand into her mother's. Larisa led them down the stairs, holding on to Dasha with one hand, and Masha with the other.

Masha walked next to the wall, and on the other side Dasha was running her hand down the banister, collecting all the local germs into her palm.

'Take your hand away from there,' Larisa ordered.

'Why?' asked Dasha.

'Because I'm telling you to,' Larisa answered.

This was not a very instructive answer, but Larisa knew her daughter well: an absence of logic worked on her like magic. As it was doing now. Dasha had taken her hand off the banister and had even put it behind her back.

It was completely different with Masha. With her you

had to explain everything in great detail, distinguishing between cause and effect and demonstrating their connection to each other.

When they finally reached the cloakroom to pick up their coats, it turned out that their tag had disappeared. They started searching their pockets and in Larisa's bag, not wanting to believe they had really lost it. Then they poked into all the compartments of the bag and their pockets one more time, but the tag was nowhere to be seen.

'I'm afraid we've lost it,' admitted Larisa, looking guiltily at the cloakroom lady in her blue overall.

'Well, you'd better go and look for it then!' the cloakroom lady commanded, and considering the audience at an end, she retreated back into the depths of her kingdom.

Larisa took her daughters by the hand once more and all three plodded off back the way they had come, staring hard at the floor as they went, and combing with their eyes every inch of the lilac-beige floor.

Near the lavatories Dasha came across a large black button with four eyes, and in Viktor Petrovich's consulting room she found a shiny wrapper from a popular brand of sweets. They carried these trophies back to the cloakroom lady but could not interest her in them.

'I'm sorry, we couldn't find it,' said Larisa, trying to appear pitiful and guilt-ridden. Meanwhile the girls looked on cheekily, grinning as if nothing had happened.

'Oh, yes, that's what they all say!' exploded the cloakroom lady. 'But I'm the one who has to pay for it!'

'Oh, I'd be happy to pay!' exclaimed Larisa gladly. 'How much does a tag cost?'

'A rouble,' the cloakroom lady declared officially.

Larisa now recollected that she had not taken her purse with her when they set off for the clinic. But there might well be a rouble somewhere in her bag. She poked around once more with her eyes and her fingers into all the compartments of her bag, and came up with four fifteen-kopeck coins, three ten-kopeck coins, a five-kopeck piece, and even five one-kopeck pieces.

During this time an elderly lady with a ribbon in her hair had walked up to the cloakroom. Her hair had been drawn from the back and the sides into a neat pony tail with the ribbon. People used to wear their hair like this before the war and this lady had obviously remained loyal to that particular style. She was a real lady; you could never have called her an old babushka. Her eyebrows were etched in with black crayon, but the lines went in different directions: the real eyebrows went downwards while the false ones went upwards.

The lady looked with great suspicion at Larisa, whose trousers were held up by a belt, and whose thick fringe came right down over her eyes. She then looked at the children, who were also wearing trousers and had long fringes, and her eyes expressed a deep concern about the youth of today, and about the future of the whole world in fact, which would one day have to be handed over to people like these. Leonardo da Vinci had probably felt the same way when he was an old man, and could not see a single pupil around him worthy of handing his paint-brushes on to.

The laws of time and biology dictated that Larisa and her children would live on after this elderly lady, and this prospect displeased her still further. She looked first at Larisa with an expression of great distrust, and then at the cloakroom lady, as if wanting to share her doubts with her.

Larisa cast a furtive look at the lady and ordered her children to move along a bit, so as not to take up all the space. Everything was perfectly polite and proper, but the age-old conflict of generations nevertheless flitted over the cloakroom like a grey shadow.

Larisa counted up her kopecks one more time and proffered the heavy handful to the cloakroom lady. But this gesture immediately followed the exchange of glances and the cloakroom lady now felt uncomfortable taking money from such a disreputable hand.

'I'm not taking your money,' said the cloakroom lady sternly.

'Why not?' Larisa asked in confusion, with her out-stretched hand still suspended in the air.

'What am I going to do with it, eh? It's the tag I want, not the money.'

By this time the elderly lady had already put her coat on and left, but the cloakroom lady couldn't change her mind now.

'Well, who I shall I give it to?' asked Larisa.

'Take it to matron . . .'

Larisa closed her fingers over the money, and, gripping the coins in her hand, walked down to the end of the corridor. The children trudged off after her, but kept a certain distance behind, like the dependants in that story by Chekhov.

A notice with the word 'Matron' on it hung from a white door.

Larisa knocked at the door and went in without waiting for an answer.

Matron, dressed in white coat and cap, like the ones they wear in Russian bakeries, was furrowing in a drawer of her desk evidently looking for something, and was very absorbed in this activity.

'Excuse me, but we have lost our cloakroom tag,' said Larisa.

'So?' said Matron, distracted from her drawer for a second.

'Here's the money,' Larisa explained.

'What have I got to do with this?'

'The woman in the cloakroom said that I could give it to you.'

'Why me?' said Matron with displeasure. She was one of those people infected with the pettiness of the underpaid.

'Who am I supposed to give it to, then?'

'Hand it in wherever you lost the tag.'

Matron again started searching in her drawer for whatever it was that she needed.

'Sorry to have bothered you,' said Larisa sheepishly as she left the office. She shut the door behind her.

'I'm hungry,' Dasha whined.

'I'm thirsty,' said Masha chiming in.

'Who had the cloakroom tag last?' asked Larisa crossly.

'She did,' said Dasha, pointing at her sister.

'Did not,' denied Masha.

'That's all we need, you two quarrelling,' Larisa said bitterly. 'What scatterbrains . . . How can you be so careless? Why is it that no one else's children ever get colds or lose anything? I'll send you away to boarding school if you don't look out.'

Dasha and Masha listened meekly. They believed her. Grief descended to their souls.

'Don't follow me!' ordered Larisa. 'Just stay right here. Don't move.'

She turned and walked back briskly to the cloakroom.

A fairly decent-sized queue had now formed at the counter, and the cloakroom lady was moving about with perspiration on her face.

'Matron wouldn't take it,' Larisa said to her over people's heads.

The cloakroom lady did not respond. She was carrying an armful of coats hoisted on to her stomach.

Larisa held out her fistful of change over the other people's heads. 'Do you think you could take it after all?'

'Don't jump the queue,' said a woman. 'There are people waiting here with children.'

'But I've already been waiting here,' Larisa explained.

'Some people have no shame,' observed someone in the middle of the queue. 'They just don't give a damn. And then they'll have the cheek to tell you it's raining outside!'

The cloakroom lady carried on silently handing out coats, pretending that she did not know Larisa, that she was seeing her for the first time in her life.

Larisa was pushed aside to the back of the cloakroom.

She looked out into the corridor. The children were where she had left them, standing underneath a poster about the dangers of alcohol abuse. Masha was sobbing quietly, but Dasha was examining the poster; she had an amazing ability to adapt immediately to new situations and not worry about anything.

'What are you blubbing about?' asked Larisa, as she went up to them. 'Come on, what is it?'

Masha hung her head, stuck out her bottom lip, and howled with even greater feeling now that she had someone to show her distress to. She cried just like Auntie Rita used to. Auntie Rita had been a distant relative of theirs, an old spinster who had ended her days in an old people's home. Well, when Auntie Rita used to cry, her bottom lip stuck out and her eyebrows wobbled in just the same way that Masha's did. Or rather, it was Masha who cried just like Auntie Rita used to, and it was impossible to work out through which mysterious channels this particular combination of chromosomes had come to be bestowed on nature.

'I'm sorry, sweetheart,' said Larisa, crouching down in front of her daughter. 'Come on, let's make it up.' Masha flung her heavy little body against her mother and sobbed into her face, breathing hot air on to her cheeks.

'There we are now, it's all over,' said Larisa, kissing her damp little face. 'All right?'

Masha nodded. She was still shedding tears, but they were light and gentle now, not bitter like before. Her eyebrows and cheeks had come out in red, nervous blotches.

Dasha stood stock still next to her, gazing avidly at the picture of a grimy old man with a red nose on the anti-alcohol poster.

Typical Prokhorov behaviour, thought Larisa. They're all the same . . .

Matron came out of her office at that point.

'Excuse me . . .' Larisa began, but Matron walked straight past her like a general might march past new recruits at a parade. Then she came back to her office and shut the door. Her broad back seemed to say: 'First they loiter about, then things just happen to disappear . . .'

'Who should I go and see?' asked Larisa, looking at Matron's inaccessible back.

'Go and talk to the doctor you are registered with,' she replied in rehearsed tones.

Obviously all the mothers went to see her about medical problems, and she sent them all to the doctors they were registered with.

Viktor Petrovich was moving the stethoscope up and down a child's back, saying, 'Breathe in . . . hold your breath.' Then he took the ends of the stethoscope out of his ears and looked up at Larisa who had just walked into the consulting room.

'What do you think?' asked the little boy's mother, taking Viktor Petrovich's eyeballs prisoner.

'There's no change, I'm afraid,' he answered, carefully withdrawing his eyes from the captivity of her pupils. 'What sort of change could there be?'

The woman said nothing. She could not reconcile the

hopes she had fostered with common sense. And Viktor Petrovich stood on the side of common sense.

'And what if we don't go ahead with the operation?' asked the woman quietly.

'But we have been through all that,' Viktor Petrovich reminded her gently. 'What else can I say? I can only repeat what I've said before.'

The woman was silent. She stood there with a calm expression on her face, but Larisa could see that this was the calmness of devastation, when everything inside has been taken out, and only the shell is left. An immovable, suffocating silence filled the consulting room.

'What do you want?' asked Viktor Petrovich, looking at Larisa.

'Nothing . . .'

Larisa went out into the corridor. People were walking past her, but Larisa did not notice them. She was trapped inside a capsule of someone else's unhappiness, like a seed in a grape, and could not move from where she was standing.

By this time the queue in the cloakroom had gone, and there was no one waiting any more. The cloakroom lady was sitting on a stool doing her knitting, and Matron was standing in front of her with her elbows on the counter, watching her hands.

'So, you have to do fifty-two stitches. Have you made a note of that?' said the cloakroom lady.

'You mean you have got to count up to fifty-two?' Matron asked.

Now the cloakroom lady did not understand her, and both looked at each other intensely for a minute.

'Fifty-two purl and fifty-two plain, or fifty-two in all?' clarified Matron, at that moment catching sight of Larisa and her children. 'Oh no! It's them . . . The Fujiyamas are back again!'

Why 'Fujiyamas' Larisa did not quite understand.

Perhaps their dark hair and eyes gave off a faint aura of the Far East?

'I'm hungry . . .' Dasha reminded her.

'Me too,' chimed in Masha.

'Look, please give us out coats. I beg you. I can't bear it any more,' Larisa pleaded gently.

'But no one is keeping you here,' said Matron in mock surprise. 'Just hand over your tag and you can go home.'

She had power over Larisa at that moment, and was probably experiencing a pleasure from exercising it with which she did not want to part.

'But you know we haven't got our tag. What are we to do? Go home without our coats?'

'But how are we going to find your coats?' asked Matron with interest.

'I'll find them for you.'

'You'll find them, will you . . .' said the cloakroom lady slowly, insinuating that Larisa might well take off the hooks coats which belonged to other people. Coats which were protected by tags, and which had not been lost.

'Do you mean you don't you trust me?'

'Why should we trust some people, and not others?' Matron asked, entirely reasonably.

As long as there are thieves in society, there are bound to be tags and cloakroom ladies. Thieves are probably essential to the general stew of life, in fact, because they enable people to distinguish between Good and Evil, by teaching them to value one and contrast it with the other. Thieves existed even when society had slaves. Thieves were no different from anyone else until they stole something.

'Well, what are we supposed to do?' asked Larisa in dismay. 'We can't stay here all night . . .'

'What do you mean, stay here all night? There's no need for that.' Matron took the ball of wool and the knitting needles from the cloakroom lady's hands. 'So is it just fifty-two or a hundred and four?' she asked, returning to her previous question.

'Why should it be a hundred and four? It's fifty-two. Look, just knit a piece like this,' said the cloakroom lady spreading out her thumb and index fingers to indicate the width, 'and then I'll finish you off when you have to drop the stitches. The main thing is the top bit.'

Matron stuck the knitting needles into the ball of wool.

'Just give them whatever coats are left over,' she ordered and then started to walk away.

'What do you mean?' asked Larisa in confusion.

'When we close, all the coats will be taken, and I dare say yours will be left.'

'When do you close?'

'Eight o'clock.'

'So you mean I've got to sit here and wait until eight o'clock?'

Matron was just walking past Larisa at that point. Larisa feared that if she left now, nothing could be changed. The cloakroom lady, being of lower rank, would not dare to disobey the order.

'Wait!' Larisa grabbed Matron by the sleeve.

Matron gave a shudder and tried to pull her arm away. So Larisa took an even firmer grip, resolving to hold on no matter what happened. Even at the expense of her own life.

And then there occurred something which takes place during physics experiments in laboratories, when a reaction is sparked off between two particles that come together.

There was a clap of thunder, and a flash of lightning, and Larisa suddenly found herself flying towards the pharmacy in the opposite corner, slithering along the floor on her tensed legs. Next she felt herself on top of Matron's soft body, and then all of a sudden she was underneath her, feeling the hard linoleum with her shoulder blades, and seeing nothing but a mass of white coat. The bronze and silver coins rolled out all over the cloakroom clattering loudly.

The woman in the pharmacy poked her head out and said, 'You ought to call the police. She should get fifteen days in the lock-up for this.'

Masha and Dasha started wailing in unison, their mouths wide open. They bawled with such intensity that their faces even started to turn blue. The cloakroom lady now began to be scared that the children might suffocate and die from a lack of oxygen. She dived into the bunches of coats, then came back and threw two Bulgarian white fur coats and Larisa's dyed sheepskin on to the counter.

Mothers with their children had been coming up to the cloakroom all this time, but they were afraid of entering the danger zone. It was not clear on whose side victory lay. Matron was definitely winning in terms of sheer bulk, but Larisa had the edge as far as temperament went.

A few volunteers threw themselves into the middle of the fray and pulled Larisa and Matron into different corners, as if they were in a boxing ring. The two women stood, breathing heavily, unable to utter a sound.

'What dreadful hooliganism,' said the woman in the pharmacy.

'This is awful,' chipped in the nurse from the reception desk. 'If they all start coming in and attacking the staff, what will be left of us, I wonder?'

Meanwhile the cloakroom lady was hastily putting Masha and Dasha's coats on. She had done up all the buttons, drawn up their fluffy hoods, and was wrapping their little scarves tightly around their necks so that they would not catch cold and have to come back again with their mother.

Larisa freed herself from the volunteers. She took her sheepskin coat and started walking towards the door, pulling it on as she went, and losing her gloves and scarf from the sleeves. Someone ran to pick them up and handed them to her.

The children shuffled off after her in their matching fur coats and fluffy hoods.

Outside it was snowing, and the ground was white and festive. The sky was hazy and also white.

Ten years ago a village with little front gardens and cherry trees had stood on this site. A whole new district of the city had sprung up here now, but somehow the snow and the sky still had something rural about them.

An old man was standing on the pavement looking down at his feet. Larisa also peered down at his feet and saw an apple core lying there. The old man raised his head and said, 'I was eating this apple, you know, and I found this worm in the middle. I've been standing here for half an hour now watching it. They're really amazing creatures, you know, worms . . .'

Larisa nodded absentmindedly and walked on. And then suddenly she stopped. She was trying to work out how she, a young woman from a good family with an MA behind her, the mother of two children, a person sensitive to literature and music, could suddenly get into a fight like any old hoodlum. They were on the point of handing her over to the police! The officer would have turned up, carted her off to the station, and asked, 'What were you fighting for?'

'I was bored,' Larisa would say. 'Bored to death . . .'

There had been youth once. And there had been love for Prokhorov. Prokhorov was still around, but the love had passed on. Everything had passed on, but there was still a lot of living to do. And she had at least thirty more years to go until the point when she could just spend her time contemplating worms like that old man. Thirty years, in which each day was like an identical heavy raindrop, falling on to the top of her head at regular intervals.

There was really nowhere that she could go. And even if there had been somewhere to go, she had nothing to go in. Fashions kept changing the whole time, and if you wanted to keep up, you had to devote your whole life to it. And even if she did have something to go in and somewhere to go, it would still be boring. Her soul was as restless as an orphaned child.

'And if I sentence you to fifteen days, won't that be boring?' the officer would ask.

'It's all the same to me . . .'

'All right,' the policeman would say. 'You'll get used to it.'

'I won't, you know.'

'Oh, yes, you will. There's nothing else to do.'

Larisa lowered her head. Her eyebrows started quivering and she could feel Auntie Rita's expression forming on her face.

The children were plodding along behind, subdued and miserable. The pavement had become pale beneath the snow and they kept on slipping. They did not actually fall, but their shoulders kept banging together.

The shift came to an end at three o'clock. Matron walked out on to the concrete steps. The post-natal session began at three, and the area in front of the clinic was completely full of prams.

Another young mother had arrived with a pram and was taking her little person out of it. The little person was dressed in a romper suit, and he was all round like a little ball, with a round little face. The sheet covering the mattress in the pram had caught on the belt of his romper suit and hung down from him like a royal train. It had to be detached somehow, but the woman did not have a free hand, so she held up her little prince on her outstretched hands as high as she could. The sheet soon detached itself and fell away, but the woman did not want to lower her hands yet. She carried on holding the child high up over her head, laughing and screwing her eyes up at him as she did so, dazed with happiness. The baby hung up there contentedly in midair, expressing neither fear nor joy, his little hands and legs dangling involuntarily from him. He was secure in his mother's arms and sure of his mother's love. So it had been from the first day of his life, and he could not imagine things being any different.

Matron glanced at the pair. If she had a warm, round little person to herself, she thought, she would not want anything else in the world. She would never utter a rude word to anybody. But that hussy, she thought, remembering Larisa, had two children, and she still got into fights . . .

It was not cold, but the wind was blowing through the holes in the delicate weave of her scarf.

The Knight cinema stood next to the clinic, and a valiant knight made of sheet iron looked out from the building's exterior over the district entrusted to him.

THE JAPANESE UMBRELLA

Near the shop called Universal Stores stretched a long queue. The people standing in it had placed themselves one behind the other, each keeping a certain distance from the person in front, and all standing 'at ease'.

I stopped and pondered a while. If I were to nudge the last person standing in the queue in the back, I thought, they would fall over on to the person in front of them. Then that person would fall over on to the person in front of them, and within a minute the whole queue would be falling flat on their faces, and it would sound like someone running their finger down the teeth of a comb.

Then I wondered what the point of pushing people over was if all it meant was that I could exalt myself over them. Why exalt yourself over people when you can co-exist with them quite peacefully?

I crossed the road and joined the queue.

I stood behind a back in a sheepskin coat and a head in a musquash fur hat. It's incredible; you'll never be able to buy a sheepskin coat in a month of Sundays, yet the whole of Moscow is wearing them. I personally wear an imitation seal-fur hat which is actually rabbit, and a gaberdine overcoat, which I made myself in 1958. Gaberdine is very hard-wearing; it lasts a lifetime. In all the years I've been wearing it, my coat has already managed to go out of fashion and back in again.

'What's for sale?'

I turned round. In front of me stood a girl in a sheepskin coat.

Good question, I thought. What *am* I actually queuing for?

'I'm sorry, I don't know,' I said politely, 'but I'll find out this second.'

I tapped on the back of the person in front of me, as if he were a door. The musquash head turned round and showed me his swarthy, large-beaked profile, which made him look like an extremely seedy-looking old crow.

'Excuse me, please, can you tell me what's being sold?'

'Japanese umbrellas.'

'Japanese umbrellas,' I relayed to the girl.

'I heard,' the girl replied crisply.

Of course she heard. She wasn't deaf. But she could have pretended that she was. She could just have said, 'Thank you very much.' Then I would have said, 'Are they any good?'

'What do you mean, any good?'

'The Japanese umbrellas.'

'They're very handy. You can collapse them and tuck them away in your bag.'

As I don't carry a bag around with me, I would have asked, 'Can you put them in your pocket?'

'Depends on the pocket,' the girl would have said.

That would have been the beginning of our conversation, a conversation which might have gone on for a whole year, perhaps three years, or even a whole lifetime. But the girl didn't even want to talk to me for more than three minutes, because I was wearing a gaberdine coat with narrow lapels rather than a sheepskin.

Clothes are the expression of one's outer self. Unfortunately the state of my outer self depends more on my circumstances than it does on me. It certainly does not correspond with my inner self. In fact my two selves exist in a state of permanent antagonism, which means I am never free to develop my own style. They deprive me of all individuality.

They say that millionaires in the West dress very modestly. Rockefeller, for example, could have put on my gaberdine coat, gone calmly about his business, and no one would have batted an eyelid. When a person can give himself everything he can possibly desire, he can certainly afford the luxury of going around in an old coat. But I am not rich enough yet to be able not to value money. Not wise enough yet to be able to stop searching for the meaning of life. Not old enough just to enjoy life as it is. And not young enough simply to surrender to an innate optimism and enjoy it for no reason at all.

I am at the middle of my life, that most tragic time, when passion is not yet a thing of the past, but weariness has already taken up permanent residence in the heart. The battle between my inner and outer selves has reduced me to a state where I have no confidence left in either myself or in others. That is why what I like doing most of all is standing in long queues. Standing behind other people's backs and behaving like everyone else.

So here I was, standing at the end of this long, reliable queue. I was feeling calm and at ease with myself. After all, that many people couldn't all be making the same mistake. They wouldn't be wasting their time and energy for nothing.

A Japanese lady in European dress brushed past me as she walked down the length of the queue. She was carrying an umbrella which had been manufactured in Moscow. It was black and sturdily built, and had an impressive wooden handle with a plastic knob.

I stepped out of the queue and stood in the way of this Japanese lady. 'Hello,' I greeted her warmly. 'Good afternoon.'

I was secretly hoping that the Japanese lady would bend over in a low, respectful bow so that I would be able to see the nape of her slender neck. Well-brought-up Japanese women have been taught always to bow to a man, regardless of who he might be. And that is all they should be taught, too. A man does not want to cope with someone else's personality. All he ever wants to find in a woman is confirmation of his own.

'Good afternoon,' the Japanese lady replied in flawless Russian. It obviously hadn't even occurred to her to think of bowing. This particular Japanese lady must have been corrupted by civilization, and when she turned her gorgeous eyes on me, she wasn't thinking about bowing – anything but. World economics probably.

'Why aren't you holding a Japanese umbrella?' I asked.

'Our umbrellas aren't built for your climate,' the Japanese lady replied, before going on her way, tripping daintily, as if she was wearing a kimono rather than a pair of trousers.

I got back into the queue, and a particle of loneliness descended on me. I began to have doubts: did I really need a Japanese umbrella which was not designed to withstand our climatic conditions? Was I right to succumb to the caprices of fashion? Maybe it would make sense to overcome my natural instincts and get out of the queue?

But the umbrella seller intruded into my reflections.

'Blue or red?' she asked.

'What?' I said, coming back into the real world.

The umbrella seller thrust a blue umbrella and a box at me.

'What's that?' I said, pointing at the box.

'Job lot. Italian platform shoes.'

'What do I need them for?'

'To keep you anchored to the ground. They come with the umbrellas.'

I didn't need either an umbrella or platform shoes, but I couldn't leave empty-handed.

'I'll just take the umbrella,' I said.

I walked a few paces away, opened the umbrella, and

suddenly felt myself being pulled upwards. I dug my heels into the ground, but my shoes proved too light and I took off into the air.

The sensation of flying was a familiar one to me and even rather ordinary. I could remember it from my childhood dreams.

The blue dome of the umbrella entered a warm air stream, and so up I flew, holding on tight, and not afraid of falling.

At first I flew quite low, only about two metres off the ground. I was fully expecting someone in the queue to grab me by the legs and bring my ascent to an end, but no one did. Perhaps they were afraid that I would wrench them from the ground and go soaring up into the clouds with them hanging on to my legs. It's everyone together as far as standing goes, I thought, but when it comes to flying, you are out on your own.

I remembered that I had not betrayed the queue even in my darkest moments of doubt. But when I had taken off into the air, no one had even raised an eyebrow. Why was that? It was because everybody needed an umbrella and nobody needed me. And that was fair enough, I suppose. You couldn't tuck me away in your bag or even swap me for anything worthwhile. I was neither beautiful nor useful. In fact I was just one long inconvenience. I had to be fed. I had to be talked to. I had to be understood.

All this time the umbrella had been gaining height. I was scared that it might carry me on to a flight path and that I'd get hit by an aeroplane – struck by a propeller.

As I flew over a nine-storey block of flats, I managed to grab hold of a television aerial with my free hand. After floundering a little in the air, I finally came to rest on the roof. I pressed the button on the umbrella handle and the umbrella suddenly became all limp, its blue dome collapsing into nothing.

I hung it on the aerial and then sat down on the edge of the roof, dangling my legs.

It was great looking at the city from up above.

Suddenly I noticed that the queue had sort of changed. At first I couldn't make out what was going on. But when I looked closer, I saw that the people and the merchandise had actually changed places. The items were stretched out in a long queue and were choosing people for themselves. And the people were sitting in cardboard boxes, like the ones television sets come in, craning their necks to get some fresh air.

'I'd like a smart one with glasses,' said a Canadian sheepskin coat.

'Just a minute . . .'

The assistant wandered about between the boxes and then brought back a bespectacled man with a drooping moustache.

The sheepskin coat gave the assistant some money, and off they went.

'We want that fat old chap over there,' requested some American blue jeans.

'But I won't fit.' The fat old chap got out of the box in his baggy satin pantaloons. 'I'm a fifty-six and they are a forty-four.'

'It's true,' agreed the assistant. 'He will be too big for you . . .'

'But we've been queuing here all day,' said the jeans indignantly. 'Do you mean to say we have been queuing up for nothing?'

A nylon toupé had a tussle after the jeans. And then it was the turn of a pair of Austrian platform boots, which kept shifting from one foot to the other.

'Choose me!' whispered a pretty blonde girl to the platform boots.

'No, me!' said a dark-haired woman with a moustache, adjusting her hair before gallumphing up in her box.

But who would choose me? I wondered, looking at all the goods. Would I be wanted by anyone?

And then suddenly I saw my gaberdine coat in the queue. During the seventeen years that I had been wearing it, it had gradually taken the shape of my body: it had the same stooping shoulders and the same stretched elbows as I did. God, how old it looked! In several places the gaberdine had worn through so much that it was as transparent as gauze. And the lining had holes the size of dinner plates.

I looked at my coat and realized that if I didn't take it, no one else would. It would stand there for ever with its threadbare sleeves sunk in its threadbare pockets.

A migrant bird landed on the television aerial. First it lowered its claws, like an aeroplane fuselage lowering its wheels, and then when it felt firm ground it let its wings drop.

'Having a rest?' asked the bird.

'It's none of your business.'

'I'm flying to Africa,' said the bird, completely unperturbed. 'We could fly there together if you want.'

'What would I want to go there for?'

'As you like,' said the bird, still unperturbed.

It lifted its little wings and fluttered them for a while, then it disengaged itself from the aerial and flew off tracing a delicate pattern in the air, as if it was writing its name.

I looked around. The roof had not been tidied up. There were bricks and pieces of broken glass lying around, and various building materials. When the builders had laid the last tile, they'd either forgotten to sweep up after themselves or they just couldn't be bothered to.

I took the heaviest brick I could find and wedged it under my belt to increase my ballast. Then I took the umbrella off the aerial and opened it over myself.

The umbrella whisked me smoothly off the roof and carried me downwards towards the shop.

I found a large empty box and got into it. Then I started to wait for my coat. A picture of a blue wine glass was printed on my box with the words: 'Fragile. With care. This way up. Don't tilt.'

THE SECRET OF THE EARTH

One morning, Elena Andreyevna Zhuravlyova – Cross-Eyed Alyona, as she was called behind her back – woke up feeling fed up with everything.

When she had become fully awake, she lay there for a while with her eyes open, becoming sure of her feelings. Once she was quite sure about them, she decided that the feelings were worth turning into words, and the words into speech. By telephone.

Nikolayev would ring her at nine. She would pick up the receiver, and say, 'Do you know something? I'm tired of all this. I'm fed up with it all. I don't want this any more.'

Usually he would ring on the dot of nine. That was his time of day. He would ring up and say, 'Hello.'

She would answer, 'Hello.'

He would say, 'Bye.'

And she would answer, 'Bye.'

And that was the whole conversation. All of four words: two on each side. 'Hello' and 'Bye'.

But it was not as little as it seems at first glance. In actual fact this conversation was much longer than those four words. In actual fact it ran:

'Hello. You are in my thoughts.'

'And you are in mine.'

'But I am busy now. I have to go to work. Bye.'

'I respect the fact that you have to go to work. For a real man work is more important than for a woman. But after work you will come and see me. I will be waiting for you. Bye.'

That is what those four words – two from each side – actually meant.

But today everything would be different.

Today when he said, 'Hello,' she would reply, 'I'm tired of all this. I'm fed up with it all. I don't want this any more.'

He would be surprised and say, 'Why not?'

She would say, 'What is the point of questions?'

Her round alarm clock of antediluvian design showed three minutes past nine. Then four minutes past nine.

Fifty-six minutes later it showed ten o'clock precisely.

Nikolayev had not called! This ran contrary to all laws and customs. It was as if the sun had risen an hour later than usual, or had not risen at all.

Alyona looked from the alarm clock to the telephone, and from the telephone to the alarm clock, experiencing a sense of general confusion. She was afraid that this confusion would undo her plans, and that instead of saying her prepared phrases, she would instead shriek into the phone, 'Why haven't you rung? I've been sitting here waiting like an idiot . . .'

She wanted to go into the kitchen and put the kettle on, but was worried that the sound of running water would muffle all other noises; that of the telephone ringing, for example.

She stood for a while longer by the telephone, then got bored of standing there and went to sit down.

Time stopped around Alyona. But perhaps it was Alyona herself who had stopped, while time continued to flow slowly round her bare feet and frail face.

Alyona looked like Audrey Hepburn. If Audrey Hepburn had been cross-eyed in her right eye, then she would be a carbon copy of Elena Zhuravlyova, teacher of singing at the local elementary school.

Singing was not a compulsory subject and the children liked to assert their personalities during this class, both for their own benefit and also for that of the class. The responsible kids, in the person of the form captain and the other monitors, would always try and keep order, but very often things would degenerate into civil war. The responsible kids would end up attacking the bullies, and vice versa.

Whenever that happened, Alyona would endeavour to hide behind the piano, because she never knew which side to join, and was afraid of getting hit by both sides.

She was staring at the telephone, but in her mind's eye she was recalling a lesson with the fourth form.

Round-eyed, round-headed Afanasyev crowed twice like a cockerel, for no particular reason other than to set a generally frivolous tone to the lesson that had just begun. So then Zvonaryova the form captain – plump little Zvonaryova (she was an early developer) took hold of her satchel and hit Afanasyev smack in his chubby face. But unfortunately the back of his head hit the radiator and a large bump started appearing right in front of everyone's eyes, just like in the cartoons. This was an obvious abuse of power on Zvonaryova's part. A rumble started at the back of the class, like that of a volcano about to erupt.

For the first second Alyona froze with fear, but already in the second she was proclaiming loudly and passionately, 'There are two mysterious deaths in history, that of the Crown Prince Dmitry and that of the composer Mozart!'

Both the first and the second deaths had ceased to be mysteries a long time ago. In fact maybe they had never been mysteries anyway. It is well known that Dmitry was killed by Boris Godunov's people, and that Mozart died of tuberculosis. But Alyona had to find some way of transferring the children's attention from Zvonaryova to Boris Godunov's treachery, or anyone else's treachery for that matter. And if that meant coming up with another mystery, she would have been quite prepared to think one up herself, and, what is more, she would have passed it off as a genuine historical event without any qualms whatsoever.

The class soon forgot about Zvonaryova, Zvonaryova forgot about Afanasyev, and Afanasyev forgot about his bruises. They sat there with their mouths hanging open hearing all about the jealous Salieri and the easy-going, fun-loving Mozart.

Twenty minutes were devoted to Mozart and Salieri. Twenty remained. Time to learn a new song.

There was a children's song on the syllabus called 'We shall not stay at home'. But the children were not going to be interested in the official school repertoire, which had not been updated for decades. They wanted to sing what the grown-ups sang.

Alyona could not afford to risk losing their attention, and so she announced that they would learn the popular folk song 'Why do you lasses love handsome lads . . .'

First she dictated the words, then she played through the introduction with great gusto and the whole class launched with great inspiration into, 'The daisies are hiding, the buttercups have drooped their heads . . .' Afanasyev stretched out his neck and sang louder than anyone, putting as much into it as he could. He had a very good ear.

Form 9 were taking an algebra test next door, but no one could concentrate on the equations. They were all sitting there listening, carried away by their thoughts to distant places.

Even the teachers poked their heads out of the staff room. They also felt like singing a good song with a rousing accompaniment.

One day Alyona had decided that she would no longer let herself be commandeered by twelve-year-old children. She decided that she was going to rule them with a rod of iron: take control at the beginning of the lesson and keep it. It was precisely in this new frame of mind that Alyona had turned up to her next lesson with the fourth form, having focused within herself all her willpower and her well-intentioned strictness. But for some reason the children were still not frightened of her. They sat there quietly enough, but they looked at her with great scepticism, and as soon as she started to shout, someone laughed. Evidently there was a certain lack of conviction about her which could immediately be sensed by children and dogs, because dogs would bite her at the first opportunity, and children were disobedient with her. Nikolayev was not at all obedient or frightened either. He treated her love like a superfluous object.

The alarm clock now showed a quarter to eleven. She was a bit peckish. She remembered the way they had said goodbye the day before. She had looked into his eyes, while he continued to gaze at something somewhere above her. The whites of his eyes were slightly yellowish and there was a dour and very unpleasant expression on his face.

She went to the telephone and dialled Nikolayev's number. After all, why should she have to wait for him to ring her? She could ring him up herself. She could ring him and tell him everything.

A long, mournful ringing tone sounded in the receiver. First one, then another. The ringing tones were going out of his office. That was where his desk stood. It was his own space, all seven cubic metres of it, separated off from the general space which everyone else inhabited.

No one answered the phone for a long time. Alyona waited patiently, seeing Nikolayev's face in her mind.

Then suddenly an unfamiliar voice said, 'Hello.' Someone must have come into his office.

'Could I speak to Nikolayev, please?' asked Alyona, feeling somewhat taken aback by the strange voice.

'He's in a meeting with the director right now. Can I take a message?'

'No, it's all right, thanks.'

She could of course have passed on via another person the message: 'I'm tired. Fed up. Don't want any more of this.' But would that be honest with respect to the love that they had once shared? The beginnings of relationships are always interesting, and endings are always exactly the same. Nevertheless, their relationship deserved a different ending somehow. It was important to have respect for one's feelings, even ones that were no longer there.

But she couldn't say all those important things through a third party. She had to say them herself. And not on the telephone, either, but in person. She should turn up at his work looking glamorous and independent. She should arrive and say everything straight out. Then turn round and leave. And as that new song went, he could appeal, but he wouldn't get her back.

The establishment at which Nikolayev worked was called the Institute for Geo-Physical Research, or IGPR for short. Lots of junior and senior research assistants worked there, churning out dissertations for their doctorates. The ultimate goal of all their activities was to extract from the Earth another secret, like, for instance, electricity, so that in about ten years or so, it would be impossible to imagine life without the discovery which IGPR was working on at the moment.

It was difficult to say what that secret would be. Perhaps they would discover a new law of time, which would make it possible to plan things in advance. Then everyone would be able to make their lives as long as they wanted. Or stay for forty or fifty years at the same age, whatever you preferred.

But the Institute had not been able to extract from the Earth its greatest secret on this particular day. Instead it was simply compiling all kinds of materials on all kinds of topics which the research associates would one day turn into dissertations. One day a genius would turn up and make sense of it all by producing one solid idea from all this chaos. But the genius had not appeared yet. Perhaps he had not even been born yet. Or maybe he had been born, but he had not grown up yet. Or maybe he had grown up, left college, and was standing in the personnel office right now, waiting to be given a job. Or perhaps he had been working there for a long time already, but had not shown any initiative yet, and the director had called a meeting to single him out as a genius amongst the rest of his milieu.

Perhaps it was Nikolayev? That was not very likely, though. Nikolayev regarded science as an engine for self-promotion. It was the same as singing lessons with Afanasyev. Afanasyev only sang better than anybody in the class because he wanted to make everyone throw up their hands and say 'Well I never!' But he was not interested in singing for the sake of art. He was only interested in crowing.

Alyona had an acquaintance called Vova, who was her four-year-old neighbour. Alyona would crouch down when she ran into him and stroke his hair. 'You're such a clever boy, Vova,' she would say. 'And so handsome. You're better than everyone else.' And Vova would stare at her without blinking. Even his eyelashes would not move. If someone suddenly said to him, 'Vova, you're awful,' he would believe it, get thoroughly upset, and cry bitterly.

That was the sort of relationship Alyona had with Nikolayev. She would stroke his hair, saying, 'You're my favourite boy. You're the only one for me. You're so much nicer than everyone else . . .' And Nikolayev would also look into her eyes, and there would be an expression of deep attention on his face.

Alyona was being sincere when she said those things. But even if she had uttered a simple, banal piece of flattery, Nikolayev would not have noticed the difference.

This need to be reassured arose from a lack of self-confidence. Despite his apparent superiority complex, he still had an inferiority complex too. He did not believe in himself. And Alyona's faith in him was essential from the point of view of his retaining some kind of gravity. It stopped him from bobbing about on the surface, or from being carried off the face of the Earth by the wind.

It was just past two o'clock, and the meeting with the director was still going on. In front of the director's office sat a neatly presented secretary, the sort of woman whose age was indeterminate. She could have been thirty, but on the other hand maybe she was forty or even fifty.

She looked at Alyona with carefully concealed disapproval.

'What can I do for you?' she said.

'I need to see Nikolayev,' answered Alyona, sitting down in an independent sort of pose, crossing one leg over the other.

Alyona was afraid that Nikolayev would leave after the meeting without dropping by his office, which would mean she would have to come another day. And she could only come on Wednesdays, when she did not have singing lessons. The three days off a week, plus the three months of summer holidays, not counting the spring and Christmas vacations, were the best things about her poorly appreciated, badly paid job.

Male and female research associates were constantly passing by reception.

Alyona divided everyone up into men and women, and women she divided into those with eyebrows and those without.

The latest fashion advised women to pluck their

eyebrows to open up their eyes more. An open eye, it was said, is seen better by other people, and also sees better when it is not curtained by heavy brows. So that even if a woman hurrying about her business chanced to walk past happiness without noticing it, happiness would see her and tap her on the shoulder.

Alyona also divided men into two groups.

The first were those openly searching for something. They were openly searching for happiness and the meaning of life. These men were not only interested in the secrets of the Earth, they were also interested in the secrets of love. But they never usually found either, because to find one, you cannot afford to be distracted by the other. But there are some men who not only manage to do both, but even excel in both areas. It is precisely these men that the girls with plucked eyebrows try to single out from the crowd.

Then there was the second category – the men who were not searching for anything. Either they had found everything they wanted, or they had never been looking for anything in the first place. These people do not usually follow fashion, because they aren't at all interested in their external appearance.

It was the women with eyebrows and the men not searching for anything who were mostly passing by the reception. As they walked past, they looked first at Alyona with a certain degree of surprise, and then at the secretary, as if to ask 'What's this?' Not 'who', but 'what'.

Alyona was dressed not as if she was visiting a research institute during working hours, but a nightclub – the sort of place that stays open all night during film festivals. She was wearing satin culottes and a silver lamé top, out of which her young body peeped in some places and actually gaped in others. She had turned up from a Saturday night, and it was a weekday afternoon. She suspected that the people at the institute were thinking that she had come from a witches' gathering rather than some glamorous party. And not everyone goes to those sorts of things.

Suddenly Alyona felt like getting up and leaving, but just at that moment the door opened and people started pouring out of the director's office. They were almost all people not searching for anything, or they were hiding it carefully if they were.

In the middle of this cluster of people there was a heavy man with slightly baggy, sagging trousers.

Alyona was convinced that people were not necessarily descended from monkeys, but from all kinds of different animals. She thought she was descended from a cat, for example, and Nikolayev from a horse – a pony though, not a full-grown horse. Perhaps even a donkey. This person in the middle of the crowd was obviously descended from a lion. He had a heavy, regal face, with imposing features. Alyona guessed that this was the director. He was not talking, but everyone's attention was nevertheless focused on him, as the needle of a compass always points to north.

Someone was talking to the director with a great show of words and gestures. He was listening, but it was clear from his facial expression that he was not interested in what the person was saying. The director looked as if he was fed up with everything too. He hadn't suddenly become fed up today like Alyona. It happened to him about twenty years ago. And then he had felt fed up every day since then. This was a chronic, advanced stage of being fed up.

What was he fed up with? With his work? No. It seemed that he loved his work. Men do not get fed up with their work.

Maybe he was tormenting a woman and tormenting himself as well? Or maybe he was tormenting two women and was doubly tormenting himself?

The director was listening to a person whispering and spluttering into his ear that he was the genius whom they had been looking for, but had not found. The director must have heard all this more than once before. He wanted to say, 'Just shut up, will you, I've had enough of all this!' But it was not easy to interrupt, so he listened patiently with leaden eyes.

Alyona got up from the chair, her eyes darting from one person to the next. Nikolayev was not there. First of all she had a feeling he was not there, and then she saw that he really was not there. She could not have missed him – he really was not there.

She pushed her way through to the director.

'Where's Nikolayev?' she asked.

The director looked at Alyona as if she was a mobile object. Not a 'who', but a 'what'.

'Which Nikolayev?' he asked blankly.

'He works in the technical information department,' prompted people behind him.

'Nikolayev . . . ah yes,' remembered the director. 'Where is Nikolayev, in fact? Why isn't he here?'

'Perhaps he forgot,' suggested the person who had been whispering into his ear.

'Couldn't have . . .' said another.

'Why on earth not?' said the director, perking up. 'It's perfectly possible for him to have forgotten. He's a young man, after all. He doesn't have any responsibilities. No sense of self-importance yet!'

'Unlike you,' said Alyona bitterly.

'What do you mean?' said the director, turning to look at Alyona. There was a spark of interest in his eyes.

'He spent three months working on a blueprint for you, and you went and lost it.'

'Which blueprint?'

'Well, it wasn't exactly a blueprint . . . more a technical drawing, but he sat up working on it from morning till night. He couldn't talk about anything else. He went quite crazy about that drawing. And you lost it.'

'I did?'

'Well, not you personally. But one of you did. Someone senior.'

'How did this happen?'

'How should I know? Maybe someone put it down somewhere, then forgot about it. Or maybe whoever it was left it in a taxi because they were drunk . . .'

'Why don't I know anything about this? Where is Nikolayev anyway?'

'That's exactly what I've been asking.'

The director looked around those present.

'I haven't seen him today,' someone said.

'Maybe he's ill,' another suggested.

'Perhaps he really is ill . . .' mused Alyona dreamily. 'He's got chronic bronchitis, after all, and he does catch cold so easily.'

'And who are you? How are you connected to him?' asked the director.

'I'm not connected to him,' remembered Alyona. 'At least not from today anyway . . . And as far as his dissertation goes, the fact that he isn't getting on with it is actually more honest, I think. Everyone is writing them these days, it seems. That's what comes of universal literacy. You can't move for Ph.D. candidates.'

The director looked at Alyona placidly, in the way that a lion might look at a cat. Maybe he felt a certain kinship with her. After all, a lion is a sort of cat when it comes down to it.

'Well, I'd better be going,' Alyona announced. And off she went, wending her way festively through all those working people. Before she disappeared behind the door, she turned and bade a polite goodbye to the secretary.

*

76

Nikolayev did not have a phone. He lived in a new district, and telephones were only going to be installed there in a few years' time.

Nikolayev's mother opened the door. She was a coquettish old lady – one of those 'eternal women'. In private Alyona used to call her Little Toad. Toad would have been rude, but the diminutive was just right.

Nikolayev was joined to his mother as if they had forgotten to sever the umbilical cord when he was born. It was as if they shared the same blood circulation even now. He was getting on for thirty-two, but he was still attached to the Little Toad's apron strings with a large safety pin.

When she was younger, Alyona used to tease boys like that that they were sissies. There was one living in their building at the moment. He probably had a name, but no one ever called him by it. Everyone called him Sissy.

Sometimes Nikolayev would rebel and disappear. The Little Toad never worried though. She knew that one day her little frog would come back to the marsh again, so she could feed him worms and maggots. And one day she would take him to meet Thumbelina. That's how it was.

'I had two children already by your age,' the Little Toad once said to Alyona, who understood exactly what she was really saying. What she meant was, 'Go and get married, start a family, and don't waste any more time with my son. Nothing will happen between you anyway.'

Alyona and the Little Toad did not like each other. For no particular reason; it was just that the chemistry between them was wrong. Or maybe there was a reason: Nikolayev. For each of them he was the sole object of their love, and they both wanted to possess him without having to share him.

'Hello,' said Alyona.

'Good afternoon,' answered the Little Toad, rather

surprised by the appearance of Alyona in her militant plumage.

'Is Sasha at home?' asked Alyona.

'He's at work,' replied the Little Toad very politely, feeling almost sympathetic that Alyona had not settled down and got married yet, and was still running after her son with no prospects at all.

'He's not at work. I've just come from there.'

'I don't know where he is, then. He told me he was going to work, anyway.'

Alyona wanted to say 'Toad' to her. But she got the better of her feelings and simply said, 'Goodbye.'

She walked down to the ground floor and went out on to the street.

The little square in front of the building was covered with greenery. A tall, angular old woman was walking round it, taking large steps round it like a monk, dragging a hose behind her.

Alyona stopped and thought for a moment. Nikolayev had gone to work, but he had not arrived. So something must have happened. Perhaps he had fallen under a bus?

She lifted up her head, searching for Nikolayev's flat.

The Little Toad appeared immediately in the window and even from there it was possible to see the look of fright on her face. She had obviously had the same thought as Alyona – certain situations produce certain trains of thought.

'Vera Petrovna!' Alyona called out.

The Little Toad leaned her head out of the window.

'You don't know where accidents get reported, do you?'

The Little Toad instantly disappeared again; perhaps she had collapsed in a faint.

Alyona waited for a while, then carried on walking, deep in thought, to the bus stop.

If Nikolayev had been run over, then he would

probably have been taken to the Sklifosovsky Hospital. She could ask for a white coat and go and visit him in the ward, and then lie down carefully next to him on the bed. Nikolayev would lie in her aura, as if he was lying in a warm bath, and would feel no more pain and no more fear. She would move her lips up close to his ear and ask softly, 'Can you hear me?'

He would open and close his eyelashes, as if nodding to say yes.

'I'm tired of this,' Alyona would whisper. 'I'm fed up. I don't want this any more.'

He would lower his eyelashes on to his cheeks. A small, opaque tear would run from the corner of his eye to his ear.

Nikolayev had gone to work but he had never arrived. Maybe something really had happened to him. Or maybe it was something else, or rather someone else.

Alyona stopped in her tracks, puzzled by the mystery of it all. She remembered that Nikolayev had not gone to work once before, when they were at the beginning of their relationship. At that time Alyona was more important to him then than all the secrets of the Earth put together. He was not afraid of getting into trouble for not going to work, nor of any punishment that might be meted out to him. Instead of going off to work that day, he had taken Alyona off to the cinema instead. Then from the cinema to a café. And afterwards they had wandered through the streets, arm in arm.

The same thing had happened today. The same behaviour; the same words. But why on earth should he have to think up new words and behave in a different way? The object of his love might have changed, but he was exactly the same. And he was bound to go on expressing his feelings in the same way.

He and the Other Woman were probably in the cinema right now, the same one they had gone to, sitting elbow to elbow, and shoulder to shoulder. He would be watching the screen, but she would be looking at him. He would turn to her and nod in the direction of the screen as if to say, look over there. But she would continue to look at him, and then he would look at her, and their eyes would twinkle in the darkness.

Who knows what a person thinks about in the last seconds of their life? No one has ever been able to talk about it. But Alyona thought it quite feasible that in her last moments she would see his bright eyes twinkling in the shadows. It would be better if he really had been run over and was in the other world, rather than in this one, with the Other Woman.

They would have just come out of the cinema and gone into a café. He would be eating with his mouth closed, with his eyes glued to the Other Woman, not understanding how he could ever have been in love with anyone but her. She would be prettier than Alyona – younger and more elegant, and the Little Toad would like her too. Nikolayev would entertain her according to his usual programme. First of all he would tell her about his childhood, in which he would portray himself as a starving urchin rather than a spoilt mummy's boy. Then would come the Institute of Geo-Physics, where he was not just a show-off, but a serious scholar, struggling with new ideas. The director had tried to understand him, but Nikolayev would not lower himself to the level where he could be understood by other people. No one could understand him . . . The Other Woman would place her delicate hand on his cheek and say, 'But I understand you. You're better than everyone else. You are the only one for me.' And Nikolayev would take her hand from his cheek and kiss each finger. And then she would lean over and kiss his hands, also finger by finger. She would know about Alyona of course. She would call her 'your little singing teacher', and he would be mute with embarrassment, as if he wanted to apologize for his past with his silence.

The words 'Your ticket please,' sounded above Alyona's ear.

She came back down into the real world to discover that two women were standing over her, and she was sitting in a bus. Alyona could not remember how she had got on to the bus, nor could she understand what these strange women wanted from her. She raised her grief-filled eyes to them, then got up from her seat and walked away without looking at anyone.

Momentarily stunned, the women stood back and let her pass.

'Shameless hussy,' someone said behind her back.

'Young too. How can people be so dishonest?'

Alyona got out at a stop called Festival Street. What sort of street was it? How had she ended up here? She must have been going in the wrong direction. Or she had got on the wrong bus. Most likely both.

A beaten-up old mongrel was lying by a lamppost near to where she was standing. A car must have hit it and someone dragged it over to the side of the road. It was large, white and dirty, and Alyona saw it as a model of her future life.

Those two were sitting in the café right now. Eating and drinking in the warm. They were there, and she was here, at the other end of town, rejected, hungry, and a shameless hussy in the eyes of society as well.

But meanwhile, life had been taking its usual course. Evening was wafting along to take the place of day, and the clouds stood majestically in the sky, indifferent to everything taking place on Earth: what is one life in the overall scheme of things anyway? Stray dogs were roaming around looking for food and affection.

What should she do? How should she stand up for herself?

Maybe she should throw herself out of the window in front of him? He would remember her then. He would not be able to forget her even if he wanted to. Her dead body would come between him and the Other Woman and drag them apart.

But why bother killing herself, when she could kill him?

Alyona suddenly felt a sharp coldness, and she started choking. Then water was pouring down her in streams.

A lorry hosing the streets was going by. The driver leaned out to shout something. It sounded as if he was angry.

The vehicle continued on its way, but Alyona was still standing by the bus stop. Her hair was drooping, her mascara was running down her face in little black streams, her trousers were clinging to her legs, and there was water dripping into her shoes. Nikolayev and the Other Woman were walking around the city and could turn down Festival Street any minute. They would walk past Alyona hand in hand, united by the joy they were both feeling.

Nikolayev would recognize Alyona and say 'Hello' to her. She would say 'Hello' to him. Then he would say 'Bye,' and she would say 'Bye.' They would walk past, but after a few moments the Other Woman would turn round and swiftly run her eyes over Alyona.

He was the one who was fed up with everything. He was the one who didn't want things to go on any more. But she was the one running all over town after him to tell him those eight words. She felt as humiliated as if their meeting had actually happened. But the humiliation soon transformed itself into a feeling of self-respect, and the new feeling would not let her stand there any longer.

She set off along Festival Street, but it was uncomfortable walking in wet shoes, so she took them off, and walked along the warm asphalt barefoot, carrying her shoes in her hand. People walking in the opposite direction turned and stared at her in amazement as she went by, feeling secretly envious. They too wanted to take their clammy shoes off, and walk along lightly and airily, as they had done in their childhood. But for various reasons none of them were free. They were all constrained by different circumstances.

The lift in Alyona's building was not working. It was not working precisely because her last strength was drained. If she had been in a good mood, the lift would have been in full working order. Alyona had been noticing such coincidences in her life for a while now, and she had even derived a law from them which she called the 'law of meanness'.

The law of meanness was in operation today, so Alyona had to walk up to the eleventh floor by foot. She felt as if she was walking on the valves of her heart rather than on her feet.

On the tenth floor, Alyona paused to catch her breath. One more flight of stairs, one last effort, and she could shut herself off from the world: from people and clouds, buses and dogs. She could walk into her unhappiness as if she was entering an empty, echoing church, and let no one in.

At this particular minute, she did not want anything at all. But when her feelings returned to her, she would not want to die or to kill anyone. She would just want to hold out.

Nikolayev was sitting on the stairs in front of her door and looked as if he was dozing. But when he saw Alyona, he lifted his head and stood up. He looked at her without blinking, his eyes just like those of a horse, or a pony. But then ponies, horses, and donkeys all have the same eyes when it comes down to it. They may be different sizes, but basically they are pretty much the same. There was something brittle and joyless about the way he looked that reminded one of a butterfly, the Camberwell beauty in particular. He exuded a kind of lugubrious charm.

Alyona swallowed her alarm, so that it would not stick in her throat. It went away for a moment, but then it came back again in her throat, and made it difficult for her to breathe.

'I've been looking for you since twelve o'clock,' said Alyona.

'And I've been waiting for you since twelve o'clock,' said Nikolayev.

'Do you know something?'

'Yes . . .'

They lurched towards each other and stood there stock still, locked in an embrace.

Alyona hugged him as if he were her own son who had left the battle zone and was shortly to return to it. She hugged him as if he were some magnificent cowboy in a broad-rimmed stetson, and there was no one strong enough to pull them apart.

She breathed in short gasps, like a child who has been crying. Like the scorched earth breathing after a rainfall. Everything was clear except for one thing: why she, Elena Andreyevna Zhuravlyova, such an attractive, forward-looking person, who was capable of steadfast feelings, why out of all the male population in the country she had to pick Nikolayev, who was a sissy and a show-off, and who also happened to be the same height as her.

This was one of the secrets of the Earth that was never going to be unravelled. But then there wasn't any need for it to be.

Nikolayev left later that evening.

Alyona waited for him to say something to her other than 'Bye, then.' She looked straight at him, but his gaze wandered off somewhere above her head. The whites of his eyes were tinted with yellow, and his expression was the one she did not like.

Then he said, 'Bye, then.' And left.

The lift was not working, so he ran down the stairs, and the rhythmic patter of his footsteps could be heard for some time.

Alyona awoke the next morning feeling fed up with everything.

COINCIDENCE

Claudia Ivanovna Prokhorenko, employee of Postal Services Centre No. 483 (otherwise known as old Claudie from the post office) stuck it out until the end of the day and then beetled straight round to the grocer's.

The grocer's was in the same building as the post office, but it was on the opposite side, while on the third and fourth sides of the building there were some shops, a dry cleaner's, a cafeteria, and a hairdresser's with a beauty salon attached to it.

All these conveniences had been installed next to the hostel for foreign students. The idea was that the students would have everything from a post office to a hairdresser's right at hand, and would not have to run all over town.

Claudie went into the grocer's. The students in their bright clothes were stalking about like tropical birds stranded in the Antarctic. What do they need a hairdresser for? thought Claudie as she looked at the curly black hair of the coloured students. They'd look the same whether someone did their hair or not . . .

There wasn't much in the meat department by the end of the day. The imported chickens in their attractive polythene packaging were frozen hard as rocks. They looked as though they had been slaughtered several centuries BC and then kept in permafrost until the present day.

Claudie scanned the counter without interest and decided to go to the market.

Going to the market always excited her, like the dance floor used to all that time ago when she was young. It was the element of choice and the possibility of something nice happening which excited her. And even now as she was passing through the arched gates of the Cheremushkinsky Market, she felt that long-forgotten tightening in her chest again.

The market greeted her with all the bounty of autumn, although just outside the entrance it was actually spring – all grimy and lacking in vitamins.

Flowers were sold just inside the door. Utterly segregated from their earthbound proprietors, they maintained a detached existence in buckets of water.

People said that those flowers had been frozen; that their crafty owners had doused them with some secret solution so they would always wilt the moment you got them home. Maybe that was true. But looking at the fragile loveliness of the peonies and roses on display, it was difficult to believe that their beauty had a life-span, and would one day fade.

There wasn't any meat at the market. The people from the collective farms had obviously sold out by the end of the morning, handed in their scales, and gone back to their villages. Claudie meandered about between the stalls for a long time without purchasing anything, then bought herself a bag of pumpkin seeds and headed towards the exit.

Right by the exit, she ran into a tall, thin woman wearing an unzipped anorak. A little chick was craning its neck to peep its head out of the anorak. It was a bit manky and rather grubby, and looked a bit like a baby eagle that had taken to drink.

'How much is that goose?' asked Claudie, removing the husk of a pumpkin seed from her lip.

The woman looked Claudie carefully up and down, from her fox-fur hat to her crêpe-soled shoes, and said, 'You're the goose, missus . . .'

*

All the seats were taken in the bus. Claudie surveyed the other passengers, hoping to catch someone's guiltily averted eye. But the other passengers were either reading their newspapers with great concentration or staring out through the dusty windows, thinking about their lives.

Claudie steadied herself and also tried to look straight ahead in a nonchalant fashion, but a sense of injury could be clearly discerned in her proud, tired eyes.

The grievance lay not in the fact that everyone was sitting down and that Claudie was standing up. That did not matter. What hurt most was that Claudie was the only person standing in the whole bus. It was just for her that there was no room. And that's how it always was.

God had probably ordained Claudie to be a failure, and in all the fifty years she had spent on Earth so far he had never let her deviate once from his initial idea.

If Claudie ever fell in love, for example, it was never with the right person, even though the 'right' person might have been standing next to her. If she was ever ill, there were always complications. If she ever stood in a queue for something, then the whatever it was would always run out right in front of her nose. And if an atomic war were ever to break out, and a bomb was dropped on Moscow, then it would definitely fall right on Claudie's head.

A young couple jumped on to the bus and went to stand near Claudie. They couldn't care less whether there were any seats or not. The boy immediately flung his right arm around the girl's shoulders, his bony elbow poised right above Claudie's ear. That sort of discourtesy upset her. She felt an uneasy sense of expectation, like before a blood test, when you know you are about to get a needle jabbed into your finger.

The bus suddenly made a sharp turn and almost keeled over on to one side. The young man tilted over with the bus, and his elbow landed squarely on Claudie's head.

'Couldn't you try to be a little more careful?' asked Claudie wearily, as if she had been expecting just such a thing to happen.

The boy glanced at her hurriedly, said 'Sorry,' and moved aside. The girl also looked briefly at Claudie and her amiable expression seemed to say, 'It must be awful being so fat and having to wear a hat like that.'

When Claudie arrived home, she took the little chick out of her bag. Its claws were tied together with a scrap of red satin.

She undid the knot, unwound the piece of material, and stood the chick on its legs, but it promptly fell over on to one side. She stood it up once more, but it fell over again, its round orange eyes staring impassively upwards.

Claudie stood for a while by the chick and then went to ring up her friend Zinaida. Zinaida also worked at the post office; she sat behind the community services window.

Zinaida had two conflicting passions in her life: love and hatred. The love for her daughter and the hatred for her son-in-law. Whenever her son-in-law was moving about the flat, Zinaida would weep silent tears of incurable, debilitating hatred. This feeling of hatred lived with her constantly and expressed itself with a raucous voice. They had tried to live apart, and even swapped their flat for two rooms in different areas of the city. But once she had lost the opportunity to hate her son-in-law, Zinaida felt a sense of emptiness in her soul, which was like a gaping hole left by a bullet. In the end, she just could not go on living with this hole any longer, and so finally she moved back in with her daughter, and went on with her loving and hating in even less space than before.

'Zin, that you?' asked Claudie, hearing a familiar voice.

'He's scoffing cheese without bread!' shrieked Zinaida. 'I said to him, I said, "Why aren't you having some bread with it?" And he said, "I don't want to get fat." That's the limit, that is. I mean any fool is going to want to gobble up everything nice without bread given half a chance, aren't they?'

'Mmmm . . .' said Claudie, making a show of sympathy. 'Listen, I bought a chicken at the bazaar, but it's ill . . .'

'How much did you get it for?'

'It was only a rouble.'

'Well, of course it's going to be ill, then,' said Zinaida. The train of her thoughts must have been the following: a chick is a small hen, which will soon grow up and be worth a lot more, so nobody in their right minds would sell you something for a rouble which is actually worth five . . . An unhealthy chick is not worth anything at all, so you're doing pretty well if you can get a rouble for something which in general has absolutely no value at all.

'They must have gone round the whole market looking for a moron like you,' Zinaida added.

Claudie remembered the sullen woman in the anorak. Perhaps she really had stood there the whole day, waiting for the only moron in the whole city to turn up. Another fat drop fell into Claudie's cup of endurance.

'But do chickens really get sick?' asked Claudie doubtfully.

'Of course they do! Their livers can even get inflamed.'

'And do they get given medicine?'

'What sort of medicine do they make for chickens, I'd like to know? Under the knife and into the soup more like. Don't even think about cooking it, anyway . . .' warned Zinaida. 'Just forget it. To hell with the rouble.'

'But what am I going to do with it?'

'Just chuck it out!'

'But it's alive!'

The two women fell silent for a moment, then Zinaida said, 'Yesterday, you know, he came out of the bathroom, then he sat down in the chair and began cutting his toenails. They were flying all over the place, and getting stuck in the carpet. And who do you think has got to clear them up? I said to him, "You might at least have put a bit of newspaper underneath . . ."'

'Look, I've got to go,' said Claudie pensively. 'I've got someone here . . .'

The chick was lying there, surrendering to its fate, its eyes half-covered by a transparent film.

Claudie got a three-litre jar of rice down from the shelf, and sprinkled a few grains into her hand. Then she lifted the chick's head and cradled it carefully in her palm. She felt its sharp little beak, the slight heaviness of its head, and the warmth only barely coming through its long, drooping neck.

The chick remained immobile, and didn't even bother to open its eyes.

'It's not eating,' Claudie confirmed. Her soul filled with a sudden sadness. She too felt like lying down like the chick and closing her eyes.

She looked out of the window. Outside there were some old ladies walking with children. The weather was dank, and the old ladies were standing motionless, with their backs to the wind, and their heads and shoulders drawn into their shoulders like penguins. Meanwhile the children ran around yelling and shrieking, bursting with all the joys of life. It seemed as if there was one kind of weather for the old ladies and another for the kids. Children live nearer to the ground, so maybe there was a different climate down there.

Claudie transferred her gaze back to the sorrowful profile of her little chick and suddenly remembered that chickens like worms.

She took from the stove the empty tin she put used matches into and got out an aluminium spoon. Then she put on her jacket and went outside.

For a while she stood around with the old women, joining in their conversation, then she contrived to separate herself from them, as if it just happened by chance. She went round the corner of the building, looked around on all sides, then took out the spoon and the tin from under her jacket.

Placing her feet apart the width of her shoulders to steady herself, she bent over, wheezing, and started scraping at the earth energetically with the spoon.

The earth was all hard, compressed by the cold and by the roots of the grass which had not started to spring up yet.

Within seconds geometric shapes were dancing before Claudie's eyes, as she was not very well suited to standing for a long time with her head bent over. She straightened up and saw through the twinkling shapes the very real figure of eight-year-old Lenka Zvonaryova.

'Are you doing community service?' asked Lenka, nodding with her head at the freshly dug hole in the earth.

'No, I'm digging for worms,' Claudie answered nervously.

'Are they to feed your fish?'

Claudie did not reply, because she didn't really want to open up her soul to Lenka.

'We buy ready-made food for our fish,' boasted Lenka. 'From the pet shop.'

There was less than an hour till the pet shop closed, so Claudie went zooming off there in a taxi.

Something had gone wrong with the system of permanent bad luck – a valve must have gone somewhere – because Claudie had an endless run of good luck that evening. The shop was still open when she got there, the fish food did not run out in front of her nose, the taxi flew over the asphalt as if it was airborne, and the taxi driver did not just sit there, detached from all Claudie's little worries, but was helpful and concerned, like a true accomplice.

True, the whole excursion to the other end of town and back cost her as much as if she had bought a healthy, fully-grown chicken. But Claudie had forgotten about all of that. She flew over the asphalt, holding two packets carefully on her lap: one seething with tiny pink maggots, the other containing some sort of powder that looked like ground-up desiccated flies.

A week went by. The chick got better and started running about the flat, scratching at the parquet with its sinewy claws.

Claudie washed it in the bath with a special baby shampoo from Poland, which had an absurdly childish name.

Zinaida's warning that chickens should never be bathed because they might die from it unfortunately came too late.

Claudie did not sleep all night. She kept lifting her head from her pillow to look into the corner where the chick was dozing, rolled up into a dark little bundle. It was sitting with its head sunk on to its breast, its claws gripping the back of the chair. That was its perch.

In the morning it became clear that the chicken had not died from having been bathed. In fact it had become extremely beautiful. Its feathers now shone a brilliant white, its claws were a beautiful pale yellow and its comb blazed with a fiery redness above its orange eyes, in which an ungrateful and wayward look could be observed.

Soon the cockerel began to develop certain habits that must have been instilled by instinct, because Claudie certainly couldn't have taught them to it. At four o'clock in the morning, for example, it would start crowing to greet the new day. Its crowing was not exactly full-blooded and virile, but actually rather rusty and squeaky, though even that was quite enough to make Claudie wake up. She would then lie for hours, waiting for the shadow from the windowpane to stretch out down to the floor.

She soon began to be frightened that the cockerel would bother the neighbours on the other side of the wall, so she put a rubber band from a medicine bottle round its beak, and only took it off when it was feeding.

She also never opened a window, fearing that her little chick would fly off like a crane into the skies, or would clamber out on to the balcony and get caught by Lusya, the neighbours' cat.

Lusya prowled up and down the balcony all day. Sometimes she would get up on her hind paws and press her whiskers against the glass door to gaze at the furniture inside with her beautiful sinful eyes.

In the evenings, Claudie would settle down with the cockerel in front of the TV. They would watch every single programme from beginning to end, their eyes glued to the set, as if they had to write a review for the newspaper the next day.

Claudie would sit in the armchair with the cockerel on her lap, craning its neck to look at the screen. It was obviously hypnotized by the grey and white blobs moving about.

They liked watching the European ice-skating championships best of all. Sometimes the cameraman would turn his camera on to the audience, and then you could see the fans: jolly old men covered with badges, neatly coiffured old ladies, and pretty young girls with flowing locks.

And then Zinaida would ring up, bringing her sorrows out to graze.

'Do you know what time he turned up last night?' Zinaida asked ominously one time.

'It's fine while he's still small,' Claudie replied anxiously. 'But when he grows up, I'm worried he's going to start pining . . .'

'Who are you talking about?' Zinaida asked with complete incomprehension.

'The cockerel.'

'To hell with you and your bloody cockerel!'

'To hell with you and your wretched son-in-law as well,' retorted Claudie as she put the receiver down.

Life carried on at its regular pace, familiar and boring. And bad moods followed good moods, not for any apparent reason, but just to maintain the correct emotional balance. Then one day while she was at work at Post Office No. 483, Claudie suddenly refused to distribute the lottery tickets.

Mr Koryagin, the post office manager, interpreted this uncharacteristic behaviour as a sign that Claudie was getting run down, so he summoned her to his office, and offered her a free trip to a sanatorium in Yalta.

It would have been good to catch up with the summer, to stand by the edge of the sea and look at the white ships and the furry palms. It would also have been good to go on holiday in spring, so that one's colleagues could take their vacations during the summer.

'I can't go,' said Claudie, looking into Koryagin's trustworthy eyes.

'Why not?'

'I've got . . . someone at home who needs looking after.' Claudie wanted to say the word 'chick' but she could not bring herself to. Koryagin might have thought that she was into animal husbandry and was breeding chickens on the side to make money.

'Who is that?' Koryagin asked, both amazed and irritated.

'Pete . . .'

'What, you mean he can't heat up things for himself?'

Claudie bit her lip.

'He's younger than you, is he?' guessed Koryagin.

Claudie stopped to think: chickens had a different life-span, so their age had to be calculated differently.

'I don't know,' she said. 'He might be younger, but then again he might be the same age.'

She went back to her department.

Zinaida was sitting on the telephone, ignoring the queue of people lined up in front of her window. Her son-in-law had been taken to hospital with a stomach ulcer. Doctors claim that the only ground for an ulcer is intense stress, and Zinaida suspected that she had ploughed that ground with her own bare hands. Now she was being plagued by her conscience, and was ringing home every half an hour and asking, 'So, how is our little poppet doing, then?'

A brightly coloured caravan of Japanese students in expensive jackets tripped past the window, looking like so many Christmas-tree baubles from a golden childhood. Some girls with fair hair who looked like Russians also walked past. Perhaps they were Russians . . .

One evening the phone rang. Claudie was convinced that it was going to be Zinaida ringing up again to moan about her son-in-law, but it turned out to be Ed, a friend from earlier days. He had actually been named Industry in the spirit of the times, but that was a bit of a mouthful, it had to be said, and not very practical for everyday use.

The phone line crackled and hissed and his voice sounded very far away. Claudie thought he must be ringing from the other side of the world; his voice seemed to be struggling through several continents.

'What are you up to?' Ed shouted, as if they had last seen each other the day before, rather than thirty-four years ago.

'You mean what am I doing?' Claudie answered with surprise. 'I'm watching TV.'

'Why don't you come over to the Hotel Yunost?' invited Ed.

Claudie could just imagine how it would be in the hotel with her in her unfashionable wool coat, and the attendant on the floor asking her where she was going.

'Actually, it would be better if you came over here,' said Claudie.

The first time she had seen Ed was before the war, at a gymnastics display. He had run around with a megaphone shouting out orders to the gymnasts, and they had obeyed him. He was dressed in a white shirt, white trousers, and a white cap. He was all white and all over the place, enthralled with the fascination of power.

Claudie had taken one look at Ed and was mesmerized by him. The problem was that she could not demesmerize herself, so she ran after him for a whole year. But he was running away from her at the same speed, so the distance between them never decreased an inch. And then even when he put his arms round her and every cell of her body tingled with joy at their being so close, Claudie could still feel that same distance between them.

And then one fine day Ed accelerated full speed ahead and simply vanished. Claudie was left behind, feeling as if a cold bullet had lodged in her stomach: she could not breathe, she could not bend over, she could not stand up straight. Then eventually the bullet somehow went away and it became possible to get on with her life again.

She sighed and put some potatoes on to boil. She wanted to put on something different to wear, but then she looked at herself in the mirror and changed her mind. Instead all she did was sprinkle herself liberally with talcum powder, which turned her nose chalk-white and her glasses all misty.

There was a ring at the door.

Claudie went to open it. On the doorstep stood a man with a briefcase in a coat that was all askew – the buttons must have been sewn on wrongly. He was also wearing a green felt hat with a wide brim, like the ones you see in the early portraits of Maxim Gorky.

Claudie did not recognize Ed, but she realized it had to be him because she wasn't expecting anyone else. They looked at each other for a while without saying a word, then Ed bellowed in disappointment, 'Good Heavens, just look at what's happened to you!'

Claudie felt embarrassed and rather upset. Deep down she thought she had changed very little. Certainly less than other people anyway.

Ed stepped inside and took off his coat and hat. He turned out to be bald, and was wearing a fashionable polo-necked sweater made out of acrylic.

'And you said you lived in Moscow!' he said reproachfully.

'It's a very nice area,' said Claudie defensively. 'There are even foreigners living here, you know, from Africa.'

'Poor blighters won't be ready for this then, if they're from Africa. All they've got out there is the Sahara Desert.'

They went inside the flat. The cockerel was standing on the windowsill on its pale yellow legs and looking out of the window. It didn't turn round to look at who had come into the room; something had evidently caught its attention.

'What, can't you buy chicken here?' asked Ed in amazement.

'Oh yes, you can,' Claudie replied.

They went into the kitchen. It was cosier in there and more comfortable.

Ed opened his briefcase, and took out a bottle of vodka and a couple of lampreys. There were precisely two of them; one for him and one for her.

Claudie had put out on the table everything she happened to have in the flat: pickled gherkins from the market, cold lamb with garlic, and some fishcakes which could pass for chicken with a bit of imagination. She drained the potatoes and then fried them up with a big knob of butter, some crushed garlic, and some breadcrumbs.

They each drank a glass of vodka.

'Dearie me, just look at what's happened to you!' said Ed again, snorting. Perhaps he thought that Claudie hadn't heard him the first time.

She wanted to say, 'You can talk!' but instead she held her tongue, and put a piece of meat in golden red aspic on a plate for him.

'You don't half live well, though!' he said approvingly.

'And how about you? How are you doing?'

'I'm in advertising. I've come up to Moscow on publishing business.'

Ed put his briefcase on his lap and took out of it a brochure with a black cover. On it were written the words 'The Garden of Happy Memories' in white letters.

'What sort of garden is this?' asked Claudie.

'It's a cemetery,' said Ed, starting to eat.

Claudie continued to look at the brochure out of politeness.

'It's a tough market,' said Ed. 'I'll be glad to get out of it.'

'Which market?' asked Claudie in confusion. For some reason she had a picture of the Cheremushkinsky Market in her mind.

'Well, my life has gone by,' said Ed. 'And it's brought nothing good.'

'There must have been some nice things.'

'Hey, do you remember being in love with me?' Ed asked suddenly.

'No,' Claudie replied firmly. 'I don't.'

'I remember, though. No one else ever loved me like you did.'

'So are you married?' asked Claudie.

Ed told her that his wife was dead and buried, and then he started crying. Claudie looked at his mouth, all horseshoe shaped, like a disappointed child's, and then she started crying too. A quiet, cosy sadness crept on tiptoes into the kitchen.

'How about getting married?' Ed asked abruptly.

'Whatever for?' answered Claudie in naïve surprise.

'So we could grow old together.'

'But I don't love you any more,' Claudie said apologetically.

'I'm not asking you to love me, just to get old with me,' Ed explained. 'Some bride you'd make . . .'

The cockerel came into the kitchen at that point. It had obviously got bored standing on the windowsill.

It started flapping its wings and then flew into the air, planning to land on the back of the chair, which was its usual perch. But the chair turned out to be occupied by the guest. So it flew a tiny bit higher than usual and landed on Ed's shoulder. Ed jerked his shoulder, which made the cockerel fall on to his plate, so then he picked it up roughly by its wing with two fingers and flung it into the corner of the kitchen.

And after that everything happened very quickly, but at the same time very slowly.

The cockerel lay in the corner for what seemed a very short time – three or four seconds at the most. Then it picked itself up, and, with its legs whirring and its neck stretched out, it made a beeline for Ed and bit him on the leg, just below the knee.

Ed lashed out with his foot, and the cockerel went flying back to its previous position, which once again gave it sufficient room for a running start.

'I've got thrombo-phlebitis! It'll peck through to my veins!' Ed shrieked. He started jiggling his legs about whilst still seated, thinking this would decrease his chances of being attacked.

Claudie rushed into the hall and grabbed her coat from the hook in order to throw it on either the cockerel or Ed, whichever was easier.

But when she got back to the kitchen, she found the following spectacle: the cockerel was flying around Ed's head, while he was flapping his arms out in front of him, as if he was trying to learn doggy-paddle. They were fighting tooth and nail, and white feathers were gliding elegantly about the kitchen.

Claudie plunged into the epicentre of the conflict and jumped back out of it again, clutching the cockerel. It croaked hoarsely in the depths of her coat and was struggling to get back into the battle.

Ed slumped on to a chair, his strength completely drained.

'Ill-bred creature,' he groaned.

'You started it,' Claudie said in defence.

That was the last straw as far as Ed was concerned. He got up and went out into the hall. He pulled on his coat, pushed the buttons through the huge loose buttonholes, put his hat on, and left.

'Some bridegroom!' said Claudie with contempt at the closed door. 'Call yourself a writer!'

She let the cockerel down on to the floor, then went over to open the window, in order to let some fresh air into the place.

Outside the window there was complete darkness.

The wind was pressing on the glass, and the blast that came in through the open window was as strong as in a storm on the open seas. People said that two winds met in the south-west area of Moscow, the southerly and the westerly, and that the vortex created where they converged was situated exactly above their block.

Claudie imagined Ed walking along holding on to his hat, his forehead buttressing into the wind. She remembered his serious intentions towards her and suddenly felt rather sorry.

On the edge of the table sat a pair of glasses in a plain dark frame, which Ed had left behind. Claudie grabbed them and ran out of the flat.

She caught up with him at the bus stop, when he was already getting on to the bus, and shoved the glasses into his pocket.

'When are we going to meet up next?' Ed shouted. 'And where?'

Claudie looked carefully at the hat which now crowned his head instead of his former white cap.

'In the Garden of Happy Memories!' Claudie shouted and ran back home, pushed onwards by the prevailing wind. The experience of running was a forgotten pleasure.

When Claudie got home, the cockerel was not there to meet her. The window was swinging on its hinges and creaking, and a small feather lay on the windowsill, white on white.

Claudie felt that everything had died and stopped within her; all her organs seemed to have ceased their usual functions.

She undid the latch and pulled open the balcony door. Dust flew everywhere, leaving bare the dirty grey cotton wool used for insulation in the winter.

She went out on to the balcony and looked up and down, but the cockerel was nowhere to be seen.

All there was to be seen was a great emptiness beneath the cupola of the sky and four identical, tall buildings. The last one had been built during the winter, while her balcony had been sealed up.

Claudie went on to her neighbour's balcony and knocked on the door.

Nothing stirred for a long while, but then the blinds were finally drawn back like theatre curtains, and Claudie's neighbours, a newly married student couple, appeared behind the glass. They stood close together, as if in front of a camera lens, and stared at the figure of Claudie looming up at them from out of the darkness, her hair sticking up on end from the wind.

'What's happened?' asked the young man as he opened the door. He held on to the balcony door with one hand, while covering his legs with the net curtains with the other. This strange apparel made him look like a Hindu.

'Is your cat at home?' asked Claudie.

'Yes, it's asleep,' said the girl. 'Why, what's happened?'

'I've lost my chick,' said Claudie.

Despite the flippancy and self-absorption of their young years, they were nevertheless able to sense that Claudie's world had been turned upside-down.

'It must have been stolen!' sympathized the girl.

'No, he went off by himself. He grew up and flew away.'

'Where did you get it from?' asked the Hindu.

'I bought him at the market.'

'Then why don't you go back to the market and buy another chick?' suggested the girl.

'But it won't be the same one.'

'Well, that doesn't matter. It'll replace the one you've lost.'

'No one can replace another being,' said Claudie. 'Even when it's just a cockerel.'

The wind was blowing in great gusts, the vortex where the southerly and westerly winds converged spiralling slowly and powerfully above Claudie's head.

The four buildings followed each other like pilgrims along the edge of the waste ground.

EENY, MEENY, MINY, MO

'Sidorov!'

'You mean me?'

'Who else?'

Sidorov got up slowly, with a bewildered and rather distrustful expression on his face.

'Go to the blackboard, please,' said Evgeny.

'What for?'

'I'd like to see how well you've done your homework.'

'But you called on me yesterday and gave me "satisfactory" . . .'

Sidorov used the word 'satisfactory', not 'average'. He obviously had great loyalty and respect for his C.

'Well, so what if I called on you yesterday?' said Evgeny firmly. 'I'm interested finding out what you know today too.'

'It's not as if I'm the only person here, though.'

'Don't argue, Sidorov.'

Sidorov extricated himself from his desk and walked up to the board, leaning over to one side and slouching badly.

He turned to face the class, then stood there with his eyes raised to the ceiling.

'Fire away, then,' said Evgeny in his fine bass voice.

'"The Prisoner". By Pushkin. No, hang on . . . Pushkin. "The Prisoner".'

'Alexander Sergeyevich,' prompted Evgeny.

'I know,' said Sidorov, rejecting the prompt. 'Alexander Sergeyevich Pushkin. The poem "The Prisoner". "I sit behind bars in my dark prison cell . . ."'

'"In my dank prison cell,"' corrected Evgeny.

'That's what I said . . .'

'Go on . . .'

'"I sit behind bars in my dank prison cell. An eagle who must in imprisonment dwell."'

'"In captivity dwell."'

'That's what I said.'

Evgeny said nothing.

'Alexander Sergeyevich Pushkin. The poem "The Prisoner". "I sit behind bars in my dank prison cell. An eagle"' – Sidorov stumbled, trying to remember where it dwelled – '"who must in captivity dwell. My mournful companion, waving your wing . . ."'

'Who is waving his wing?'

'The companion.'

'Which companion?'

'Well, the eagle . . .'

'Right,' said Evgeny. 'Go on.'

'I can't do it if you are going to keep interrupting me.'

'Begin from the beginning again then.'

'Alexander Sergeyevich Pushkin. The poem "The Prisoner". "I sit behind bars in my dank prison cell. An eagle who must in captivity dwell. My mournful companion, waving your wing . . ."'

Sidorov now ground to a complete halt.

'Did you really learn it?'

'Yes, I did.'

'Did you or didn't you?' asked Evgeny, at that moment feeling someone giving him a hard tap on the back of his neck.

He shook his shoulders and looked around.

Neither the class nor Sidorov were there any more.

Instead he was in a room with pretty pinkish-mauve wallpaper and a sofa which looked comfortable even to the eye – like the sort you find in millionaires' living rooms. And in the middle of the room stood Kasyanova with her mauve fringe, wearing faded jeans and a striped T-shirt.

'Where are you?' asked Kasyanova, anxiously scanning his face with her eyes.

'At school,' said Evgeny.

'Why?'

'Yesterday Sidorov just managed to inch his D up to a C. But I called on him again today.'

'All these Cs and Ds . . . what about me?'

'You too,' said Evgeny, looking into her worried eyes.

'Do you love me?'

'Yes.'

Evgeny could not imagine the time when Kasyanova was not in his life; nor could he imagine being without her some time in the future. He felt the same way about his daughter. It was impossible to believe that six years ago she did not even exist, and it was also impossible to believe that one day, a long time after his life ended, hers would too . . .

'If you really love me, why do we have to part every day?'

'But we see each other every day,' he said, and she was aware of him trying to get out of a tricky situation.

Kasyanova knew Evgeny's face and his soul so well that she could tell what was going on in his soul from the expression on his face. This meant she could not be lied to, and Evgeny felt uneasy being perpetually spied upon.

'What is it you want?' he asked.

'I want your life. In exchange for mine.'

'But I told you, I need time.'

'You only say you need time because you don't want to have to make up your mind right now.'

'Don't keep on at me. I'm tired.'

Evgeny's eyelids flickered. He half-closed his eyes in order to remove them from the direct aim of her pupils.

His irritation and faint-heartedness were all too plain for her to see though, and a feeling of doom rose up in her throat like nausea. She felt as if a vacuum had formed round her heart, and her heart was expanding and expanding to the point when she thought it was suddenly going to burst with a great bang like a balloon. She turned round and, carefully, so her heart would not break, walked out of the room. Evgeny saw how unsteady her steps were, and he also noticed how childish the pocket on her jeans was, with its buttons and little picture.

The room became empty. Evgeny immediately started missing her so he went shuffling off after her into the kitchen.

His mother often used to take him to the shops with her when he was a kid, but she would never let him go inside with her. She did not want her child breathing in germs from all those people milling about, so she would leave him outside by the doors. He would always stand by there by the doors obediently waiting for her, but in the depths of his soul he was convinced that his mother would leave by another exit and not come back for him. He would wait there patiently every time, feeling sick in the bottom of his stomach with fear and worry. Evgeny could still vividly remember that aching loneliness even now, some thirty years later. He felt something faintly similar when he was without Kasyanova for a long time.

Kasyanova was standing over the stove staring hard with her eyes, trying to hold back the tears.

Evgeny did not believe that she had any real reason to be suffering, but she really was suffering. He went up to her and patted her hair in a clumsy way like a dog, and his hand actually was rather round and heavy like a dog's paw.

'How shall I kill you?' Kasyanova asked, looking at him trustfully.

'You could poison me.'

'No, that's no good. I'd get sent to prison,' she said.

'OK. Then give me the poison and I'll poison myself. I'll come home one day and swallow it all.'

'You'd never do that. You're far too much of a coward. Or else you'd change your mind. I know you. You are far too lily-livered, and you're also far too much of a ditherer.'

'So don't you feel sorry for me?' asked Evgeny, feeling hurt.

'No. Not at all.'

'Why not?'

'Because I've gone as far as I can go with you. These days I'm just starting to hate you more and more.'

Evgeny looked at her with his eyelashes half lowered. There was an inspired and lofty expression on his face, which made him look as if he had just walked out on to the steppes.

'You don't believe me, do you?' Kasyanova said. 'I'm serious, though.'

It was getting dark, and the snow had piled up in high drifts. A narrow, trodden-down path ran from the bus stop to the apartment block with tall banks of snow on either side. It was not easy to walk down it; you had to put one foot in front of the other as if you were a tight-rope walker.

People were feeling their way along the path, balancing with both arms, while glowing yellow windows beckoned them onwards, one for each person. The lilac-coloured snow and the yellow lights in the building opposite made everything seem very mellow.

Meanwhile, behind his back, Kasyanova was standing there suffering, and the fact that she wanted to poison him was also a very necessary and good thing.

*

By the time Evgeny got to school, lessons had already begun. The school had the quiet solemnity and resonance of a church.

Evgeny had pulled off his Soviet-made sheepskin coat and was just hanging it up in the cupboard when he suddenly caught sight of Larisa Petrovna, the headmistress. The kids had shortened her name to an acronym, as if she was an institution. They called her Larpet, or Larpetka when they wanted to be less formal.

Larpetka came out of her office, turned the key twice in the lock, left it sticking out of the keyhole, then set off in the direction of the cloakrooms.

Whenever Evgeny was late and he happened to run into one of his colleagues, he would usually make two giant steps to the side, one step backwards and end up squashed between the door and the cupboard, feeling the cold, paint-covered wall against his back.

He performed the same routine today, but after doing his two steps to the side and one step backwards, he felt the warmth of someone's stomach instead of the cold of the wall against his back. He looked out of the corner of his eye, and recognized Sidorov, who was also late for school and was also hiding.

Larpetka strode past briskly, the clear outline of her steps echoing in the corridor. Evgeny remained standing there for a while, leaning against Sidorov and feeling his breath on his neck, then he peered out of their hiding place. The corridor was empty and calm.

Evgeny came out from behind the cupboard and straightened his jacket.

'Why are you late?' he asked Sidorov sternly.

'I was in the trolleybus, sir, but it ran into a bus, so I had to walk the rest of the way,' replied Sidorov, looking with devotion at his teacher.

'Is that so?' inquired Evgeny.

'Yeah, honest, sir . . .'

'Whose fault was it?'

'The bus's of course . . . The trolleybus was attached to the cables but the bus could have gone anywhere it wanted to.'

Evgeny shook his head disapprovingly, and walked down the corridor to his classroom.

Sidorov followed him, a few paces behind.

When they got to the door, Evgeny halted and said, 'Let me go in first. You can come in a little bit after me.'

'Promise you won't call on me?'

'Don't push your luck, Sidorov . . .'

Evgeny went into the classroom.

The children started getting up from their seats, banging their desks and making a lot of noise.

'Sit down!' said Evgeny, waving a hand at them, not bothering to wait for them to stand up properly and get into order.

The class started sitting down again, making so much noise banging their desks and scraping their chairs that it seemed it would never end. Evgeny stood patiently by his desk, longing passionately for the holidays.

'Composition!' he announced. 'I'm going to give you a choice of subjects.' He went up to the blackboard, picked up a piece of chalk, and started writing above the damp patches.

1. My favourite hero.
2. How I would like to live my life.

'But we've already written on "My favourite hero",' Kuznetsova the form captain informed him in her gentle voice.

Evgeny decided he had better pick another topic. He picked up a dry, chalk-covered rag and rubbed out what he had written.

After thinking for a while, he wrote, 'What I would do if I were a millionaire.'

At that moment the door slowly opened and Sidorov appeared.

'May I come in?' he asked in a humble and obsequious voice.

'Sit down!' Evgeny replied curtly without looking at him, thus denying him any complicity.

Sidorov made his way carefully to his desk on tiptoes.

Evgeny put down the chalk and went over to the window. A richly textured humming sound started up immediately behind his back. He was able to distinguish all the different shades and tones in this hum, like a good mechanic listening to an engine ticking over.

He knew in advance that no one would write about being a millionaire, because they did not know what his official position on the subject was, and because they would not actually know what to do with all that much money anyway.

They would almost all write about how they would like to live their lives. They would all want to journey far and wide, without ever going back. It would be just like in one of Pakhmutova's famous songs: 'I've gone to the sultry steppes, while you explore the snowy taiga.' But why couldn't they go together to the steppes or to the taiga? And sometimes it was a very good thing to retrace one's steps. Not only a good thing, but actually essential.

There was a bare grey-green tree outside the window. Its branches were covered with a host of little grey birds, all looking in one direction and singing at the tops of their voices. They were probably learning a new song.

'Stop the car!' ordered Kasyanova.

'OK, that's enough of your little games,' said Evgeny, refusing to react.

Kasyanova grabbed the door-handle and flung it open while the car was still moving along. The car immediately became dark and cold, and somehow unreal. It was as if a large bird had flown into the car and was flapping its wings.

Breaking all the laws, Evgeny managed to get over into the right lane and bring the car to a halt up alongside the pavement.

Kasyanova bent over and started pulling off her warm winter boots, first one then the other. She tossed them aside, then jumped out of the car into the snow in just her socks.

It was minus 34 degrees, and even the children were not going to school.

Somewhat alarmed, Evgeny started following behind her slowly in the car. She was walking barefoot. He shouted something to her, and people turned to stare at them.

Evgeny could not remember what they had been arguing about that time. There was some battle going on between them which felt like a tug of war.

He lay down on the ground, on the sticky, scented pine needles, and started gazing up at the sky, his hands clasped beneath his head. He felt he had been made a fool of and he wanted to cry.

Kasyanova was sitting at the other edge of the clearing. She was looking at him with pity in her eyes.

'If you are so jealous, if you don't believe me, why don't you just come and look into my eyes?'

Evgeny said nothing. His nose was itching, and his eyes and lips were swelling with despair.

'Just look me in the eye, and everything will immediately become clear to you.'

'That's all I need,' muttered Evgeny.

'Well, if you don't want to, I'll come over to you, then.'

Now it was her face that was hanging over him instead of the white sky. He could hear her breathing, as light as a child's, and he could see her eyes. He suddenly realized that they were not dark brown, as he had always thought, but light brown: coffee-coloured streaks across a green field. Her pupils first positioned themselves above his right eye, then moved slightly to take up a new position over his left eye. She could not look into both of his eyes at once, and neither of course could he, so their pupils bobbed from one to the other. These few seconds were the Truth. The highest meaning of existence.

He held his face beneath her breath, like under a warm shower of rain, but found he could not breathe properly. And he found that he could not meet her gaze for very long when he looked at her either. Suddenly he felt the sky drawing him upwards.

He flung his arms out on to the grass, conscious of the earth and sky pulling him in opposite directions.

The bell rang.

Evgeny gave a start and turned back to face the class. On the corner of his desk, in a neat and tidy pile, stood the collected exercise books containing his pupils' compositions.

The children were sitting quietly with their hands in their laps, looking at their teacher.

'Write down the task for tomorrow.'

Evgeny went up to his desk, opened the textbook and started to dictate.

'One. What aspiration does the poet express in the poem? How is this aspiration strengthened by the image of the eagle languishing in captivity?'

'But we've written this down already!' shouted out Sidorov gleefully.

'Since when were you allowed to shout?' said Evgeny, ticking him off. 'If you want to say something, put up your hand.'

Sidorov raised his hand.

'Right, that's the end of class,' said Evgeny.

'Homework. Go over what we did today. I'll deal with all questions next time . . .'

. . . Anyuta was running about the square at the back of the apartment block with her friends. Evgeny recognized her from far away. She was a head taller than all of them, and looked a lot older then her five years.

She was wearing a fluffy hat, but there were strands of hair trailing down by her face. Her hair always got in the way, and she was always pulling funny faces to try and get it out of her eyes. It had become a habit now, and her little face would twitch nervously even when her hair was carefully tied back.

When Anyuta had caught sight of his car, she had rushed off towards it with a whoop and a yell as if she was an Indian on the war path. Evgeny had got out, and now Anyuta was hanging from his shoulders, letting her legs dangle. She had round eyes, a round little nose and a round mouth. Even her teeth were round; she was like a jolly little pagan god who had come down to earth.

'What have you brought me?' asked the little cherub in a businesslike manner. Anyuta had got used to extracting a tribute from her father, even if her love for him was purely unselfish.

Evgeny got out a box from the back seat and proffered it to her. She untied the string excitedly and took out of the box a German doll in a checked dress and little plastic boots.

'But I've already got one like this. Daddy Dima gave it to me.'

Anyuta looked at her father with her round eyes, and her little feminine soul comprehended something.

'Well, never mind,' she said soothingly. 'They'll be twins like Yulka and Lenka. It'll be even better for them to grow up together. That way they won't be so selfish.'

Evgeny brushed the hair away from her face, and felt the soft vulnerability of her cheeks beneath his fingers.

'So how are you?'

'All right,' said Anyuta. 'How are you?'

'I'm all right too.'

In two years she had already got used to the fact that she did not have one father like everyone else, but two. And she had got used to not asking questions.

Anyuta examined the doll.

'Do you think her hair can be washed?'

Evgeny thought about it seriously. During these brief meetings he wanted to be of maximum use to his daughter.

'Yes, I think it probably can,' he decided.

Anyuta looked around to her friends. She couldn't wait to show off her new doll to them, but she felt awkward about running off from her father.

'Do you want to go for a drive?' suggested Evgeny.

'No, let's play hide and seek.'

'All right. Start counting, then,' said Evgeny.

'Eeny, meeny, miny, mo . . .' Anyuta began, counting by the syllables rather than the words, with her little hand in its mitten going back and forth like a shuttle on a loom. 'Catch a tiger by his toe. If he hollers let him go, eeny, meeny, miny, mo . . .'

On the word 'mo', she stopped her hand half-way down and tucked it into her fur coat. She did not want to do the seeking; she wanted to go and hide.

Evgeny pretended that he hadn't noticed this bit of cheating, and covered his face with his hands. He counted in his head to thirty and then warned loudly, 'One, two, three, four, five. I'm going to come and get you. Six, seven, eight, nine, ten. I'm going to come and find you.'

Evgeny took his hands away from his face. Anyuta was standing right next to him, looking across to the far corner of the square, screwing her eyes up as if the wind was hurting them.

Evgeny followed the direction of her gaze and saw Daddy Dima out walking with a dog on a lead. He looked as spruce and elegant in his sports gear as a mime artist. The hand holding the lead was cocked at a capricious angle, and the dog was long-legged and also exceedingly elegant. Evgeny felt nauseated by such copious quantities of elegance.

The dog was pulling on the lead and barking in their direction.

'Chilim, good doggy!' exclaimed Anyuta affectionately.

'Why not go over to them if you want,' said Evgeny, hiding his jealousy.

'When are you coming next?' asked Anyuta.

'I'll ring you,' said Evgeny.

'I'll ring you, too.'

Anyuta ran over to the dog, kicking out her legs. Evgeny watched the dog jump up and lick her face all over.

He got into the car, backed a little, then turned round and drove down the streets he knew so well.

Their district had changed so much . . .

When he and his wife had first come out to look at their future home and had got out of the Underground, the first thing they had seen was a horse and cart, and a farmer in a sheepskin jacket sitting in it. Beyond that quaint scene lay the village of Belyaevo all shrouded in mist, with its Rexes and Rovers crouching behind crooked fences. And in the foreground a solitary high-rise apartment block reached up into the sky like a signpost.

Seven years had passed since that time. And now when you came out of the Underground you found yourself in the middle of a small town, with as many people living in it as in some small state. And then you realized that seven years was an awfully long time in a person's life.

And what had he done in those seven years? He had destroyed everything that he had built until then, and now he was having to start from scratch rebuilding his life again.

Kasyanova was standing by the furniture shop, waiting to catch sight of the bonnet of his little Zhiguli.

When she saw Evgeny framed by the edge of his windscreen, she waved to him as if she was in a First of May parade, and then rushed over to greet him. Her eyes shone as clear as aquamarine, and her sheepskin coat looked bright and festive with its colourful Ukrainian embroidery.

She opened the car door and collapsed on to the seat next to him. The car suddenly became brighter and smelt of expensive scent.

'So, how are you feeling?' asked Evgeny, jealous of her as always. He even found it painful to think that Kasyanova had been standing in the middle of the road at the intersection of other people's glances.

'Pretty awful!' Kasyanova answered, smiling happily. That meant they would start trying to sort out their relationship again today. First would come the arguments, then they would make up, going through the entire spectrum of human emotions along the way.

It was snowing. Wet snowflakes were hitting the windscreen, becoming flat and then sliding down in uneven streams. The windscreen wipers moved back and forth evenly and rhythmically, like someone breathing.

Evgeny was looking straight in front of him and seeing Chilim the dog putting its paws on Anyuta's shoulders and licking her face all over. Anyuta had brought out the doll so Chilim could say hello to her too, but the dog only sniffed at its unfamiliar scent.

Kasyanova was asking about something. Evgeny did not answer.

He was remembering how he used to give Anyuta her bath. How he would work the shampoo in her hair into a lather, and then rinse it out under the shower. Anyuta would sometimes swallow some water and start choking, and then she would get scared as she struggled for breath. But she never cried; she would just demand that they wipe her eyes with a dry towel.

Then Evgeny would whisk her out of the bath, sit her down on his knee and envelop her in a bath towel. Anyuta would gaze down from her new height at the bath with its little islands of grey foam and always say the same thing: 'The water was clean. Now it's dirty. Anyuta was dirty. Now she's clean.'

Whenever he took her out of the fug of the bathroom, he would always think that the flat had become very cold, and would be convinced that his child would be bound to catch cold.

Next they would sit down together on the bed, and his wife would bring over a small pair of scissors, a hairbrush, and a clean pair of pyjamas. They would always sit down together to carry out this simple ritual, and his wife's blue eyes would shine with happiness.

Why had they ruined all that? Why had they destroyed it?

Perhaps it was because Evgeny was unable to exercise self-restraint in certain areas, and his wife couldn't tolerate certain things. Or perhaps neither of them had been tolerant enough?

A dark-coloured rag was lying in the road. Its ends fluttered nervously in the breeze, while the middle of it was stuck to the asphalt.

'It's a cat!' shrieked Kasyanova, covering her face with her hands.

'It's only a rag,' said Evgeny.

Kasyanova believed him and returned her hands to her lap, but then she sat for a long time without saying anything, as if in the embrace of someone else's tragedy.

'Where were you just now?' Kasyanova asked quietly.

'At home,' Evgeny replied after a moment's hesitation.

'What were you doing?'

'Bathing Anyuta.'

'And are you ever with me?'

'I was with you today at school.'

'But why can't you ever be where you actually are? Why can't you be at home when you are at home, at work when you are at work, and with me when you are with me?'

'What is it you want?' asked Evgeny.

'I want to know why you can't be where you are.'

'I am incapable of living in the present,' said Evgeny, after hesitating a moment.

'That means you can never be happy.'

'No, almost never.'

'It's a shame,' said Kasyanova.

'For me?'

'And me. It's more of a pity for me.'

They had got to the end of Leninsky Prospekt, and were about to turn on to the Sadovoye ring road.

'Stop the car,' Kasyanova requested.

Evgeny looked warily at her boots, and Kasyanova understood his glance.

'Don't worry,' she said. 'I'm going to leave you with my boots on.'

She got out of the car, but before shutting the door, she said, 'I don't want to kill you any more.'

'Why not?' said Evgeny, feeling offended.

'Because you are going to kill yourself.'

She closed the door carefully, then banged it shut and walked off throwing her bag over her shoulder. She walked with a confident and detached air, as if teasing him with how little she had to do with his life.

Evgeny watched her as she walked away and experienced a feeling of relief mingled with pain.

He didn't have the strength to overstrain his nerves today. He didn't want to argue and he didn't want to patch things up. He just wanted a little bit of peace and quiet: the solitude which every adult human being needs from time to time.

He turned on the ignition abruptly and the little Zhiguli gave a snort. Then it lunged forwards, ready to carve its way through the traffic.

First Evgeny drove on to the Sadovoye ring road, which was full of noise and fumes like a factory shop floor, then he turned off into a quiet street which had retained its old Moscow name. Kasyanova was far away, standing at the intersection of other people's glances.

They were past the time of their first rows now, when it always seemed that everything was final, and he would go completely numb with horror. Once he had even lost consciousness behind the steering-wheel, and had to be taken home by a policeman.

Lately he had started to get used to their rows, and was even learning how to adjust to them. He knew that in a day or two they would make up again and not fight any more, because their souls had become as one.

He still did not know that she had left him today for good, and that he would be left all alone, like a child abandoned in front of the shop. Many years would pass before he would once more experience the relief he felt today.

RELATIVES FOR LIFE

An autumn wind was blowing in from the Neva.

Two men were standing on the bank of the Swan Canal gazing into the distance, as Pushkin and Mickiewicz had once done in their time.

Man is part of nature. He is not only indissolubly linked to it, but he is also subject to it. The two men standing there on the bank of the canal that day were subject to the wind, to autumn, and to the low clouds. Their conversation was moving towards frankness.

'Irka is stronger than I am,' said the first man. 'She earns one and a half times more than I do. And it depresses me. Do you know what I mean?'

'Yes, I do,' agreed the other.

'Also, she has a very flexible timetable, so I never know where she is or what she's up to. It's me who has to go to the laundry, beat the carpets and bathe the kid. She's been trying to turn me into a woman for ten years now, but I'm a bloke! Truth be told, she's a bloke too. We don't have a woman in our house. And when I think we've got to go on like this for maybe twenty or thirty more years, it makes me want to just give up and not bother going on with my life.'

A little passenger boat was chugging down the Neva, and its frozen passengers, all hunched up with their heads drawn into their shoulders, were standing on the deck looking as if they had gone on their Sunday outing just to spite someone.

'But Vera just worships me. Even when she hears me sneezing her eyes fill with tears! And when she sees me eating, she just laughs and says that I open my mouth really wide. I had never noticed before how I sneezed or how I ate. I never thought that all that could be of interest to anyone but me. Do you know what I mean?'

'Yes, I do,' said the friend. He also had always thought that he chewed and sneezed exclusively for his own benefit.

'Now look: I don't want to put either myself, Irka, or my new love in a false position with regard to this new situation that has arisen,' the first man continued, spurred on by how understanding his friend was being. 'It would just be humiliating for all three of us. So I have decided to tell Irka that I am leaving her. The thing is, it's going to be a terribly awkward conversation, so I'd really appreciate it if you could come with me.'

'Where to?' asked the friend.

'To my place.'

'What for?'

'I just told you: I want to tell my wife that I am leaving her.'

'If you want to tell your wife that you are leaving her, you would be better off coming over to my place rather than going to yours.'

'Why?' asked the man, not understanding what his friend was talking about.

'Because your wife left you for me this morning. She's my wife now.'

Just then some seagulls came swimming up the Swan Canal. They were as big as ducks, and speckled rather than white. The man had never seen seagulls like that before. He guessed that they must have flown up the mouth of the Neva from the Gulf of Finland, and had then managed to work their way across to the Swan Canal.

The man watched the seagulls swimming by, while trying to assimilate this new piece of information into his nervous system.

'How come I didn't know about this?' he asked after a short pause.

'I brought you here specifically to tell you. Now you know everything.'

'Why didn't you tell me straight away?'

'I wanted to but you've been talking the whole time. I couldn't get a word in edgeways.'

'Some friend you are,' said the man peevishly. 'And to think I trusted you.'

'But I've done nothing wrong,' his friend declared. 'I've loved Irka for a long time, but I never expressed my feelings to her in any way. Irka hadn't the faintest clue that I was in love with her before I told her.'

'So what do you see in her?' the man asked, taking an interest all of a sudden.

'She's very beautiful.'

'Who? Irka?'

'Her expression is always so endearingly naïve, and she asks such silly questions.'

'Really?' said the man reflectively, as if he was trying to summon his wife up from the depths of his memory. 'Are you sure you aren't making a mistake?'

'No. I'm pretty sure of it.'

'Strange . . . Why did she walk out, anyway? What does she say about that?'

'The same things you've been saying.'

'Yes, but what exactly . . .' said the man, trying to wheedle everything out of his friend.

'She says that she wants to be a woman, but that she is forced into being a bloke. She says she has a flexible timetable and that you give her plenty of freedom, but she says that all that freedom you give her is actually loneliness when it comes down to it. And when she thinks that she's got to live like that for another twenty or thirty years, she gets very depressed and just wants to curl up and fall into a deep sleep for all of that time.'

'How mean!'

'What is?'

'To go on about her own husband like that!'

'She doesn't talk about you to everyone. Only to me.'

Across from the Swan Canal you could see the Engineers Fortress, where Paul I was murdered. And to one side stretched the Summer Garden with all its statues. An old-style pot-bellied tram, which people always called the 'American', was rumbling past.

The tram, the garden, and the fort all seemed deeply indifferent to the individual fate of one particular person. 'So what?' their expression seemed to say. 'You're miserable. So what?'

'Let's go,' said the man. So the rivals strode off in the direction of the Fontanka River, which always used to be called 'the stream without a name' during Peter the Great's time.

Irka was sitting in an armchair with her legs wrapped up in rug, reading André Maurois' *Literary Portraits*.

When the two men came in, she put a marker in the book so she could find the page again easily.

'So you're settled in here just like at home, I see!' the man said, obviously feeling quite galled.

'Well, of course I feel at home here,' said Irka. 'This is my home now, after all. And this is my new husband. You're our friend.'

'I insist that you explain your behaviour!' the man demanded.

'Hasn't he said anything to you?'

'He has got nothing to do with this. I've got nothing to say to him. But you are my wife. And you're the one I'm asking.'

'Well, to put it bluntly, I love him,' said Irka. 'There you have it.'

'Rubbish!' said the man. 'You don't love him. You may be in love with him, but it's me that you actually love.'

'No, in actual fact I hate you!' Irka confessed. 'I'm fed up to the back teeth with you.'

'Yes, you may hate me,' agreed the man. 'But you still love me. We've lived together for twelve years, don't forget, right from when we were young to now. We have a child who belongs to both of us. We have property which belongs to both of us, and a life that we have ruined together. We are relatives for life now, and you can't just go and ditch relatives or swap them for other people whenever you feel like it.'

'I still love him, though,' said Irka firmly.

'Don't be stupid! Love is one thing and life is another. You can't mix the two up.'

'Don't listen to him, Irka,' said the friend. 'Love equals life and life equals love. Love and life are precisely what need to be mixed up.'

'But what about our twelve years?' asked the man. 'Are you planning to just shake our ruined life off, like snot from your fingers?'

'What a disgusting thing to say!' reproached Irka.

'And what a disgusting way to behave! Come on, get your things together and let's go home.'

'And what are we going to do at home?'

'The same things we always do. I'll watch hockey on the box, and you'll blather on to your friends on the phone.'

'Does that mean you are going to watch hockey and let your slipper swing on the end of your foot?'

'Probably.'

'God, how dismal . . .'

'Listen, have you ever noticed how you breathe?' the man asked.

'No. Why?'

'Well, that is what family life is like. It's got to be as habitual and unnoticeable as breathing is. Then it can release a person's creative energies. Only complete idlers live off undiluted passion.'

'Don't listen to him, Irka,' said the friend. 'Look, why don't we go down to the Neva and take a boat trip?'

'Listen, if you start messing with my wife, I'm going to beat you up,' the man warned.

'And I'm going to beat you up too,' warned his friend.

'Look, if you two are going to start fighting, I am afraid I will be forced to take the side of my first husband.'

'Why?' said the friend, feeling very put out.

'Because he is hungry.'

'So what? I haven't eaten anything since breakfast either.'

'But I've lived with him for twelve years, and for only three and a half hours with you.'

'Let's go,' insisted the man. 'I can't wait any longer. Spartak are playing against the Soviet Army in twenty minutes.'

'Oh, God . . .' sighed Irka, unwrapping herself reluctantly from her rug. 'My foot's gone to sleep,' she said as she limped into the hall. The man and his friend followed behind her.

She pulled on her raincoat then put a scarf over her head. She crossed the ends of the scarf and started to tie them at the back of her neck, but the ends were short and slippery, and her slender fingers got all mixed up. At one point it looked as if she were about to tie her fingers into knots.

'I'm ready,' she declared finally.

'What about your things?' asked the man.

Irka went back into the room and returned clutching André Maurois' *Literary Portraits*.

'That's everything!' said Irka.

'What about me?' asked the friend, as genuine tears started springing to his eyes.

'Come with us!' said the man. 'There's no point in you sitting here in this mood!'

'You're taking away my wife and I'm supposed to come with you?'

'Don't be stubborn,' said Irka.

Their apartment block stood on Liteiny Prospekt, a street which had always had the same name.

The man felt surer of himself as he went in through the doorway, now that he was stepping back into his own territory.

'You're a fine one,' he said to Irka. 'Carrying on with my friend, behind my back . . .'

'Well, what am I supposed to do? Are you going to tell me I've got to go out dancing if I want to have some fun?' objected Irka. 'I'm not seventeen, you know. I've got a job, and a family, and a house to look after. When am I ever going to get the time to go out? I won't find anyone better than your friend, and you know that very well.'

A Siamese cat with blue eyes was sitting on the stairs between floors. It sat there watching them as they went past with a fawning look, and its ingratiating expression was not at all something you would associate with the proud, half-wild animal it was supposed to be – almost a tiger even.

'It's homeless,' commented Irka. 'Someone must have lost it.'

'This is too much! Even your stair cats are Siamese!' said the friend in distressed tones.

'Come on now, don't be upset,' said Irka.

The friend started crying.

'If I hadn't brought him over to our place, you wouldn't have left.'

'You've got to think constructively,' advised the man. 'It's no good thinking about what would have happened or what wouldn't have happened. You've got to think about what is going on right now, and what can be done to change the situation.'

'And how can I change the situation?' asked the friend.

'It's not within your capability.'

'What am I supposed to do, then?'

'Just don't think about it.'

'Irka, you've got to leave him. See how unpleasant he is?'

'Oh, I agree, he's extremely unpleasant,' said Irka.

By their familiar front door there was a familiar doormat, which had seen better days as Irka's jacket.

Near the doormat stood a suitcase. And on it sat a girl with big eyes, her slender, delicate hands folded in her lap.

'Vovik,' said the girl, getting up from the suitcase. 'I've been waiting and waiting and you never showed up . . . So I decided to come here myself.'

'This is Vera,' said the man as he introduced her.

Vera held out her slender hand to everyone.

'Irina,' said Irka.

'Stanislav,' said the friend.

'The thing is, you see, Vera,' began the man, 'I thought I was unattached. But it turns out that I'm married. This is my wife.'

'Irina,' said Irka once more.

'I've been deceiving you,' continued the man. 'Not on purpose, though. I've been deceiving myself too.'

'You poor thing,' said Vera, her eyes brimming with tears of sympathy. 'But don't get too upset. I'll still love you.'

'Yes, but the uncertainty of it all will start eating at your feelings,' said Irka. 'You will end up suffering for it.'

'What am I going to do, then?'

'Get married.'

'To my friend,' said the man.

'Who gave you the right to start giving out orders all of a sudden?' interrupted Irka.

'But you know as well as I do that she'll never find anyone better than him. We have no reason to be ashamed of him.'

Vera looked trustingly at Irka.

'He really is a wonderful person,' Irka confirmed truthfully. 'He demystifies everything for you. You see so much around you when you are with him; more into yourself and into other people too.'

Vera went up to him and lifted up her head to examine him more closely.

'Yes, he is wonderful,' she said. 'But I won't see anything when I'm with him because I don't love him. And he doesn't love me.'

'No, I don't love you,' agreed the friend. 'And you don't love me. But who knows. Maybe in about ten years' time we will become relatives for life.'

The man got out his keys and opened his front door.

His friend picked up Vera's suitcase and led her by the hand down the stairs.

Vera obediently followed him, at the distance of her outstretched hand. She twisted her head round to look back at Vovik one last time.

The Siamese cat was dozing on the radiator.

When it heard the sound of people coming down the stairs, it opened one eye. The expression on its face seemed to say: 'Maybe from the point of view of other more fortunate Siamese and Siberian cats, my life might seem pretty frightful. But from the point of view of ordinary stair cats, I am absolutely thriving. I have a staircase that is swept regularly and well ventilated, the little boys here are all very kind to me, and I have as many tasty leftovers as I could ever wish for.'

A CUBIC CENTIMETRE OF HOPE

There were never all that many patients, and most of them were old ladies. The old ladies thought that vitamins were good for the blood and helped it to run smoothly through their tired veins. The hyaloid membrane, they thought, would absorb all their harrowing thoughts about death, so that when they woke up, they would not have to think about their health any more and could go back to leading normal lives.

The most important thing was not to think about your health when you got up in the morning. Everything else you had was sheer happiness. Young people had their idea of happiness. Old ladies had theirs.

There were two nurses called Lora and Tanya who worked at the clinic treating these old ladies. One of them worked mornings and the other worked afternoons.

Lora was a quiet and trustful sort of person who believed in the existence of some kind of universal justice in the world. If, for example, a brick were about to fall on her head and she managed to think about something before it hit her, she would think, 'Well, this was obviously meant to happen . . .'

Lora believed in people. She also believed in words, and in medicine. Each injection she gave was a cubic centimetre of hope, as far as she was concerned.

But for Tanya, each injection she gave was just another old backside.

Tanya was married. Deep down, though, she was convinced the situation she currently found herself in was not the one that was going to make her ultimately happy.

She never admitted it to anyone around her, or even to herself, but she was really waiting for a new man to appear in her life.

She was too busy to look for this new man, nor did she know where to look for him anyway, so she was waiting for him to find her. One fine day she was sure she would open the door and he would come in, take her by the hand, and whisk her off to an interesting life.

But instead of that, the door would invariably open, and the next old lady would come in and lift up her dress. And so it was, day in and day out. From month to month and year to year.

She was bored with elderly faces and knitted underwear that came down to the knees.

The patients could sense this and became timid and nervous as a result. The needle would not go easily into their tensed veins and sometimes even broke, which meant that it would have to be exchanged for a new one.

But nevertheless the old women scuttled out of the consulting room looking all pink and rosy-cheeked, having been made young again by their confusion and fear. Only an irrepressible desire to live induced them to come back again.

Tanya was irritated with her life in the way that one gets irritated with shop assistants who put the wrong things on the scales and then try to cheat you while they weigh them. An expression of irritation and distrust had now frozen permanently on her face. If the new man were really to open the door and come in now, he would be unable to discern her face beneath this hardened expression. He would just say, 'Excuse me . . .' and shut the door.

Tanya was living with one man, but waiting for someone else, and this double existence was playing havoc with her nerves. People are as finely tuned as musical instruments, after all. They're like guitars, for example.

How could one possibly play a guitar like Tanya? And even if one were to try and play something, just think what would it sound like!

There were about fifty more people in the bus than it could comfortably accommodate. And there were about thirty more people than one could actually even imagine squashing into it.

Lora was standing up, compressed by bodies on all sides. The back pressed against her face, however, smelt of something smoky and was actually very pleasant.

Lora was on her way to a shop called Leipzig, where they sometimes sold German bras for six roubles fifty. It seemed to her that every single passenger on the bus, including all the children and all the men, was also going there to buy bras.

Suddenly the bus braked sharply. A cat or a dog must have darted out across the road, and the driver was unwilling for his soul to bear the sin of running it over.

The passengers all fell forward together, and those standing up at the front must have experienced some uneasy moments, because they could easily have ended up squashed against the driver's cabin. Those who were standing at the back turned out to be standing in the best place at that moment.

Then the bus jolted sharply again before proceeding on its journey, and this time everyone shot backwards, which meant that those at the back now exchanged places with those at the front: it was the people at the back who were suffering now, while the ones at the front were all right. There was a sort of poetic justice at work. People cannot always be having a good time, but then neither can they always be having a bad time.

Those people like Lora who were standing in the middle of the bus, however, experienced pretty much the same discomfort on both occasions. They were neither terribly comfortable, nor were they terribly uncomfortable.

Next the bus turned down a street on its route, and all the passengers fell to one side.

Lora arched her back, trying to stay upright, but she found she was unable to, and she ended up collapsing on to the knees of someone sitting down. The knees were hard, rather bony, and, to judge from those particular attributes, masculine.

The bus kept making turns, and Lora just could not get up from the person's knees. In fact on the contrary, she was pressed right up against the person's chest, which was really rather improper.

'Sorry,' murmured Lora without being able to see anything. 'I can't get up.'

'It's all right, you can keep sitting,' said the person.

Lora raised her eyes and saw that this person really was a man.

Sometimes on television they show programmes about scientific expeditions which go out to sea to study underwater life, on little boats looking more like rafts than ships. Half-naked golden-tanned men with blond hair roam the decks, their beards turned platinum by the sun, their minds full of the sea, the sun, and serious scientific problems. And yet they are modest and handsome too. It is when you look at people like them, that you realize that women are born for love and that people are born for happiness.

Lora looked into this person's eyes. They were clear, blue, and honest. He could have told a pack of lies in a courtroom and got away with it.

Lora felt as if someone wearing fluffy mittens had taken her by the shoulders and was quietly pushing her towards those eyes. But no one of course had taken her by the shoulders, particularly someone in mittens. Who would be wearing mittens in June anyway? And no one was pushing her in any direction – who on earth would ever do something like that? But there is an expression to feel 'drawn' to someone. Lora felt drawn in the strictest sense of the word, and if there had not been any other people present, and if such behaviour was not considered publicly indecent and generally reprehensible, she would have put her head on to the man's chest, shut her eyes, and said, 'I'm happy.'

Happiness is when you feel at peace with things and you don't want anything other than what you have at the given moment.

And he would have hugged her and said, 'Me too.'

It was time for Lora to get up from his knees.

'I'm just about to get up, so you can carry on sitting in my seat,' he suggested.

'Oh no, really!' said Lora in embarrassment. 'There's no need.'

She was as embarrassed as if the bus seat belonged to him personally rather than to the general public.

'I've got to get off anyway, though.'

Lora nodded submissively. Happiness never lingered about her for long. Either other people seized it from her, or it got up and left of its own accord.

'I have to go. I have people waiting for me.'

For some reason he considered it necessary to explain himself, although he was perfectly entitled to leave without any explanation whatsoever.

'These people waiting for me depend on me, you see.'

But does it really matter why happiness is leaving if it has made the decision to leave?

Perhaps it did matter. The reason for leaving would at least have significance in her memories. And memories form part of one's life too.

Lora transferred all her energy on to her legs and,

tensing her calves, she managed to get up from the gentleman's knees.

The false witness also got up and at that moment their bodies were thrown towards each other.

'Let's meet,' he said suddenly.

'Today,' said Lora quickly.

'Where and when?'

'The Kazakhstan cinema. Five o'clock.'

'Why the Kazakhstan?'

It would have been more correct if he had asked 'Why five o'clock?' It was an odd day, and Lora was supposed to be working from three to seven. Her old ladies would be lining up to see her at five o'clock.

'I work there.'

'Where? The Kazakhstan?'

'No. In the clinic. It's next to the Kazakhstan.'

The bus stopped and the doors opened.

The false witness carved his way through the crush of people like one of those famous ice-breakers, the buttons dripping from his shirt like raindrops as he did so.

He jumped out of the bus at the last moment, or maybe even a second later.

Apart from him, no one else got off. They all stayed in the bus. And that is how it always was in Lora's life. The unnecessary people always stayed, and the necessary person always left.

Lora pressed her nose against the window. The false witness was standing by himself on the pavement, holding on to his now buttonless shirt with his hands to keep it from flapping in the wind. He was twisting his head in different directions like a bird.

He didn't seem like an ice-breaker any more to Lora. Now she thought he looked more like a poor little orphan boy, all lost and abandoned.

Lora suddenly lost all interest in the Leipzig shop and

its bras, and she got off the bus at the next stop. She crossed the street by the underpass and got on to another bus going in the opposite direction: towards the Kazakhstan cinema.

'He won't come, you know,' said Tanya, gazing at Lora with a mixture of pity and contempt.

There were no patients waiting to be seen and Tanya was sitting on the examination couch, knitting a hat to a fashionable design.

Half the couch was covered with a sheet, and the other half with a piece of oilcloth. The oilcloth was put underneath the patients' feet, so that they would not waste time by having to take their shoes off.

'Why won't he?' asked Lora.

'Either he won't come or he'll turn out to be a complete wretch. One of the two.'

'Why do you think so?'

'They're all like that.'

'But this man's really nice,' said Lora, not believing her. 'He'll definitely come. I'm positive of it.'

'How can you be so sure?'

'Because I saw his eyes.'

'And what do you think you could see there?'

'I saw them close up. I was sitting on his lap.'

'You were what?' said Tanya, not understanding. 'One minute you become acquainted and the next you are sitting on his lap?'

'No. First I was on his lap and then we got to know each other.'

Tanya put down her knitting and looked at Lora with increased interest.

Lora was looking out of the window. From where she was standing she could see the House of Furniture shop and the Kazakhstan cinema.

She was going to have to explain why she could not work that day and why Tanya was going to have to sit through the second shift, which would mean she would work about fourteen hours all in one day. But how could she explain about the boat that looked more like a raft, or about him looking like an orphan? Words are not the only form of expression, nor are they always the best way of expressing one's feelings. One can use gestures, for example, or music. But Lora could neither dance nor sing, and besides, how could she possibly suddenly start singing right in the middle of the treatment room?

Lora and Tanya were about as similar as a dog and a goat. Obviously the two animals share some similarities. They are roughly the same size, for example, and they both possess four legs and a tail. But a dog is still a dog. And a goat is a goat. And what is obvious to one is absolutely incomprehensible to the other.

And so Lora stood there mute and acquiescent, all too painfully aware of her dependency on Tanya.

At five o'clock the old ladies would start turning up. They would go and sit in the waiting room meek as lambs, clutching their cubic centimetres of hope in their hands. It was not a good idea for them to miss their injections, because the body can never be deceived; it would understand and take offence. It would stop rinsing away the salt and then the pain would come back again, together with all those agonizing thoughts about death. And all because Lora wanted to be happy. At any price.

'I'll work for you tomorrow,' promised Lora. 'I'll work two whole days in a row if you like.'

'He'll never come.'

There was a knock at the door and a middle-aged lady stepped into the treatment room. She was not old, but not exactly young either. To be more accurate, she was both young and old; it just depended on how you looked at it.

The old ladies would certainly think she was young, anyway.

'What's your name?' asked Tanya sternly as she slid awkwardly off the couch. She went up to the desk where a large book in a black binding lay open.

'Why won't he come?' asked Lora.

'Just look at yourself in the mirror,' Tanya suggested. There was no mirror near by, but Lora had a pretty good idea of what she looked like without one. She had the sort of face which was very common in central Russia. She was always reminding people of someone.

'Well, be honest. Who in their right minds is going to go after us because of who we are?' said Tanya.

The woman smiled in an ingratiating way, as if she was participating in the conversation, but Tanya looked at her sternly, as if to call her to order, and the woman became serious again.

How the river sparkled. It was as if little people from the sun were running across the water, an innumerable number of them, like Chinese. They kept running and running, and more and more of them kept appearing. There seemed to be no end to them.

Seriozha, Lora's lawful wedded husband, got out of the river dripping water and said, with his teeth chattering, 'Ah, this is what true happiness is . . .'

Then they went for a stroll along the river bank. Lora was nineteen at the time, and she used to wear her hair in a long plait. Seriozha held her plait rather than her hand.

A week later there came a knock at the door.

Lora went to open it and saw a woman standing there with a flat package under her arm.

'Is Seriozha at home?' asked the woman coolly.

'He's at work,' explained Lora, somewhat taken aback by the unfriendly tone.

'Give this to him, will you. He left his slippers at my place.'

The woman held out the package. It turned out to contain a pair of slippers wrapped in newspaper.

The left-behind slippers and the little people from the sun seemed so incompatible to Lora that she could just not equate them in her mind. She simply did not understand.

'You really shouldn't have gone to all this trouble! He could have come round and picked them up himself . . .'

She looked earnestly at the woman, who then for some reason suddenly decided to strike her on the cheek with the slippers. It was all very strange.

Seriozha did not deny that they were his slippers. But he was upset by the unfriendly behaviour of the woman. Invading his family with a direct accusation of treachery . . . Friends didn't do things like that!

Seriozha said that if it were possible in our society to have two wives, then he would marry them both. He would have housed and fed both of them, because he liked them both. Each for different reasons.

But in our society you can only have one wife. You have to make a choice. Seriozha did not know who he should stay with, but the other woman did. She was a strong person and she knew how to insist on her happiness.

After he left her, Lora started losing several pounds a day in weight. The flesh just dropped off her, and finally she just got into bed and never wanted to get up again. She was wasting away, because Seriozha had been her whole life. If there was no Seriozha, there could be no life for her.

Tanya saved helpings of food from her family meals to bring to Lora. She forced her to eat and talk, but did most of the talking herself.

★

The big town clock showed half-past six. The small watch on Lora's hand showed the same time.

The false witness was now one and a half hours late, and what was most unpleasant of all was the fact that Lora could see the treatment room from where she was standing, and Tanya's face kept bobbing up in the window from time to time. Lora could not make out her expression from where she was standing, but she could guess what it was anyway. It was as if Tanya was saying, 'What, still standing there? Well, go on then, carry on . . .'

Perhaps he had met the same strong woman with the earrings in her ears. Perhaps she had taken him by the hand and said, 'Come with me.' But he would gently free his hand and say politely, 'Strong women are for weak men. But I'm a strong man. That's why I'm off to meet Lora.'

Lora looked carefully round once more. An old man in overalls was putting up a poster for a new film. First he put up a board on which there was a picture of the actor Ulyanov's face. The edge of his cheek and his ear were missing, but his eyes, with their earnestly demanding and slightly impatient male squint, were nevertheless able to look out on to the world. The workman put up one more section and attached Ulyanov's ear to his cheek.

Over to the left was the House of Furniture. Cars kept driving up to the shop.

There were some rather hefty swarthy-looking men standing a little to one side of the entrance, who looked as if they were real men about town. They had both money and a goal which they were confident of reaching. If they didn't have a goal for some reason, they would have thought one up, and if they didn't have any confidence, they would have bought some.

Womanizers and wheeler-dealers like these men tend to eat a lot and their guts expand. The stomach raises the diaphragm two or three centimetres, and the diaphragm

presses on the heart, which gives them breathing difficult-
ies. They also have roving eyes. They are constantly
scouring the world with their eyes, looking for something
else to buy.

Lora was at the cemetery once. Some grave diggers
had sauntered past her in workman's jackets, with shovels
thrown over their shoulders. They wore their jackets with
a sort of casual elegance, and there was a youthful spring
in their step. Behind them trod some of those heavies in
sheepskin coats; they were getting a grave ready for one
of their mob. As they walked past Lora they ran their eyes
over her. And when she left the cemetery they were
waiting for her at the gate. Under no circumstances would
they let anything pass them by. And Lora could almost
feel their critical gaze on her even now, as they eyed her
pert breasts, her smooth pink face, and her strong legs.

But when *he* arrived, he would take Lora by the hand
and lead her away from all those leering eyes. And the
thugs would watch them as they left, incensed for a brief
moment by their impoverishment.

Seriozha had left Lora in the summer and two years later,
also in the summer, the senior partner at the clinic fell in
love with her. He was forty, she was twenty-two. He was
the most important doctor at the clinic, and therefore
highly respected, and Lora was proud of him.

The senior partner said that Lora was the woman of
his dreams, but that he could not betray his son. Let his
son finish school first and get a place at university, and
then the head physician would marry Lora and condemn
himself to happiness for the rest of his life.

Three years later the son left school and got a place at
an institute.

The senior partner said, 'Small children mean small
problems. But big children mean big problems.' If he left

his family now, he said, he would leave his son without a father, and then the boy might fall prey to bad influences and become a criminal or a drug addict. Let his son finish at the institute and find his feet, and then he would consider he had done the duty bestowed on him by God. Four long years passed.

So Lora had to sit at home all by herself in the evenings and weekends, even on New Year's Eve. When the Kremlin chimes rang out on the stroke of midnight, Lora would quickly write out her wish on a piece of paper, swallow it, down a glass of champagne, and go straight to bed, while all around her the walls shook and music jangled as other people greeted the New Year.

The senior partner forbade Lora to go alone to parties or to the theatre. He was very jealous, and asked her to put herself in his shoes. Lora was included in his good times, but not amongst his responsibilities. Time went by. The son had almost finished at the institute and was in his last year now, but it was just at that point that a small African state acquired its independence. The senior partner was invited to go to Africa, set up a clinic, and offer some friendly support.

The senior partner asked Lora to put herself in the shoes of the African state.

Strong people were strong because of their strength.

And weak people were strong because of their weakness.

All that was left for Lora was to believe in divine justice and wait for Someone Decent to come and include her in his orbit of good times and responsibilities. Then neither of them would have to put themselves in each other's shoes because their lives and destinies would be shared.

Lora had the sort of face one often came across. There were dozens more like her. Her ideal man would be drawn to her because she was Lora. For no other reason.

The eight o'clock showing was just beginning, and the space in front of the cinema became empty.

The House of Furniture had shut and those evil men had left.

Tanya had finished work and left the clinic.

It was pointless to carry on waiting, but Lora stood and waited. An inertia of loyalty had built up.

A nanny with a baby walked up to the cinema. The nanny looked about eighteen. With her round face and long straggly hair, she looked a bit like a coconut.

The girl stood there for a while, gazing dreamily over the child's head as if peering into the foggy contours of her future.

She stood there for a bit longer then left. The area around Lora became empty again. And there was an emptiness inside her too.

Do you really exist, divine justice? Or was everything just a meaningless accumulation of chance happenings? If a brick were to fall on you, was that also chance? The brick did not have to fall. It could fall on someone else even. Why did it absolutely have to fall on her? What was the reason?

'I knew you would wait.'

Lora gave a shudder and turned round.

He was standing in front of her, young and bearded, like Pushkin's Prince Guidon in jeans. Where had he sprung from? Perhaps he had been hiding behind the poster . . .

'Were you hiding on purpose?'

'No, I'm just late.'

'Why are you so late?' asked Lora, still not understanding, but sensing that this was happiness.

'I forgot it was the Kazakhstan. I could only remember it was somewhere in Central Asia. Somewhere warm . . .'

'So how did you end up here?'

'I wrote down all the cinemas with suitable names:

Kirghizia, Tbilisi, Alma Ata, Armenia, Tashkent,' he said ticking off the fingers on his right hand, then crossing over to the left hand when he ran out of fingers. 'Erevan, Baku, Uzbekistan . . .'

'But the Uzbekistan is a restaurant.'

'Yes, but there's a cinema too. In Lyanozovo. The Ashkhabad is in Chertanovo, the Tbilisi is on Profsoyuznaya Street – I've been on the road for four hours.'

'But Tbilisi isn't in Asia.'

'It's hot there, though.'

He fell silent and looked at Lora. He looked just like Prince Guidon does in the fairy tale, when he wakes up and suddenly sees the town with all its battlements and belfries stretching out before him.

'I knew you would wait.'

'How did you know?'

'I saw your eyes.'

HAPPY ENDING

I died at dawn, somewhere between four and five in the morning.

At first my hands and legs turned cold, as if someone had put wet stockings and gloves on to my feet and hands. Then the coldness went higher and reached my heart. My heart stopped, and I felt as if I had sunk to the bottom of a deep well. It's true that I had never lain at the bottom of a well before, but then I'd never been dead before either.

My face stretched into a mask and I could no longer control it. I felt neither pain nor regret. I just lay there, without thinking about what I looked like.

At eight o'clock I heard the shuffle of footsteps along the landing. It was my son Yuranya coming out of his bedroom.

Barefoot, I thought. He always walked barefoot, like a half-wild child of the forest, and I would always say 'Feet!' to him.

He shuffled along the landing until he got to his father's door. My husband coughed and turned over.

The door squeaked. Yuranya must have half opened it. 'Are you up yet?' he asked in a plaintive whisper.

'What do you want?' my husband replied in an irritated voice. He didn't like it when people bothered him at the weekend.

'I need to get to the cinema. I've got a subscription. It starts at nine,' said Yuranya, still whispering.

Yuranya thought that if he whispered he would not actually wake his father up.

'Go and wake up Mum,' ordered my husband.

He did not like it when he got lumbered with other people's duties. Although he also hated his own.

The door to my room creaked open.

Yuranya was silent at first, then he said, 'She's sleeping.'

'Never mind. She'll get up soon,' said my husband.

'She's sleeping,' repeated Yuranya. 'And she looks very pale.'

I was taken to the hospital at twelve o'clock and was handed back the next day.

They put my long dress on me. It had been brought back for me from Paris a year ago, but having a smart evening dress just added to all my problems, because there was absolutely nowhere I could wear it to. And so it just hung in my cupboard glittering and rustling, like an unnecessary reminder of all the good times I was supposed to be having.

Our neighbour from the sixth floor said, 'They won't take her in the next world. She was too young.'

'Left a little boy, too, didn't she? sighed another neighbour. This woman had seen her son through till he went on his pension, while I had not seen mine past primary school. She sketched out in her mind the rest of the journey I would now never complete, and shook her head.

Yuranya came in and out, feeling very pleased with himself. Everyone was being nice to him and he was flattered by all the attention. He wasn't feeling too bad, because the day before I had warned him, 'If I'm not there tomorrow and people say that I have died, don't believe them.'

'Where will you be then?' he had asked.

'I'm going to nestle on a cloud and watch over you from up above.'

'Oh, all right,' he said.

Our caretaker Nyura was surprised at all the pretence. After all, just the day before she had seen me in the street with a shopping bag and even heard me talking to our neighbour. 'Efim, whatever do you think you look like?' I had said to him.

'What's the matter?' he asked in surprise.

'Well, you look so dolled up. Just like a young lady.'

'I always dress like this,' said Efim, highly offended.

'Men ought to look rugged and scruffy,' I said as I ran down to the underpass.

Only yesterday I had been here with everyone, and now I was goodness knows where. I was obviously experiencing some sort of displacement. And if this displacement had happened to me, it meant it could happen to anyone, even to Nyura.

My husband had never believed in my illnesses before, and now he did not believe in my death either. Deep down he thought I was just acting up.

The flat was full of people. For some reason I thought fewer people would come. I didn't actually think there would be anyone to bury me, to be honest. I had got used to always doing everything myself and to doing it all by myself, and I had also got used to not depending on anyone. If I could have buried myself, I would have. But strangely enough, they seemed to cope all right without me. They even managed to reserve a place at the cemetery and fill in all the right forms.

The official at the registry of births, deaths, and marriages, a woman in a grey cardigan, gave my husband a certificate and demanded my passport in return. When he handed it to her, she looked at it without any interest, then tore it in two and threw it into the wastepaper basket.

When my husband saw my passport being torn up, he realized that I really had departed from this life and that nothing could be changed now. He was free now, but he did not know how to deal with his freedom yet. Or even whether he wanted it in the first place. Whatever you say, there were more advantages to having me around than there were disadvantages.

My husband came from home from the registry office looking as if he had been drugged – as if he too had entered the kingdom of eternal sleep.

My friends Alya and Elya came round during their lunch break. They are both very attractive women, but I was the only one able to perceive Alya's beauty; everyone thought Elya was beautiful.

Alya lived by herself, without anybody to love or a family to look after. She thought that I was really successful, and could not understand how I could possibly have wanted to throw it all up in exchange for my present state. Whatever was wrong with your life, surely anything was better than this . . .

Elya was as 'successful' as I was, and she had the same problem with the evening dress she could never wear. She was also equally tired of searching for alternative solutions to her problems. Actually, it wasn't so much that she was tired of trying to find a way out, more that she felt assaulted and burnt out by the whole process. But now at least she realized that she could never take her life by her own hand. She knew now that she would have to drink her cup to the dregs.

Alya and Elya looked at my mask-like face in bitter silence.

My death was a lesson for both of them.

I had become friends with them separately, and they had never got on well together. They always had some sort of moral pretensions towards each other, but now, as they stood by my coffin, those pretensions seemed totally groundless.

'We are all guilty before her,' said Alya. 'No one

wanted to know what was really going on inside her. No one wanted to help.'

'But how could anyone help her when she didn't need anyone?'

The telephone rang quite often. My husband would pick up the receiver and say that I couldn't come to the phone because I had died. Then a long pause would obviously follow at the other end. People were so shocked that they couldn't say a word. Nor did they know how to react: should they ask questions or not? Those who rang up generally remained silent. My husband also remained silent, then he would say goodbye and put the phone down.

But had *he* rung up? Probably not. He was waiting for me to ring him. Last time we had decided that love was not a sufficient reason to disrupt the lives of our children and we had started trying to find a solution to make everybody happy.

We struggled like flies beating against a window pane and we could even feel ourselves hitting the glass, but we still could not come up with an answer.

'I think we should part,' I suggested.

'But how will we live?' he asked.

That I did not know. Nor did he.

'Well, let's stay as we are, then,' I said.

'But that's not a life.'

'Do you have any better ideas?'

'The best solution would be if I died in a plane crash.'

'And what about your children?' I asked.

'They will have to love my memory.'

I wondered whether in fact he had called. Or whether he would ring up in two days' time like he always did.

'She's dead,' my husband would say.

He would not say anything. Nor would my husband. And then my husband would say goodbye and hang up.

And that would be all. No need to look for alternative solutions any more.

Death is boring precisely because it does not offer the possibility of any alternatives.

Towards evening my mother arrived from another city.

She told my husband that she would not leave him a single plate or pillowcase. She said she would rather smash and tear everything to pieces than leave it with him.

He got cross and said, 'Stop talking nonsense.'

My mother retorted that he was responsible for my death, and that he was the one who should have died, not me.

'That was only how she looked at things,' my husband replied. 'From the point of view of his mother,' he added, 'things were better the way they were now.'

By ten o'clock, everyone had gone. The flat became empty.

A clock ticked high up far away from me. Then I heard a rushing sound, as if someone had turned on a tap. I guessed that my husband was watching soccer on the box.

My mother came in and asked, 'How can you sit here and watch football?'

'What else is there for me to do?' he answered.

Indeed, what else was there for him to do?

I was buried two days later.

The snow had almost gone, and there were little streams everywhere. The earth was damp and heavy and this had a depressing effect on those who were living.

There were some fresh graves near to mine which had been decorated with artificial wreaths covered with cellophane. When the rain and the dirt finally disappeared they would take the cellophane off and the graves would become all festive.

The soil hit my coffin with a thud.

The little mound which formed was barely noticeable. They sprinkled it with fresh flowers, which were better than artificial wreaths, although less practical.

And then I saw God.

He was young and handsome.

I went up to Him in my long, glittering dress and looked into his eyes.

'Forgive me,' I said.

'People ask me to leave them on earth longer and you got up and left of your own accord. Why?'

'I couldn't see a way out.'

'Was this a way out?'

'At least there aren't any options this way. I was tired of all the options.'

'Couldn't you have put up with things the way they were?'

'No. I couldn't resign myself to them, and I couldn't change them either.'

Something disturbing from my previous existence suddenly made me anxious and I started crying.

He stroked my hair.

'Don't cry. I feel sorry for you. You see – I feel sorry for you.'

'I called you. I was waiting for you to decide. Why didn't you hear me?'

'I did hear you. And I answered that you should bear everything patiently, and that it would all come to pass.'

'Would it have?'

'Of course it would. Everything would have worked out fine.'

'Really?'

'Yes. Even better than before.'

'Then why didn't I hear you?'

'Because Love in you was stronger than God was. You were listening to Love.'

God passed his hand down my cheek, wiping away my tears. He was tall, with long hair, and looked rather like young people today. Only his eyes were different.

The starry galaxy twinkled above us, like the sequins on my dress.

'What do you want most?' asked God.

'I want to see *him*.'

God took me along the Milky Way. Then he stopped, waved his hand, and released my soul.

For a long time my soul flew in darkness, then it plunged into light. It circled above his house and flew in through an open window, coming to rest on the windowsill.

He was sitting at the table with his daughter playing cards.

I went up to him carefully and looked at his hand.

He was about to lose. And I couldn't even tell him.

He rang two days later, as per usual.

I picked up the phone but he did not say anything. I knew it was him though. I said, 'I'm going to die, and you are going to squander your life away.'

'You're not going to die,' he replied. 'What nonsense . . .'

We fell silent again. We could be silent for a long time and still not be bored. We stood at opposite ends of the city, listening to each other's breathing.

THE HAPPIEST DAY
OF MY LIFE
(A Teenager's Tale)

We were set a composition to write in class on 'The Happiest Day of My Life'.

I opened my exercise book and started wondering which was the happiest day in my life. I chose Sunday, four months ago, when Dad and I went to the cinema, and afterwards went round to my granny's. That was an extra nice day. But our teacher Marya Efremovna says that we can only be really happy when we are helping others. What use was I to other people when I was at the cinema or at Granny's? I could have ignored what Marya Efremovna said, but I had to get higher marks. I could have just gone and got a C+, but then I wouldn't move up to the fifth form, and I'd be sent to technical school. Marya Efremovna warned us that there were too many intellectuals in the country at the moment, and not enough people in the working class, so they were going to use us to create a pool of qualified workers.

I looked over at the exercise book of Lenka Konovalova, who sits next to me, and saw she was scribbling with incredible speed and enthusiasm. Lenka's happiest day was when she became a Pioneer.

I started remembering the day when we became Young Pioneers at the Border Guards Museum and there weren't enough membership badges to go round. The leaders ran all over the place looking for a badge they could give to me but they couldn't find one. I told them 'Never mind, it doesn't matter . . .' but I was in a bad mood after that and stopped paying attention. We were taken round the museum afterwards and told all about its history, but I don't remember anything except that we once shared some little river with the Japanese and even fought over it. But it didn't get as far as war, I don't think. Or maybe I've got it wrong. I never remember those sorts of things. They don't interest me at all.

Once my mum and I took an old drunk home. He had lost one of his boots and was sitting out there in the snow with only a sock on. Mum said we couldn't just leave him out there in the cold. Maybe something terrible had happened to him. So we asked him what his address was and took him home. There was probably a lot of good in that probably, because the man ended up sleeping at home rather than in a snowdrift, so his family did not have to worry. But you could hardly call that the happiest day of your life. All we did was take him home after all.

I leaned over to my right and peered into Masha Gvozdeva's exercise book. She sits in front of me. I couldn't make anything out, but Masha was probably writing that her happiest day was when their broken synchro-phasotron blew up and they got given a new one. That Masha is just crazy about diagrams and formulas. She's got outstanding mathematical ability, and she already knows where she is going to go to university. She's got some purpose in her life. But all I have, so Marya Efremovna says, is a large vocabulary, which I am able to use well. That's why I get to do the talks at the music school about the lives and works of composers. The music teacher writes out the talks and I just read them out. For example, 'Beethoven was a plebeian, but everything he achieved in life he achieved through his own effort . . .' I also announce the programmes at concerts. For example: 'The sonatina by Clementi will be played by Katya Shubina, who is studying with Mr Rossolovsky.'

And it sounds convincing enough, because I am tall, have a good complexion, and I wear foreign clothes. The good complexion and the foreign clothes I got from my mum, but I don't know where I got my height from. I read somewhere that these modern prefabricated apartment blocks which don't let any air in create conditions similar to those in a greenhouse, so children tend to grow in them as fast as hothouse cucumbers.

Masha Gvozdeva will certainly become an intellectual because there is much more use in her brains than in her hands. But I haven't got good hands or brains, just a big vocabulary. It's not even a literary ability; I only know a lot of words because I read a lot. I get that from my dad. But it's not as if you need to know lots of words. The boys in our class get by quite happily with about six words: right on, OK, cool, wicked, and radical. And Lenka Konovalova will sustain any conversation with two phrases: 'Well, yes, you're right really . . .' and 'Well, of course, that's right . . .' And that turns out to be quite sufficient. Firstly she lets the other person talk, and that is always nice. And secondly she shares their doubts: 'Well, yes, you're right really . . .', 'Well, of course, that's right . . .'

A week ago I heard a programme on the radio about happiness. They were saying that happiness was when you got something you wanted. And true happiness was when you got something you really wanted. Although once you got what you wanted, happiness had to come to an end, because it was the process of trying to achieve something which brought happiness, not the actual achievement itself.

What do I want? I want to move up to the fifth form and I want a sheepskin coat. My fur coat is too big for me, and I look as if I'm walking around in a big wooden box in it. It's a bit risky wearing a sheepskin to school, because the boys in our school slash the sleeves with a razor and cut off the buttons in the cloakroom, but I never go anywhere else, so I don't know when else I'd wear it.

But what do I really want? I really want to move up to the fifth form, and I want to get a place at Moscow University to study languages, and become acquainted with the actor K.K. Mum says that it's normal to fall in love with actors at my age. Twenty years ago she was also madly in love with an actor, and the whole class went mad about him. But now he's as fat as a pig. You'd be amazed what time does to people.

But my mum doesn't understand me because I'm not actually in love with K.K. It's just that he plays d'Artagnan and he's so brilliant at it that it seems as if he really is d'Artagnan – clever, dashing, and romantic. Not like our boys with their 'right ons' and their 'OKs'. Plus they're an inch smaller than I am.

I've seen *The Three Musketeers* six times. Rita Pogosian has seen it ten times. Her mum works at the Hotel Minsk and she can get you any tickets you want. Not like my parents, who can't get anything, and live just on their salaries.

Rita and I once waited for K.K. at the end of the show. We followed him as he left the theatre, got into the same compartment as him on the Underground and then just stared at him. When he looked at us, though, we immediately looked away and started giggling. Rita has managed to find out through her friends that K.K. is married and has a small son. A good thing it's a son and not a daughter, because people always love little girls more. Less affection is wasted on little boys, so a tiny bit of every man's heart is always free for new love. It's true that there is a big difference in age between K.K. and me – twenty years in fact. In five years' time I will be eighteen and he will be thirty-eight, but that's his problem. Youth has never got in the way of anybody before.

Rita says that K.K. is very ambitious. In America people shoot presidents for the sake of their careers. It's not that big a deal. Well, of course it's bad, but at least things like that aren't done here for the sake of careers yet. It's difficult to tell whether that's a bad or a good thing. My dad, for example, isn't ambitious, but I don't see the mark of great happiness on his face. He has no real incentives and a tiny salary. But grown-ups treat money like school grades. In class recently I had to give a talk about the political situation in Honduras. To be honest, what on earth do I care about Honduras? And what does Honduras care about me for that matter? But Marya Efremovna said that apolitical people won't get moved up to the fifth form. So I did my homework dutifully and churned out all the required political information. I'm not going to take risks for Honduras.

Lenka Konovalova has turned the page and has already scrawled her way through half an exercise book. While I'm still sitting here mulling over in my mind exactly when my happiest day was.

I remember the following phrases from the programme about happiness: 'The prospect of sleepless nights behind the wheel of a combine harvester'. Maybe that combine harvester driver was also career-minded.

If I am going to be really honest, my happiest days are when I come home from school and there is no one at home. I love my mother, I really do. She doesn't put pressure on me, she doesn't make me take music lessons, and she doesn't make me eat bread with my meals. I can do whatever I want when she is there just as much as when she isn't there. But it's not quite the same though. For instance, she always puts the needle down on records the wrong way, and it makes a horrible screech in the speakers. It always feels as if the needle is scratching my heart. I say, 'Can't you put the needle on properly?' and she says, 'I am doing it properly.' It's like that every time.

When she's not at home there's always a note on the door: 'Key under the mat. Food on the stove. Home at six. You're a nutcase. Love, Mum.'

I read in the newspaper that Moscow has the lowest crime rate in the world. That means Moscow is the most peaceful capital in the world. And it's true. I've found that out through my own experience. If ever the very worst amateur burglar, or even a curious person with bad habits, chanced to come up our stairs and read Mum's note, he would receive very precise instructions. Key under the mat: open the door and come in. Food on the stove: heat it up and have some lunch. And the occupants will be back at six. So there is no hurry, and you could even relax with the paper in an armchair before leaving around six, taking Dad's jeans, his leather jacket, and Mum's Alaskan wolf-fur coat with you. There's nothing else valuable in our flat because we are from the intelligentsia and we live only on what we earn.

Mum says that when a person is afraid of being burgled, they will definitely be burgled. Whatever a person is afraid of always happens, so one should never fear anything. And it's quite true. Whenever I am frightened of getting called on in class, I always get called on.

Whenever I get out of the lift and see Mum's note, I am pleased, because it means that I can live how I want for a bit and not have to fit in with other people. I go into the flat, and instead of heating my lunch up, I eat straight from the frying pan with my fingers, standing up in my fur coat. It is always much better cold, because it loses its taste when it's hot.

Then I turn the record player on full blast and invite Lenka Konovalova over. We pull all Mum's dresses out of the wardrobe, and begin trying them on and dancing in them. We dance in her long dresses with the group Blue Bird belting out: 'Don't be cro-o-oss with me, oh don't be cross, and don't regret what I have done, I'm no great loss.' And the sun comes streaming in through the window.

Then Lenka goes home, and I go and sit in the armchair, wrap myself up in a rug, and read. I'm reading two books at the moment: Julio Cortazar's short stories and the plays of Alexander Vampilov. They were given to my mother by the people who suck up to her at work.

I like this bit in Vampilov: 'Dad, we have a guest plus someone else.' And Dad replies, 'Vasenka, a guest plus someone else means two guests . . .' When I read, I start seeing K.K. in my mind, and it makes me sad to think that he is married and that there is such a big difference between our ages.

In Cortazar's story 'The End of the Game' there are the words 'inexpressibly beautiful'. These words have such an effect on me that they make me stop and think a while. Sometimes it seems to me that life is inexpressibly beautiful. And than at other times everything seems completely boring and I ask Mum, 'Why do people live?' 'To suffer,' she tells me, remembering Gorky's lines. 'Suffering is our normal state.' But Dad says, 'That's only for fools. Man was born to be happy.' Mum says, 'You've forgotten to add "like a bird is born to fly". And you could also say that pity humiliates people.' Dad says, 'Of course pity humiliates people, but only fools rely on pity. Clever people rely on themselves.' And Mum says that pity means compassion, taking part in people's suffering. That is what holds the world together, she says, and it is also a talent which is not something many people have, even if they are clever.

But my parents don't argue often, because they see each other so rarely. When Dad is home in the evenings, Mum is always out. And vice versa. If Mum is out, Dad sits at home reading the paper and watching ice-hockey on the TV. (We once had a nanny who could not pronounce the word 'hockey'. She used to call it 'thockey'.) Then when he's done that, he demands to inspect my school journal. And then he begins shouting at me as if I was deaf or was in the next-door flat and he wanted me to hear through the wall. When Dad shouts I never get frightened for some reason. I just understand less. I want to say, 'Don't shout. Please speak calmly.' But instead I just blink and say nothing.

Sometimes Mum comes home quite late, but still earlier than Dad. She is thrilled when she sees that his coat is not on the hook. She rushes to get into her pyjamas and we start dancing on the carpet in the middle of the room, kicking our legs up in the air like loonies, both barefoot and in our pyjamas. Mum's pyjamas have diamonds and mine have spots. We make whooping sounds with our mouths wide open, but only in a whisper, and we find it inexpressibly beautiful.

But when Mum has study days and she spends the whole day at home, cooking up food for the next few days ahead, and when Dad doesn't come home till late at night, she comes straight into my room, ignoring the fact that I have to sleep, and shouldn't be chatting, and begins getting me all wound up.

'I think he has left us,' she says.

'What about his leather jacket and his jeans?' I say. 'He wouldn't leave without taking them.'

'He could come and get them later.'

'Rubbish,' I say. 'He won't ever leave me.'

I am afraid, though. I start feeling sick in the bottom of my stomach and my nose itches. I cannot imagine life without my father. I'd sink to Cs and Ds. In fact I'd give up school altogether and go to pieces. I only get good marks because of my father; it's just so he will be pleased. I'd be content with Cs. And Mum would be too. She reckons that C is satisfactory. 'That means the state is satisfied.'

'I'm going to divorce him,' Mum says.

'Reason?'

'He doesn't help me. I have to work to earn my living, and I also have to stand in the queues and cart shopping bags around.'

'Were things different before?'

'No. It's always been like this.'

'Then why didn't you divorce him earlier, ten years ago?'

'I wanted to be able to give you a good childhood.'

'So when I was young and didn't understand anything, you wanted to give me a childhood. And now, when I have grown up, you want to take away someone close to me. That's treachery.'

'That's the way it has to be.'

'No, it doesn't. Then I'm not going to have anything to do with you in that case.'

'You've got your whole life ahead of you. But I want to be happy too.'

I cannot understand how anyone the age of thirty-five who has a child could want any other happiness for themselves. But it wouldn't be tactful to say so. So I say, 'When you have you seen anyone who is a hundred per cent happy? Look at Auntie Nina. Granted she is five years younger than you, and twenty pounds lighter, but she has to live without a husband. She has to use two forms of transport to get to work every day, and it's an hour and a half each way. And she only works at the chemical manufacturing plant just so she can earn enough to live on. But you work just across the road, you love your job, and everyone respects you. You've found your place in life. That is fifty per cent already. I am a successful child, and I'm healthy and well developed. That's another forty-five. I don't have any illnesses – that's another one per cent. So you've already got ninety-six per cent happiness, which means only four per cent is left . . . But where have you seen anyone who is a hundred per cent happy? Just name me someone.'

Mum is silent, thinking about who she could name. And in fact there isn't anyone who is a hundred per cent happy. 'There are creaking floorboards in every house.' Or 'there's a skeleton in every cupboard', as I read somewhere. But Mum is not consoled by other people's lack of happiness. She wants that four per cent rather than the fifty she has got. She sits on my bed shivering like an orphan, so I say, 'Lie down with me and I'll send you to sleep.'

So she lies down with me under the blankets. She has cold feet and presses them selfishly against my legs. But I can put up with that. She sheds a tear which falls on my eyelid and I can put up with that too. I love her very much. Everything actually hurts from all the love inside me. But I know that if I start to pity her, she will become even more pathetic. So I say, 'Go and look at yourself in the mirror in the light of day. Who else would want you except for me and Dad? You have got to live for us.'

But generally, I think that people have got to be selfish, to be honest. Selfish and ambitious. If they want to live well, that is. Because when people feel happy, other people around them start feeling happy too. Just like if one person feels bad, then everyone around starts feeling miserable. You never see anyone burning on a funeral pyre with their relatives dancing all around, after all.

We hear a scraping sound. It is Dad carefully putting the key in the lock so as not to wake us. He goes into the hall on tiptoes and stands there for some time. He must be taking his coat off. Then he goes into his room, still on tiptoes, while the floorboards creak guiltily. Granny said once that Dad hasn't found himself yet. Whenever he is tiptoeing about, I always think he is walking around looking into all the corners, trying to find himself without turning on the light. And I feel awfully sorry for him. Perhaps I won't find myself until I am forty years old and won't know what to do with myself.

Mum calms down when she hears Dad's footsteps, and falls asleep on my shoulder, breathing into my cheek. I hug her and hold on to her as if she were a treasure. I lie there and think: If only she could hurry up and put on some weight . . . I dream of my parents getting old and fat. Who would want them then? Only themselves. And me. But now they are slim and they wear jeans, and they are always rushing around everywhere in a hurry. It seems to me sometimes that one of their legs is buried in the ground, while the other is trying to run off in various directions. But where can you run with one leg buried in the ground?

Lenka's mother doesn't have a husband at all, by the way – just three children, all from different fathers, plus a blind grandmother, two cats, and a puppy. But their home is always noisy, messy, and fun. Perhaps it's because Lenka's mum never has the time to do anything about the mess. When people have spare time, they start thinking. And if you start to think, you invariably end up thinking of something to worry about.

A year ago a little boy from our street got run over by a car. Everyone ran over to look, but I just ran home. I was terrified – not for myself, but for my parents. I am still frightened. What if something were to happen to me? What if I got run over? What will happen when I grow up and get married? Who could I leave them with? What would they do without me?

Zagoruiko went up to Marya Efremovna and handed in his exercise book. His happiest day will probably be when the Beatles get together again. Zagoruiko knows all the current foreign groups: Kiss, Queen, Boney M . . . All I know is 'Beethoven is a plebeian', the notes of a serenade by Schumann, and a few things by ear.

I looked at my watch. Sixteen minutes to go. I couldn't think any more or I'd get a D, then I wouldn't get moved up to the fifth form and I'd have to become a lathe-adjuster or a sewing machinist. A seamstress with a big vocabulary.

I decided to write about how we planted trees around the school. I read somewhere that during one's lifetime each person should plant a tree, have a child, and write a book about the times in which they lived.

I remembered dragging over a bucket full of black earth to put into the hole, so that the tree would take root better. Zagoruiko came up to me and said, 'Let me give you a hand.'

'No, I can manage,' I said, hauling the bucket further. I sprinkled the earth into the hole and patted it down with my hands. The handles of the bucket had made a deep blue imprint on my palms. My shoulder ached and even my insides ached.

'I'm whacked,' I informed everyone with tragic dignity.

'Of course you are!' rejoiced Zagoruiko spitefully. 'First of all you had to show off, and now you want to boast about it.'

Zagoruiko is horrible. He says exactly what he thinks, although people are educated so that they can hide their real feelings when they are out of place.

But despite everything, that tree took root and will be there for future generations. Marya Efremovna would give me an A for content and I hardly ever make grammatical mistakes. I have an innate ability to spell words correctly.

I looked at the clock again. Eleven minutes left. I shook my pen (I use a fountain pen rather than a ballpoint), and started writing about how Dad and I went one morning to the cinema and then went on to Granny's. Let Marya Efremovna give me whatever mark she wanted.

I'll never be really selfish or ambitious. I'm going to live on my own means.

I wrote that the comedy film we saw was terribly funny; it had Louis de Funes in the main role. We laughed so much that people turned round to stare at us and someone tapped on my back with a crooked finger, as if they were knocking on a door. And it was the same as always at Granny's. We sat in the kitchen and ate some delicious fish (although Mum always says that Granny's fish is unsalted and tastes of ammonia, as though it had been marinated in urine). But it wasn't what we ate that was important, it was the sort of day it was. Everyone was very affectionate towards me and said nice things about me that day. And I felt as if I loved everybody a hundred per cent and was making people happy too. I have my dad's eyes, and Dad has Granny's eyes: brown with arched eyebrows like rooftops. We looked at each other with the same eyes and felt the same things. We were like a tree: Granny was the roots, Dad was the trunk, and I was the branches reaching towards the sun.

And it was inexpressibly beautiful.

Of course that wasn't the happiest day ever in my life. Just a very happy one. My happiest day hasn't happened yet. It is yet to come.

A WEE DROP
TO CALM THE NERVES

The window threw off a golden orange light, and in the midst of this scattered golden light a girl was visible. She was sitting on the edge of a chair, leaning a harp against herself, and its silver sounds were floating out over the courtyard into the evening air.

Nikitin, who was a junior research assistant, was sitting in the building opposite in his one-room flat. He was looking out of the window with his arms on the windowsill and his head on his arms.

Almost all the girls that he knew smoked, wore their jeans rolled up over their boots like pirates, drove cars, and swore like troopers. This all had its own kind of charm and was actually rather fashionable. It was quite chic at that time in fact to be a bit of a tomboy, to play the *enfant terrible* (which in translation of course just means 'terrible child'). But this girl in the building opposite was neither a tomboy nor a pirate, just a girl. There was something angelic about her, though. Even her accessories (like her harp, for example) had something angelic about them.

Nikitin stared and stared. He was sitting in complete darkness so he would not be seen from the other side.

Suddenly she stood up, stretched like any normal person would, and went over to the window. She started looking across to where Nikitin was sitting, and in a flash he had slid down from the windowsill and was crouching on the floor, rooted to the spot. Finally he dared to look up. The curtains in the gold window had been drawn.

He stood up, the joints in his knees cracking as he straightened himself out, and turned on the light. The light revealed a one-bedroom flat belonging to a person who was obviously something of a radio enthusiast, as there were bits of metal and wire of all shapes and sizes lying around everywhere. Nikitin himself looked as if he was standing amongst the debris of a plane crash, and his face bore the expression of a pilot who had just crash landed on a desert island.

He went on standing there for a while, then went over to the telephone and dialled seven digits in quick succession. He held his breath.

'Hello,' said the voice, all silvery like a harp.

Nikitin did not say anthing.

'I can't hear you,' said the voice confidently.

'I'm not saying anything,' said Nikitin.

'Why is that?'

'Well, you see . . . You don't know me at all . . . You wouldn't even be able to imagine . . . The thing is, I'm your neighbour . . . from the building opposite . . .'

'Why can't I imagine? You have striped curtains. You do exercises at seven fifteen every morning with dumb-bells. And at seven thirty-five you drink milk straight out of the carton.'

'So you can see me too?'

'Yes, I can.'

'In the evenings as well?'

'In the evenings as well.'

Nikitin wiped his forehead with his sleeve.

'What's your name, Mr Opposite Neighbour?'

'Zhenya . . . I mean, Evgeny Pavlovich . . . Well, Zhenya really.'

'I'm Natasha.'

They fell silent.

'What are you doing tonight?' Zhenya asked, growing bolder. 'Would you like to go for a walk?'

'Why don't you come over and we'll talk about it. Yes, maybe a walk would be nice.'

'But when, though?'

'How about now?' suggested Natasha.

'Staircase five, flat twelve?' verified Nikitin.

'How do you know?' asked Natasha in amazement.

'I calculated it. I'm a mathematician, you see. I've calculated your address too, and your phone number.'

'What about me?'

'Can it really be possible to calculate a dream?' Nikitin replied, half answering, half asking.

'Well, I'll be waiting for you,' said Natasha quietly before putting the phone down.

Nikitin stood and listened to the dialling tone, still not quite understanding, but nevertheless sensing that happiness had arrived.

In twenty minutes he had left his flat, wearing a Polish striped shirt, a Yugoslavian tie, which was pink with black spots, and a Finnish blue suit. He had done up all three buttons on the jacket.

As he was about to run down from the third floor, he glanced hurriedly at his reflection in the window, and this detained him for a few seconds. He touched his tie nervously. Then just as nervously, he went down one more flight of stairs and went over to a door which was insulated with dark red leather and and decorated with shiny knobs. He rang on the bell, which gave out an amusing jingle.

The door was opened by Professor Gusakov, clad in a quilted dressing-gown, such as were worn at home by lawyers in pre-revolutionary Russia. Gusakov was a member of the Academy of Sciences, a fellow of four Royal Societies, and Director of the Institute where Nikitin worked as a junior research assistant. Gusakov's flat was number 69 and Nikitin's flat was 96, and so the postman often got their letters mixed up.

Gusakov got about six hundred times more letters than Nikitin did. He was a important figure both here and abroad, in each of the four countries which had societies that he was a member of, and so Nikitin appeared in front of his padded door fairly often. They got quite used to him in fact. Gusakov's wife Isabella maybe even thought he worked for the Post Office. Each time she saw him she would give him a thin smile, and he would smile politely back, trying to work out her age. She had to be either thirty or sixty.

'Good evening, sir!' said Nikitin.

'Hello, Zhenya,' said Gusakov, noticing that Nikitin had come empty-handed.

'I hope you'll forgive me, but there's a rather odd question I want to ask you. May I?'

'Please, go ahead!'

'Valery Felixovich, you've travelled all over the world. Could you tell me, does this tie go with this shirt?'

'About as well as a saddle on a cow,' reckoned Gusakov frankly. 'You need to wear a plain one with it.'

'A plain one?' repeated Nikitin, feeling a little lost.

'Why don't you come in?' asked Gusakov, proceeding to retreat back into his flat. Nikitin followed him inside.

The walls of the flat were completely covered with keys of varying sizes and descriptions; everything from warehouse keys to the keys of the city of Antwerp.

'Going on a date?' Gusakov asked with interest, as he walked past the keys.

'Yes,' confessed Nikitin.

'Are you in love?' Gusakov asked with envy.

'Well, you know . . . she's different from everyone else.'

'It always seems like that at first.'

'Oh, no,' said Nikitin, stopping dead in his tracks, and making Gusakov stop as well. 'Everyone else is everyone else. But she's something special.'

Gusakov opened a cupboard. His wardrobe, to be frank, was rather larger than Nikitin's, and the choice of ties considerably greater. He had fourteen plain ties alone.

'Try it on!' said Gusakov, offering him a tie from his collection.

'I don't know if I should . . .' said Nikitin.

'It's a present!'

Gusakov evidently rather enjoyed playing Father Christmas. He tied a wide, opulent knot round Nikitin's long, scraggy neck, then took a gold-coloured suede jacket from a hanger.

'And this would go very well with the tie.'

'Hey, come on! I couldn't wear this! What if I spilt something on it?'

'Well, just make sure you don't.'

Gusakov got Nikitin dressed up in the jacket and took a step back to look at him, screwing up his eyes as he did so. The Nikitin standing before him now was completely different to one who had knocked on his door ten minutes earlier. The new Nikitin gave off an air of having a quite different life style. He looked as if he had just got back from the most beautiful country in the world, and had a brand-new pair of crystal slippers (size five) sitting in his briefcase.

'It looks very good on you, I must say,' said Gusakov enviously. 'It's a tiny bit too small for me . . .'

'I'll return it tonight,' said Nikitin hastily. He was scared that he would get given the jacket now, and then his heart would be unable to cope and would burst with gratitude.

'Or tomorrow, if you like,' said Gusakov, reassuring him. He was playing the role of Father Christmas after all, not that of a complete madman, and he had absolutely no intention of giving away a jacket made of antelope hide. There was no label anywhere to tell you it was made

172

of antelope rather than pig hide, but the noble origins of the jacket could nevertheless be felt, and somehow elevated the wearer into another social bracket.

Isabella poked her head round the door.

'He's fallen in love,' said Gusakov, to explain what was going on, 'and he's going out on a date.'

'Really?' said Isabella in her soft, deep voice, examining Nikitin as if trying to find some sign that he was one of the elect. 'That's wonderful. So why are you looking so glum?'

'I'm terrified,' Nikitin confessed. 'To be honest, we barely know each other . . .'

Gusakov opened the drinks cabinet and poured two half-measures of whisky. He held one out to Nikitin.

'Thanks,' said Nikitin, 'but I don't drink.'

'No one is asking you to drink. This is just a mild sedative. Like medicine.'

Nikitin drank it down obediently and then started coughing. He stood there for a minute in a state of paralysis, then left, still in a state of paralysis. He shut the door behind him.

'What a weird chap,' said Isabella.

'Yes, he is a bit strange,' agreed Gusakov. 'Capable, though. And he is more devoted to his work than he is to furthering his own career, which is a good thing.'

'Why don't you give him Koshelyov's job?' asked Isabella.

'What would I do with Koshelyov?'

'Make him retire. Or promote him.'

Gusakov looked at his wife, or rather, through his wife, thinking over the possibility.

'Don't you think it's a bit early?' he asked doubtfully.

'People ought to get things in life early on. While they still want them, that is. All the cabinet ministers in Cuba are young, you know.'

'Yes, but Cuba is a quite different kettle of fish,' said Gusakov thoughtfully. 'They've got a different climate there, you see. They've got bananas growing there.'

Nikitin meanwhile had walked across the courtyard. He had marched decisively over to staircase five, gone up to the third floor and walked straight across to flat number twelve. He had stood there for a while, then had turned round and, just as decisively, marched back down again.

The word 'Bluebird' was written in blue letters on the corner of the building, and beneath the letters there was a drawing of a bird, only you could not tell what sort of bird it was. Nikitin did not have time for birds. He went into the café and beckoned to the waitress.

'Have you got anything to drink? A wee drop of vodka, perhaps?'

'This isn't a bar, you know,' answered the waitress haughtily.

'Oh, sorry. Where is the nearest bar, then?'

'In the shop next door.'

There was a long queue in the wine and spirits section, but it was moving quite briskly, and Nikitin soon found himself standing in front of Nyura the shop assistant. Nyura was wearing a blue beret and a white overall, and she had a bruise below her eye which had almost faded. Maybe she had come to blows with an undisciplined customer.

'Could you tell me please, do you have any miniature bottles?' asked Nikitin, indicating the size of bottle with his thumb and forefinger.

'Ah, you mean a tiddler,' someone said behind his back.

'Yes, a tiddler,' confirmed Nikitin.

'No, we don't!' replied Nyura, as if affronted by the impossible request.

'Well, how about one a bit bigger?'

'That's a middler,' he heard behind his back.

'Yes, a middler.'

'Nope, we haven't got any of these either!'

'Get a move on!' people in the queue were demanding. 'There are people here who have got to go to work!'

Nikitin obediently stepped aside from the counter. He was totally confused.

'How about going halves on one?' asked a nice-looking man with a beard who had come up to Nikitin. He looked like a member of the Duma, the old tsarist state council. Or perhaps a former member. 'I don't need a whole bottle either. Let's get one and split it.'

Nikitin turned back to Nyura.

'Get into the queue!' said the voices behind his back.

'But I've been standing here! Haven't I been standing here?' Nikitin asked Nyura in an attempt to establish some sort of justice.

'Let the queue decide,' Nyura commanded. She decided nothing on her own, seeing herself as part of the loose collective that went under the name of 'the queue'.

Nikitin said goodbye to justice with a wave of his hand and went to stand at the end of the queue.

'It's outrageous!' the man with the beard fumed. 'I just need a bit of spirit to make a compress. But they won't give you any in the chemist without a prescription.'

That was when Fedya appeared.

You could read the entire story of his past and current life from his face and the clothes he was wearing.

'Let me get it!' suggested Fedya, plucking the five-rouble note out from between Nikitin's fingers.

Without waiting for an answer, and evidently not needing one anyway, Fedya took the money and went to the front of the queue.

'A bottle please, Nyura!' he said, holding the money over people's heads.

'Get into the queue!' the queue demanded.

'It's for someone who's sick,' explained Fedya as he took the bottle from Nyura, also over people's heads. He and Nyura obviously had some sort of racket going on between them.

Fedya brought the bottle back to Nikitin with a rouble forty change. 'Let's go,' he commanded. 'I've got a glass.'

The three men left the shop.

On the street, vehicles and pedestrians were passing continually. Street life was moving at its regular pace.

'Let's duck into this yard over here,' suggested Fedya, heading towards an archway.

They stopped by a sandpit in a children's play area. Two little boys were making a tunnel in the sand.

'I don't think this is quite the right place,' said Nikitin. So they carried on further round the corner of the building, where there were some large rubbish bins full of domestic refuse.

The man got out his purse and started poking around for some change.

'Here,' he said, giving Fedya three coins. 'Here's sixty kopecks. I only want a tiny drop.'

Fedya fished the glass out of his pocket and wiped it with the corner of his jacket. Then he opened the bottle and poured it out a little into the glass. He inspected the glass, then pondered the matter a while. The result of all these deliberations was that he poured half of it back accurately into the bottle.

'Here,' he said. 'That's about sixty kopecks' worth.'

The man took the glass and was all set to depart.

'Hey! Where do you think you're off to?' exclaimed Fedya in surprise.

'I need to get home. I've got to make a compress for my dog. The cat scratched her,' explained the gentleman.

'Well, what about the glass? Do you think it's one of nature's gifts? It cost money too, you know.'

'How much do you want?'

'Fifty kopecks.'

The man once more burrowed for his purse. He found fifty kopecks, gave the money to Fedya and left.

'The cheek of it!' protested Fedya. 'The dog gets to drink out of a glass, while we poor mortals have to drink out of the bottle!'

He marked his share on the bottle with his fingernail and started drinking. Then he checked the level of the bottle, took two more swigs and handed the bottle over to Nikitin.

'Here!'

'I don't think I could,' said Nikitin awkwardly.

'Just take a deep breath,' instructed Fedya. Nikitin obediently breathed in.

'Keep it held in!'

Nikitin held it in.

'Now drink!'

Nikitin took a few gulps.

'And breathe out!'

Nikitin started coughing.

'Here, have a sniff of this!'

Fedya got out a dusty bit of gherkin from his pocket and shoved it under Nikitin's nose. He held it there for a moment, then put it back in his pocket.

'Well? Can you feel it spreading out inside you?' he asked solicitously.

'Yes,' he replied uncertainly.

'How about going to get another one?' suggested Fedya.

'Er, no thanks. I don't usually drink actually . . .' Nikitin confessed.

'No, nor do I.'

'No, really. It's just today that I'm drinking. To calm my nerves.'

'What, got to go to court or something?'

'Oh no . . . Just imagine: her window is right opposite mine. It's night time. The stars are out. And she's playing *Scheherazade*.'

Nikitin started running his fingers over imaginary strings to demonstrate how she played.

'I'm starting to get a touch of the shakes too,' said Fedya. 'Come on, let's get another bottle.'

'I need to think about it.'

'OK, think it over,' Fedya agreed.

'No! No more! That's it!' said Nikitin, carving the air with his hand. 'I'm not afraid! I'm going to get up now and go!'

'Where to?' asked Fedya, puzzled.

'To her place.'

'Have you been invited?' verified Fedya.

'Yes!'

'Well, you can't go empty handed! You better get a bottle to take with you!'

'That's a good idea . . .'

'A bottle and a tin of sardines,' said Fedya, completing the idea.

'Of perfume!' interpreted Nikitin. 'How come I didn't think of that before . . .'

There was a woman already standing at the counter at the perfume shop, but Fedya, being incapable of standing in queues, nudged her aside with his shoulder.

'Excuse me,' he apologized. 'But we've got a plane to catch.'

The woman looked at Fedya in his tatty nylon anorak, then at Nikitin in his elegant suede jacket, and lines of concentration appeared on her face. She was trying to join these two people together in her mind, but she could not quite make the connection. In the end she just shrugged her shoulders and walked off.

'Could you tell me what your best perfume is, please?' Nikitin asked the saleswoman.

'Get the eau de cologne,' suggested Fedya.

'*Clemas*. It's French. It costs fifty roubles,' replied the saleswoman.

'How much?' asked Fedya in disbelief.

'Fifty,' replied the saleswoman calmly.

'Crikey! I'll get into a box myself for that much!'

'It's unlikely anyone would want to buy you though,' said the saleswoman doubtfully, eyeing Fedya up and down, from his scruffy hair to his sneakers.

'Do we pay you or do we have to go to the till?' asked Nikitin.

'Pay at the till.'

Nikitin went up to the till. Fedya rushed after him.

'You shouldn't spoil her, Zhenya, you really shouldn't. She'll pull a fast one on you later, take it from me. Get the eau de cologne. It's all out of the same barrel anyway. Believe me . . .'

'She's a harpist,' said Nikitin, raising a finger.

'An artist . . .' repeated Fedya with scorn. 'Oh, I know what they're like. You've got to give them caviare and diamonds all the time. Where are you going to get diamonds from? What sort of job have you got?'

'I'm a mathematician.'

'Well, I'm a mathematician too. Look, work it out . . .'

Meanwhile Nikitin had paid for the perfume, handed over the receipt, and received in return a bottle of *Clemas* in an emerald-coloured box. Fedya realized that the deed was done, and that it was too late to change anything.

'Very nice,' he said approvingly. 'Now we had better go and have a drink to celebrate.'

The Havana restaurant was decorated inside with all kinds of ornaments and carvings designed to create a Latin American atmosphere. Exotic curtains completely covered up the great Leninsky Prospekt that stretched out in front of the restaurant, and Nikitin felt as if he really was in Havana rather than Moscow.

A singer behind the window was singing 'Bessame mucha' – 'Kiss me, girl', to those who don't know Spanish.

'There's so much good in people,' said Nikitin, feeling a need to philosophize. 'Take us, for example. We hardly know each other, and look how kind you've been to me. How concerned you've been . . .'

Fedya modestly pushed a plate of salad towards Nikitin.

'Or what about Valery Felixovich?' continued Nikitin, putting his elbows on the table. 'He's an academician. He belongs to four Royal Societies! I ask him: Does this tie go? And he gives me this jacket. Why? Because he's a real intellectual, that's why. What is education all about anyway? It's got nothing to do with the amount of knowledge one possesses, you know. People know everything these days. What education is really all about is kindness! Let's face it, most people are fine until they fail to do something for you in return. How about you and me for example? We're practically complete strangers, and yet look how good you've been to me, wasting your time listening to me go on. It's because you're a proper, educated person.'

'I am that,' agreed Fedya. 'But as for that jerk . . . A dog . . . I mean a dog gets to use a glass, while we people have to drink straight out of the bottle! I don't care for those sorts of people. I've got no respect for them!'

'Me neither,' agreed Nikitin without hesitation, as he knocked back half a glass of wine.

'And that boss of yours, he's a crook too!' said Fedya. 'Palmed his jacket off on you, didn't he? And now he'll be on about it for the rest of your life.'

'What do you mean? He wouldn't . . .'

'He'll do it with his eyes,' said Fedya, opening his eyes wide. 'I gave you that jacket, I gave you that jacket – that's how he's going to let you know all the time . . . Look, I borrowed a fiver off old Petrovich the other week, and I told him, "When I get my paycheque I'll pay you back." And he says to me, "Oh, it's all right. You don't have to bother." Well, I didn't give it back, right? And so now he's after me with his eyes, to keep reminding me how I have to keep saying "thank you" to him. Jesus Christ! If I'd known, I've had given it back! That's what your boss is like.'

'He really isn't like that,' said Nikitin in his defence.

'Isn't like that . . .' Fedya said, mimicking Nikitin's educated tones. 'Well, why did he give you a jacket with a stain on it then?'

'What stain?' exclaimed Nikitin, starting to inspect himself.

'Here, look . . .'

There really was a damp spot on the elbow which had just appeared.

'It wasn't there before,' said Nikitin in surprise. 'What am I going to do?'

'You'll get it out, don't worry,' said Fedya reassuringly. 'You just need a bit of alcohol.'

Fedya took his napkin, dipped it into the glass of wine and started rubbing the sleeve with it. The stain now turned from pale grey to dark brown.

'There you are! It'll dry out and you won't notice a thing,' promised Fedya.

'There's a bit here, too,' said Nikitin, showing him a tiny stain near the pocket.

Fedya gave the jacket a rub there too.

'Listen, am I your friend?' asked Fedya.

'Definitely!' said Nikitin, nodding his head vigorously.

'Well then, listen to me. Give him back the jacket. Let him choke on it.'

'You're right,' agreed Nikitin. 'I had better give it back to him now, though, otherwise I might get it dirty.'

'Waiter!'

Fedya snapped his fingers in the air like a true Cuban. 'We'll have another bottle and a tin of sardines to take with us!'

The friends walked up to the front entrance.

Nikitin examined the jacket again with the aid of electric light. There were some stains shining on it that looked as if they had been rubbed. They were almost black in colour, and similar in outline to the shape of the Caspian Sea.

'You can still see them,' said Nikitin disappointedly.

'It's just that they haven't dried out yet,' said Fedya reassuringly. 'Once they dry out, you won't see a thing.'

'You know what, Fedya, how about you taking it back?' asked Nikitin. 'It's just that I'm, well . . . Look, tell him I'm ill. And that it will definitely dry out. And say thank you to him. Could you?' Nikitin's face assumed a pained expression.

'All right,' agreed Fedya readily, 'where have I got to go?'

'Up on the third floor by the lift. On the right-hand side.'

Fedya took the jacket and went inside.

The lift was not working, so Fedya set off up the stairs on foot. But he counted the floors by the flights of stairs, so the third floor for him turned out to be actually only the second floor.

Fedya rang on the door by the lift. A little old lady wearing a headscarf opened the door. She was small and neat, like a garden gnome.

'Is the professor at home?' asked Fedya.

'What professor?' asked the old lady, not understanding.

'You know, your old man.'

'No, he ain't.'

'Oh. Well, take this anyway,' said Fedya, holding out the jacket. 'It's from Zhenka.'

'You what?'

'You what?' said Fedya, imitating her rather down-to-earth speech. 'Are you blind or something? It's a junket, innit? It'll dry out, and you won't notice a thing. We are most obliged to you . . .' Fedya shoved the jacket into her hands. 'Oh, by the way, Zhenka's got the flu. He's in hospital. So ta very much then . . .'

Nikitin was standing on the exactly the same spot where he had just parted with Fedya, and was looking up at Natasha's window. The window was giving out its golden orange light like a ripe vine in the sun. It seemed that a quite different sort of life was going up there – pure, innocent, and full of noble purpose. As Nikitin looked up at the window, he felt both jubilant and melancholy at the same time. He had never felt like this before. Actually, he had also never been this drunk before either.

Fedya suddenly appeared.

'It's all done!' he said with great pleasure. 'I've given it back!'

'How did he react?'

'He wasn't at home, so I gave it to his old woman. A right one he's landed himself with, too! So where's the bottle, then? Drunk it all, have you?'

'Of course not! It's here.' The bottle stood on the ground near Nikitin's feet. 'And there's Natasha!'

Nikitin pointed to the window. Out of politeness Fedya looked in the direction of the finger.

'Hey, what about taking Nyurka with us?' suggested Fedya merrily. 'We can sit around a bit, have a few drinks. You know . . . Yours can do some playing and mine can sing along.'

'Let's do that another time. It's just that today . . . well, you see, Natasha and I don't know each other that well, and if I suddenly turn up with two other complete strangers, I would feel a bit awkward . . .'

'Oh, no, that's quite all right. I understand. Nyurka doesn't have to come with us,' said Fedya, not at all offended.

'No, Fedya, you don't understand. It would still be a bit awkward,' objected Nikitin gently but firmly. 'Look, thank you for everything. I've got to go now. Goodbye.'

Nikitin turned and walked away.

'Hey, Zhen, wait!' Fedya ran after him and stood in his way.

Nikitin stopped.

'Zhen, am I your friend?'

'Yes, of course.'

'Well, then, listen to me. Don't go. She'll lure you into marrying her. Mark my words – she'll get you to marry her.'

'But that would be terrific!'

'Zhenya!' said Fedya, putting his hand on his heart. 'Listen, I'm older than you. I've got experience. I've already worked this bird out. I know what your life will be like. You'll come home from work every day, tired as hell, and she won't even let you in the door. She'll turn up her nose at all the friends you bring home, and she'll hide the children away from you as if you were Hitler . . . Oh, and there's another thing I'll tell you: she'll take you to court and force you to go to an alchohol abuse clinic. Don't go, Zhenya! That's my advice to you – don't go!'

'But she's not like that,' objected Nikitin. 'She'll be glad to see us. "Hello," we'll say. "We've been so lonely without you." "And I've been so lonely without you," she'll say. "We've brought you some perfume," we'll say. "It's a present from France."'

'A fat lot we'll be bringing her,' Fedya said, correcting him. 'We left the perfume behind in the junket. You put it in the junket.'

This time when Fedya rang the doorbell at the Gusakov's flat it was answered by Isabella, dressed in velvet trousers. She did not look at all similar to the old lady with the headscarf. She was in a completely different age bracket, for one thing, and wanted completely different things out of life. But Fedya did not notice any of this.

'Hi, it's me again,' he said. 'Look, Zhenka left some perfume behind in the junket. Go and get it for us will you, love?'

'What perfume? Which Zhenka are you talking about?' said Isabella, looking at Fedya in astonishment.

'You know, the one who's got the flu. I told you about it. Run off and get it for us, will you? We've got this bird waiting for us, see.'

'I don't understand what this is about,' said Isabella. 'I've never seen you before in my life.'

'I suppose you are going to tell me I never gave you the junket?'

'You didn't.'

'I see,' said Fedya gloomily. He turned round and ran back down the stairs.

Isabella shrugged her shoulders, shut the door, and went back inside the flat.

Gusakov was sitting at his desk, tapping on a foreign typewriter.

'Who was it?' he asked, without looking up.

'Either a drunk, or a complete crackpot.'

The doorbell rang again.

'Not again!' said Isabella. 'You open it this time. I'm scared of him.'

Gusakov took off his glasses, put them down on the desk and went slowly to meet this uninvited guest.

He opened the door.

A dishevelled Nikitin without a jacket was standing in the doorway. His tie was twisted over to one side, and his shirt was hanging out of his trousers. A scruffy-looking fellow was peering over his shoulder: only his cap and one eye were visible.

'Zhenya?' exclaimed Gusakov in surprise.

'And she said he wasn't at home,' Fedya said, accusing Isabella. 'She was lying all the time.'

'I've got something very serious I want to talk to you about. May I come in?' asked Nikitin.

'I'm rather busy, actually.'

'It'll only take a minute,' promised Nikitin. 'Come on, Fedya!'

They all went inside.

The strange keys made no impression on Fedya.

'Well, what's all this about, then?' asked Gusakov, settling into a deep leather chair.

'I gave your wife a junket, Comrade Academician, sir, and he's my witness,' said Fedya, pointing at Nikitin, 'but she says I never gave her it.'

'I don't understand,' said Gusakov, frowning. 'Which jacket are you talking about?'

'Your jacket, Valery Felixovich!' interrupted Nikitin.

'The suede one. The one you gave me. We left some perfume in it, and we really need it back.'

'Goodness! What jacket is this they are talking about? What perfume?' asked Isabella indignantly. 'What are you listening to them for? Can't you see that they're both completely drunk?'

'Did you hear that?' said Fedya, also wanting to object. 'You mean that I took the junket myself? What would I do with it, eh? Eat it? Put it in my pocket?'

Fedya turned out his pockets, out of which flew the fifty kopecks he had earned from selling the glass. He bent over and started looking for the money.

'Lift up your foot!' he ordered Gusakov.

'What for?'

'Zhen! Tell him to lift his foot up! He's stepped on my money.'

'Here's your money! Take it!' Isabella picked up the coin from the floor, and flung it at Fedya in disgust.

'Wanted to rob me too,' said Fedya suspiciously, putting the fifty kopecks back in his pocket.

'And now just get out of here!' Gusakov ordered Fedya. 'Or I'll call the police!'

'Go ahead! Why *don't* we do some investigation?' agreed Fedya defiantly. He turned to Nikitin. 'See? They're pulling a fast one on us!'

'Valery Felixovich! Isabella Petrovna!' said Nikitin firmly. 'Excuse me please, but you are insulting a man's dignity. The dignity of my friend. And I must protest!'

'Zhenya! Why don't you go home and sleep it off! We'll talk about it tomorrow,' Gusakov advised Nikitin.

'Valery Felixovich! Where I sleep and when I sleep is my own private concern. Even if you do happen to be my boss, it does not give you the right to interfere with my personal life. OK, Valya, old boy?'

'I'll have to throw you both out, then!' said Gusakov, getting up.

'It's in there!' Fedya said, randomly pointing his finger towards an open door. 'Come over here,' he said, beckoning to Isabella.

Utterly perplexed, Isabella followed after Fedya, while Gusakov followed after his wife and Nikitin followed after Gusakov. They all ended up in the bedroom.

There was an emerald-coloured box of *Clemas* sitting amongst the cosmetics on the dressing table.

'That ours?' asked Fedya.

'Sure is,' confirmed Nikitin.

'And she said she didn't take it, the bagagge!' said Fedya reproachfully, opening the box. The bottle had already been used. 'Huh! She's already drunk some as well! Oh, well, never mind. We'll top it up with water. Come on, let's go!'

Fedya confiscated the perfume, and marched out of the Gusakovs' flat. Before he left, he turned round in the doorway and said to Isabella in a good-humoured rebuke, 'You may be getting on, but you're a dishonest old so-and-so.'

'Goodbye,' said Nikitin magnanimously.

They went out, shutting the door behind them.

The Gusakovs stood for a while in complete bewilderment, not knowing how to react.

'Well,' said Gusakov. 'What do you say to that?'

'It was only to be expected,' said Isabella calmly.

'What exactly were you expecting?' asked Gusakov, not understanding.

'You should never do any good deeds. There hasn't yet been a good deed that has not backfired.'

Meanwhile the friends had left the building and were now striding across towards the block opposite.

'He is a crook,' said Fedya, confirming his previous suppositions.

'Never mind, I'll have a talk with him tomorrow,' promised Nikitin, at that moment suddenly tripping up and crashing headlong into a puddle, despite the fact that the ground they were walking on was perfectly even. At that same moment a shaggy little dog started yelping in fright. What had happened was that Nikitin had got tangled up in its lead, which could not be seen in the darkness.

'Watch where you're going!' said the dog's owner sharply, upset about what had happened to his pet. 'Come on, Jack!'

Jack cowered behind his owner, then looked around warily.

'Miaow,' said Nikitin.

Jack did not understand this, and looked up in surprise at his owner. The owner shrugged his shoulders in bewilderment.

Nikitin got up and rubbed his shirt with his hand, trying to wipe off the dirt.

'And now I've fallen over,' he said in dismay. 'How can I go looking like this?'

'We'd better get you cleaned up,' Fedya advised. 'I know! Let's go and see Vitek! He works in a boiler house round here.'

Natasha was standing gazing at the window opposite. The lights were off. She felt as if the lights had been turned off inside her too. Her neighbour from the opposite building had not come, she thought, because he had got sidetracked on to something more important, and had forgotten someone so insignificant as her.

Her opposite neighbour, she imagined, was a brilliant young aeronautics engineer like a Tsiolkovsky or a Lomonosov, only without the wig and much skinnier. He had probably designed a rocket or was preparing to make a discovery which would one day revolutionize life on earth. But that was all to come. Now he was still young, and lived in a one-bedroom flat, drank milk out of the carton in the morning, and sat up in the evenings leaning on his windowsill, looking at the stars.

All the young people she had ever met were only ever interested in having fun. They drank vodka, joked about, and never ever seemed to think about what was going to happen the next day, or the day after that. Their lives were not illumined by the prospect of the work they were going to do, or the love they were going to bear someone. Each day passed, and that was all there was to it.

Natasha did not understand this. She was always preparing for something; either for entrance exams, or for finals. At the moment she was preparing for a competition, and the whole of her future life would depend on the outcome. Half of her future life, at any rate. The other half did not depend on her at all, and that worried her a lot.

She went to the telephone and dialled the speaking clock. 'Twelve o'clock precisely,' said a female voice without emotion. The voice was completely indifferent to the second half of Natasha's life.

She sighed, went over to the couch, and took the cushions off to make her bed. And at that moment came a long, triumphant ring on the doorbell.

She gave a start, then put the cushions back hurriedly and ran into the hall.

She opened the door.

Before her stood three people: Nikitin, Fedya, and Vitek, Fedya's friend from the boiler house.

'This, chaps, is Natasha!' introduced Nikitin loudly.

'Pleased to meet you. Vitek,' said Fedya's friend, holding out his hand steadily. It should be pointed out that Vitek was about sixty years old.

'Fedya,' said Fedya, introducing himself.

'Come in, chaps!' said Nikitin, inviting them in and walking into the flat first. 'Natasha! Where's the kitchen round here?'

Natasha stood in the hall, looking in bewilderment at these strangers who had arrived on her doorstep.

Nikitin managed to make his way to the kitchen by himself. He went over to the sink and turned on the tap. Then he put the bottle of *Clemas* under it and filled it up with water. He put the lid back and took it to Natasha.

'This is for you!' he said gallantly. 'A present from France!'

Natasha took the gift and did not quite know how to react.

'Please come in,' Fedya said to her.

Natasha went inside her own flat.

The men sat themselves down at the table. Fedya brought out the bottle and the sardines, and Vitek got out a knife and started opening the tin.

'Natashenka, dear, can we have a few glasses, please?' asked Nikitin as if he was at home.

Natasha went to get some crystal glasses out of the sideboard.

'Oh, they're far too small,' said Fedya disgruntedly. 'We'd better use teacups.'

Natasha put both the glasses and the teacups on the table.

'Sit down!' Nikitin ordered her.

Natasha sat perched on the edge of a chair.

'Do you like sardines?' asked Nikitin.

Natasha nodded uncertainly.

'See?' said Nikitin, turning to Fedya. 'And you were saying caviare and diamonds! Friends, I want you all to drink to Natasha!' he said raising his glass. 'This is a person who will never hide my children from me, nor will she ever turn her nose up at my friends!'

The men all downed their glases together.

'Ah! I can feel it spreading out inside me!' said Fedya contentedly. 'Hey, Natash, why don't you play us a tune!'

'How about this,' suggested Vitek, starting to sing: 'My friends want us to part, they say you have no heart, but I'm content to stay, around your door all day . . .'

'Ah, I love music!' said Fedya, deeply moved. 'Come on, Natashka, play us something!'

'No!' declared Nikitin. 'Natashenka! Don't go near your harp! I'll be jealous of it! I'll smash it to bits! I'll throw it out of the window! It would be better if you chaps did the singing, and we'll dance.'

Fedya and Vitek sighed loudly and then started bawling out a song which they found extremely moving: 'For you I'll study hard, to become the district nurse, oh darling I'll be true, my life is all for you . . .'

Nikitin stood up and bowed chivalrously to Natasha. 'May I?'

The sun was shining and the birds were singing. The net curtains fluttered in the light breeze. Nikitin opened his eyes. He saw first the sun, then the curtains, and then a bare leg in front of him. A tag was attached to the ankle. It was his own leg. He sat up and shook his head. Then he saw another foot with a tag opposite him. This one belonged to Fedya. And besides them, he could see about twelve other people, all with tags on their legs.

'Where am I?' asked Nikitin quietly.

'In the clinic,' replied Fedya gloomily, looking at Nikitin with extreme disapproval.

'Which clinic?'

'The sobering-up station, of course. Are you blind or something?'

Fedya was evidently not pleased with something. Nikitin could barely recognize him. He barely remembered who

Fedya was, and now he seemed like a complete stranger. And he could not understand why this stranger was being so rude.

'Whatever for?'

'I'll tell you what for!' snapped Fedya. 'What did you have to throw that harp out of the window for? That's no balalaika, you know! It was worth ten grand!'

'Who threw the harp out? I did?'

'Who else? I was hardly likely to . . . Now they'll report me at my work, and I'll have the social activists breathing down my neck. They'll have my guts for garters. If you can't hold your drink, you shouldn't drink! I don't like people like you! Got no respect for them!'

A year went by.

Nikitin and Natasha now had a little boy, and Natasha's mother came to live with them so she could help out.

The Nikitins exchanged their two one-roomed flats for one three-room flat and finally settled down in Natasha's building, two floors up.

The harp was mended, but there was never any time for Natasha to play, so they took it apart and stored it in the attic.

The boy grew up to be a chubby little lad with curly hair, just like a little Cupid. And the mother-in-law turned out to be quiet and obliging.

Nikitin got promoted to Koshelyov's position, and people even started sucking up to him at work. Everything worked out remarkably well really; things could not have been better. There was just no comparison with before. But from time to time, when everyone was going to bed, Nikitin would go into the kitchen and look across at his old window. An amateur photographer had moved in, and the walls were covered with photographs now. There were new pictures always drying on the floor and there was never anywhere you could put your foot. An enlarger stood near the window on a table, giving off a red light.

Nikitin would sit on a stool, put his arms on the windowsill, his head on his arms, and then stare for ages at the red light, which blinked like a small lighthouse in the night.

Then Natasha would come in and ask, 'What are you looking at?'

Nikitin would give a start, then answer, 'Oh nothing. Nothing in particular.'

And it was true. He really was looking at nothing in particular.

ZIGZAG

One evening, a junior research assistant named Irina Dubrovskaya arrived home from a date. She walked straight into her flat without taking her coat and boots off, then went over to the window and started crying.

Endless repairs were being done to the stairs behind her front door. The management had decided to put things into order and do a bit of painting and decorating, and now the stairs were splattered thickly with whitewash and covered with great daubs of green paint. It seemed to Irina as if they would look like that for ever, and that nothing would ever change.

A few scarce lights shone in some of the windows of the building opposite – four out of the whole building. Everyone else was sleeping soundly except for Irina, who was standing there and crying into the arms of her unhappiness. There was no one she could go to who could take her unhappiness away and stand in its place. There was just no one. In fact not only *was* there no one, it seemed that there never would be anyone. There would be no point in there being someone anyway. There was no point to anything, because her life was just one endless repair job, where one thing was constantly breaking down and something else was being built. And it would invariably turn out that whatever had broken down need not have broken down in the first place, while whatever had been built need never have been built.

And when Irina suddenly saw herself – all lonely and tearful – as if from an outsider's point of view, she started to feel doubly sorry for herself. She sobbed into her fur sleeve, so as not to wake her neighbours on the other side of the wall, and it was just then that the telephone started ringing. She picked up the receiver and drew a deep breath.

'Hello . . .'

'Is that Igor Nikolayevich?' asked a distant male voice.

'You've got the wrong number.'

She put the phone down, and was just about to continue celebrating her unhappiness when it started ringing again.

'Is that Igor Nikolayevich?' asked the male voice again.

'Well, does it really seem likely to you that I could be Igor Nikolayevich?' exclaimed Irina irritably. 'Do I sound like Igor Nikolayevich or something?'

'Why are you so cross?' exclaimed the unknown person in surprise.

'Why do you keep ringing up?'

'Did I wake you?'

'No, I wasn't asleep.'

'Have you got a cold?'

'Why do think I've got a cold?'

'Your voice sounds as if your nose is all bunged up.'

'Well, I don't have a cold.'

'So why does your voice sound like that?'

'Because I've been crying.'

'Would you like me to come round?'

'Yes,' said Irina. 'But who are you anyway?'

'Oh, you don't know me. My name wouldn't mean anything to you. What's your address?'

'7 Festival Street, flat number 11.'

'That's easy to remember. All odd numbers.'

'Where are you?' asked Irina.

'I'm standing on Gorky Street. There's a load of tanks going past at the moment, and there's a tank driver with a helmet on in all of them. Can you hear them?'

Irina listened. In the distance there really was a

rumbling sound, as if there were some big manoeuvres going on. Moscow was getting ready for the parades.

Within twenty minutes he had turned up at her doorstep. Irina looked at him and was pleased that he was the way he was, and not different. She would not have liked him so much if he had been different, even if he had been more handsome.

He had glasses that made his eyes look bigger, and his magnified eyes made his face look strange but rather beautiful. He looked at her sitting with her coat on as if she was at a railway station, and made the following decision: 'You shouldn't stay here. You need a change of scene. Come with me.'

Irina got up and followed him. Where were they going? And what was the reason?

When they got outside, he hailed a taxi and took her to the airport.

After arriving at the airport, he bought some tickets. Then he put her on a plane, and took her off again in the city of Riga.

It was now four o'clock in the morning, so they went to a hotel.

Irina went up to the window in her room. Beyond the window a grey dawn was breaking, and you could feel the closeness of the sea. Or maybe you couldn't, and it was just that Irina knew that the sea was near and thought that she should be able to feel it. She also knew that the climate should be continental there, and a grey dawn was pretty continental really.

She stood and waited. She had interpreted the unexpected phone call in the middle of the night and this unexpected trip to be the imaginative beginning of male interest. And where there was a beginning, there ought by rights to be some development. If one followed that particular line of logic, it meant that in a few minutes' time, he would come knocking, cautiously and furtively, on her door. But either that line of logic was faulty, or the male interest was nonexistent, because no one was knocking at her door. She waited a little longer without understanding quite how to react to this state of affairs. Then she decided not to react at all, nor to engage in the self-analysis so characteristic of the Russian intelligentsia. Instead she decided simply to get undressed and go to sleep.

A tram was clanging as if a fire bell had gone off. But Irina slept soundly and happily through it, smiling in her sleep.

In the morning he called her on the phone and suggested they went down for some breakfast. They ate little pies with smoked fish and a dish made with whipped cream and wondered why you could only find these delicacies in the Baltics. It is as difficult to invent a culinary dish as it is to go through the mental processes required to make any big discovery. But if someone had already thought up pies with smoked fish, why not grasp the initiative? However, dishes made of whipped cream belonged to the Baltics, Georgian *Lobbio* belonged to the Caucasus, pasta belonged to Italy, *Soupe à l'Oignon* belonged to France, and good old bortsch belonged to Russia.

After breakfast they got on to a local train and went out to Dzintary, the local seaside resort.

First they went over to the children's area and started playing on all the amusements. They swung on the swings and slid down the wooden slide with their legs straight. It was fun but ever so slightly scary, and Irina squealed with delight and fear. Then they went over to the bars to do pull-ups. But Irina wasn't able to overcome her own weight, and so she ended up hanging from the bars like a sack of potatoes. He tried to lift her up, holding on to her by her knees, but that made her just giggle uncontrollably.

In the end she exhausted herself from laughing so much and had to get down.

They set off for a walk along the beach. The sea had not frozen over, so there were lots of grey waves with white horses running towards the shore. And the air was full of ozone. Near the water's edge, the sand became quite bare, except for clusters of small, round pink shells lying here and there. Irina felt an uncontrollable desire to step on them, and feel them crunching under her foot. So she really did step on them. And they really did crunch. Suddenly she felt as if she had done that at another time in her life. But when? Where? Was it during her earliest childhood? Or maybe even earlier, before her childhood? Perhaps a distant ancestor in the form of some prehistoric dinosaur creature had come out of the sea and espied those piles of shells. It had seen them all that time ago, and she had recognized them . . .

Along the shore stood pine trees with red trunks warped by the wind. The pattern the pine needles made against the background of the grey sky was reminiscent of Japanese greetings cards.

In the afternoon they went to the Dom Cathedral to hear the Mozart 'Requiem'. Irina felt distracted during the first movement, and kept looking round at the walls of the cathedral and at the people singing in the choir, who seemed as ancient as the cathedral itself. They all seemed to be about seven hundred years old, and even the young ones singing soprano looked as if they had been taken out of a trunk full of mothballs. Irina also cast a sidelong glance at him, seeking some sign that he was attracted to her – a certain look or some accidental physical contact. But there was nothing like that – no special look, no brushing against her as if by accident; not one single sign. He was sitting, leaning back in his wooden chair and listening to the music, his gaze focused somewhere in his past. He was far away and unattainable. He belonged to no one.

Irina felt slightly surprised and rather hurt. But suddenly she found herself forgetting both her surprise and her hurt feelings. The choir was singing the 'Lachrymosa', and it was no longer sixty separate individuals singing a score, it was Mozart himself lamenting, his sacred, holy self. Irina's soul ascended upwards and choked on something. She burst into tears, and as the tears ran down her cheeks, it seemed as if all the pain inside her heart was leaving her too. Which is why her tears turned salty and her heart grew light.

They returned to Moscow that same evening.

He took her all the way to her front door and then took off his hat.

'Do you feel better?' he asked.

'Of course I do,' said Irina. 'If the sea, Mozart, and you exist, then life is not only necessary, but beautiful too.'

He kissed her hand and went down the stairs.

Irina stood and watched him leaving footprints shaped like huge broad beans on the white, paint-splattered stairs.

He travelled as far as Yugo-Zapadnaya on the Underground, and on to the 44th district by bus. Then up in the lift to his front door, which he opened with a key.

His wife was standing in the hall with their one-year-old daughter in her arms. Both his wife and daughter had round faces and scruffy hair with loose strands flying out all over the place. They looked like adorable little wild animals.

'Been off on one of your zigzags again?' asked his wife, fixing him with her eyes, which were round and small like the heads of nails.

He did not answer, and took his coat off without saying a word.

By 'again', his wife meant his previous jaunt to

Siberia, to the Biisk vitamin factory. Someone had urgently needed some oil of sea buckthorn, and he had naturally stepped into the role of magician.

'You like impressing people, don't you?' his wife said. 'You miserable show off. While I'm stuck here all alone with the kid. Running round and round in circles like a dog on a ferry.'

He looked at his wife, trying to imagine how a dog would behave on a ferry. He supposed that it might get anxious, because it did not know whether it would get taken on board. So it would run up and down barking, afraid of being left behind by its owner.

'You're wrong,' he said gently. 'You are my dog, and I am your master. You know that.'

'All the same,' his wife said. 'I'm fed up with this. You're only too keen to make the rest of mankind happy, but you won't lift a finger to do anything for me. I mean, let's face it, you can't be bothered when it comes down to me. You'd find it boring.'

'What do you want me to do?'

'You could at least take out the rubbish bin. The rubbish won't fit into it any more. I've flattened it down with my foot four times already.'

'But couldn't you take it out yourself?' he said in surprise. 'You can see how tired I am.'

He sat down in the armchair and took off his glasses, shutting his eyes.

His wife looked at him with sympathy.

'It's not that I have anything against you and your miracles,' she said. 'By all means let people become healthy and happy with your help. But why does it have to be at my expense?'

He opened his long-sighted eyes once more.

'At whose expense do miracles happen in fairy tales?'

His wife thought for a moment.

'The fairies',' she remembered.

'Well, there you are then. You are my fairy.'

His wife wanted to say something in reply to that, but while she was gathering her thoughts he fell asleep. He really was tired.

The fairy put her daughter to bed. Then she put her husband to bed. Then she took out the rubbish bin. Then she did the washing up. Then she cooked some macaroni, so it would be easy to heat up in the morning.

On Monday morning at half-past seven, junior research assistant Irina Dubrovskaya woke up in her flat. As she stared at the ceiling, she started to wonder whether 'yesterday' had really taken place or not. On the one hand, she remembered the taste of that dish with the whipped cream and the pattern of the pine branches against the grey sky so clearly that it had to have happened. Of course it happened. But on the other hand, there were no traces of it, not even a label on her suitcase. Then suddenly she remembered the footprints on the stairs.

She jumped out of bed, dashed into the hall, flung open the front door and . . . But things like that only happen when you are a child of course. When you run home after school, for instance, and walk into the sitting room to find a Christmas tree standing in the corner. Or when you are meandering along a well-trodden path in the woods and you suddenly come across a white mushroom.

There were no footprints. No traces at all. No paint. No repairs in progress. The decorating was all finished, and old Auntie Masha had been up early that morning washing the stairs. The squares on the floor were now bright red and they matched the skirting board. The skirting board was red, the walls were pale green, and the ceiling a brilliant bluish-white.

The stairs looked as festive as a Christmas tree and as unexpected as a white mushroom. And it seemed that was how they would always look and that nothing would ever change.

THE TALISMAN

It was form time in class Lower 5A, and Nina Georgievna, the form mistress, was going down the register alphabetically, commenting on behaviour and progress. Alexander Dukin (Duke for short) was a D, so his turn came up very quickly. No one had got tired yet and they were all sitting quietly and listening carefully to what Nina Georgievna had to say.

'Dukin, just look at yourself,' she was saying. 'You don't do your homework properly. You don't do any out-of-school activities. You don't even get into trouble.'

This was all quite true. Duke did not do his homework properly, and he never did any out-of-school activities; he had not an ounce of public-spiritedness in him. At the beginning of the year he had been made monitor of the third form, but no one ever told him what he was supposed to do. He certainly didn't have any idea. And also, he wasn't able to like all the children anyway. He could only like a few of them – one, or at the most two at a time. Liking the whole lot of them was quite out of the question; he was even rather afraid of them.

'At least if you were a troublemaker I could understand you. It wouldn't be a good thing, but at least it would be a sign that you had some personality. But you just don't seem to exist at all. You're an empty space. A nonentity.'

Nina Georgievna stopped talking, expecting Duke to stand up for himself and say something in his defence. But he remained silent, staring down at the tops of his boots. His boots came from America, and they had a thick grooved sole, like the tyres of a lorry. He had got them from his mum's friend Irina, who had married an American with the same size feet as him. The American had bought these boots in a sports shop and had gone hiking in the mountains in them for about five or six years. Then they had been handed down to Duke, who wore them all year round without ever taking them off. He would probably go on wearing them for the rest of his life. No doubt he would still be wearing them when he went on his pension. Then he would bequeath them to his children, and they in turn would pass them down to theirs.

These thoughts had nothing to do with what Nina Georgievna was interested in, but Duke was deliberately not paying attention to her questions. He was thinking that when he grew up, he would never humiliate someone in front of other people just because they were under age, or because they couldn't earn their own living yet and couldn't stand up for themselves. Duke could have said all this to Nina Georgievna's face, but then she would lose all her authority. The idea of a teacher without authority was so unthinkable, Duke would probably end up ruining her career; perhaps even her whole life.

'Why aren't you answering?' asked Nina Georgievna.

Duke transferred his eyes from his boots to the window. Outside a white mist hung in the air, and in the distance a white high-rise apartment block floated in this winter mist like a great ship in the fog.

Everyone had turned round to stare at Duke, and as they sat there quietly, they began to believe what Nina Georgievna was saying: that Duke really was a nonentity and just an empty space. And he became horrified as he too began to have a creeping suspicion that he really wasn't capable of doing anything with his life. He could of course take one of his boots off, hurl it at the window, and shatter the glass. That would at least confirm him in the public eye as a delinquent. But you need to have a certain kind of disposition to do things like that, and they have to take control of you, not the other way round. That way it would be organic. As it was, Duke just stood there as if he was paralysed, unable to move either his legs or his hands.

'Well, go on, say something!' demanded Nina Georgievna.

'What do you want me to say?' asked Duke.

'Who are you?'

Duke suddenly remembered that his mother had called him her 'little talisman' ever since he was a little boy. And he remembered that ever since he was a little boy, he had always been very frightened, and would sometimes howl for hours on end at the horrifying thought he might have been born to their neighbour Auntie Zina rather than to his mother, in which case he would have to have lived with her family, like Larisa had to.

'I'm a talisman,' said Duke.

'A what?' asked Nina Georgievna, actually frowning as she tried to work out what on earth Duke was talking about.

'A talisman,' repeated Duke.

'What's that – an Olympic souvenir?'

'No. A souvenir is for remembering something. A talisman is for luck.'

'How does it work?' Nina Georgievna asked, rather intrigued now.

'Well, it's like a pebble with a little hole in it. You wear it round your neck, on a chain. So it's always with you.'

'But no one could wear you round their neck.'

The class chortled.

'No,' said Duke with dignity. 'You just have to take me with you. If you have something important to do and you take me with you, it will work out well.'

Nina Georgievna looked at her pupil with a mixture of dismay and genuine interest. The rest of the class also did not know quite how to relate to this statement: whether to snigger into their sleeves or roar with laughter like a herd of rhinoceroses. In fact they continued to sit there silently, staring at Duke. Those who were sitting at the front had to twist their bodies round to look at him, but those at the back of the class were able to look at him while sitting comfortably in their seats. Even the smart Honin was unable to come up with a witty remark, although he was racking his brains in an effort to think of one.

'All right, Dukin,' said Nina Georgievna. 'This is a classroom, not a club for clowns and buffoons. I didn't want to offend you, Dukin, but you've really got to do some hard thinking about yourself and start making a bit of an effort. You've a long life ahead of you and I don't want to see you ending up as a good-for-nothing layabout who doesn't care about what happens to him. Your family does not seem to take any interest in you either. Your mother hasn't been to Parents' Evening once. Why is that? Surely she must be interested in knowing how you are doing?'

'She knows how I am doing,' said Duke. 'She signs my school journal every week.'

'Your school journal isn't going to tell her very much. Isn't the opinion of your teachers important to her?'

'Completely unimportant,' Dukin wanted to say. 'She has her own opinions.' But he couldn't say that, so he said nothing.

'All right. Sit down,' said Nina Georgievna. 'Eliseyeva.'

Olya Eliseyeva got up from her desk and straightened her dress.

'You were absent from school for a week,' said Nina Georgievna, 'and you brought a note from your parents instead of bringing a doctor's certificate. How am I to respond to that, please tell me?'

Eliseyeva shrugged her round shoulders.

'Everybody stays behind to wash the floors and clean the windows but you're not allowed to get your hands wet. Everyone else can, but you can't.'

'I've got chronic bronchitis,' said Eliseyeva with a slight haughtiness. 'I need to take precautions.'

'Do you know how children in Sparta were brought up?' asked Nina Georgievna.

'Yes,' Eliseyeva replied. 'They threw the weak ones off a cliff.'

It was not a very good example, because it meant that there was nothing to save Eliseyeva from being shoved off a cliff to prevent the contamination of mankind. Nina Georgievna decided to take a more contemporary example.

'In America, you know, the children of millionaires work as cleaners and waiters in their summer holidays, so that they can earn their own living. Children are brought up very strictly in the West.'

'But in Japan children are allowed to do anything they want!' the bright Honin retorted merrily. 'And the Japanese are still the most civilized people in the world.'

Honin was not only clever, but erudite. He was constantly displaying the depths of his knowledge to everyone, but girls didn't like him because his face was covered in volcanic adolescent spots.

'What do you suggest, then?' asked Nina Georgievna.

'Me?' asked Honin in surprise. 'What on earth could I suggest?'

'What educational method would you favour if you were in my position?'

'The one they use in the circus. Modern dressage.'

Everyone except for Nina Georgievna started laughing.

'You mean using a stick and carrot?' asked Nina Georgievna.

'Oh, no, that method's gone out of fashion,' replied

Honin. 'Modern dressage employs the observation method. You observe an animal for a long time, find out what it likes, and then develop and encourage exactly what it likes. That way you use a minimum of force.'

Nina Georgievna looked at her watch. There was no time to observe, find out, and encourage. Twenty minutes had gone just on Dukin and Eliseyeva alone, and there were still thiry more children to go. If ten minutes went on each person, that would work out at three hundred minutes in all, or five hours. Nina Georgievna didn't have five hours. She still had to run to the shops, buy some groceries, dash over to the hospital to see her mother, then come back and fetch her little daughter from the kindergarten. And in the evening there was homework to mark and food to cook for tomorrow, because her mother had just undergone an operation and could not eat anything that had been cooked earlier than the day before.

'Well, all right,' said Nina Georgievna. 'Sparta, Japan, America, the circus, I don't know . . . Just make sure you turn your Ds into Cs, your Cs into Bs, and your Bs into As by the end of term. Otherwise you'll get me into trouble!'

She gathered up her books and walked out of the classroom.

Everyone jumped up from their places, and started getting their briefcases out of their desks. Svetlana Kiyashko went over to talk to Duke.

'Last year I lent Lenka Mareyeva a record; it was Abba's latest album, and she hasn't given it back to me yet.'

Mareyeva had been in their class, but had transferred to another school which concentrated on mathematics. As it turned out, Mareyeva herself had no particular aptitude for maths, she just had to travel further now. Duke was convinced that if something was going to reveal itself in a person, it would reveal itself anyway. And if not, then no school was going to make the slightest bit of difference. That's why it was better just to sit tight in one place and wait patiently.

'So?' asked Duke, not understanding.

'Let's go and see her together,' suggested Kiyashko. 'Then maybe she'll give it back.'

'Why do I have to come?' Duke asked in surprise.

'Well, you're a talisman, aren't you?'

'Aah . . .'

Duke suddenly cottoned on. He had quite forgotten that he was a talisman. He wanted to say, 'Well, I was joking, wasn't I? How could I possibly be a talisman?' But then Kiyashko would have asked, 'Well, who are you, then?' And it would turn out that he was a nothing. A nonentity. An empty space. And no one wants to admit to themselves that they are an empty space, especially if it might actually be true. Nature must have been having forty winks when it came around to him. If only he could run fast like Buleyev, or be clever like Honin. Or good-looking like Vitaly Reznikov from Upper 5B. If only there was something which made him stand out from the crowd – talent, brains, or good looks . . . But Duke had none of those. He was just his mother's pride and joy; her talisman. Perhaps that was enough for his mother, but it wasn't enough for him. And it wasn't enough for anybody else either.

'All right,' said Duke. 'Let's go, then. But tomorrow, not today. I can't go today.'

Lenka Mareyeva opened the door to him. She had a pretty face but a rather plump figure. In fact, she was exactly the shape of a number eight: one circle on top of another.

A little white fluffy dog immediately came running up to her feet. It got up on to its hind legs and started crossing its front paws one over the other to keep its balance.

Evidently that made it easier for the dog to stay standing up.

'Ladka, get down!' said Lenka, shooing away the dog.

'What does she want?' asked Duke.

'She wants you to like her,' explained Mareyeva.

'Why?'

'No reason. Just to put you in a good mood. What have you come round for?'

'There's something I want to talk to you about.'

'You'd better come in, then,' she said, inviting him inside.

But Duke refused. All he could see through the half-open door were some kitchen units.

'What is it you want to talk to me about?' asked Mareyeva, since Duke was hedging and did not know how to begin.

'I want you to give Kiyashko back her record,' he said, beginning with the most important thing.

'No way,' snapped Mareyeva curtly. 'I like dancing to it. It's groovy.'

'But what if Kiyashko likes dancing to it too?'

'It's my record. Kiyashko gave it to me for my birthday. And then she came and said that her parents had told her off and she started demanding that I gave it back. You can't behave like that.'

Duke was confused. Taking presents back really wasn't a very nice thing to do. But then nor was keeping them by force either.

'You could have got really upset,' suggested Duke.

'I did get upset,' said Mareyeva. 'I stopped being friends with her.'

'But you could still have given her back the record,' hinted Duke.

'Not likely! Then I'd end up without a friend and the record! At least I've still got the record!'

Duke realized that the prospects did not look good.

Mareyeva would not give back the record, and she was right in some ways. Getting it back was therefore going to be an impossible task, at least by the next day. And so tomorrow people would discover that he was not a talisman at all, but a complete nonentity, and a braggard with it.

'Let's do a swap,' suggested Duke. 'I'll give you a foreign belt with a "Wrangler" buckle. And you give me the record in exchange.'

'Where's the belt?' asked Mareyeva with curiosity.

'I'll go and get it now for you. I'll be back in just a second!'

Duke ran down the stairs (since there was no lift in Mareyeva's five-storey building), then across the road and down two blocks; past the school, past the kindergarten, past apartment block number nine, and past the rubbish bins. He finally reached the entrance of his building, and crept quietly into his flat, as if he was on secret business.

His mum was talking on the phone. She could talk for four hours in a row, and find all four hours extremely riveting. She raised her hand with her palm upwards when she saw Duke, which could mean either 'Hang on, I'll just be a minute,' or 'Don't interrupt, let me have my own interests.'

Duke nodded to her, as if showing loyalty to her interests. Only a year ago, however, mention of the word loyalty would have been unthinkable, while they were still terrorizing each other with love.

Duke went on tiptoes into the other room and got out of the wardrobe the belt he shared with his mother. She used to wear it with her denim skirt. Incidentally, both the belt and the skirt had been sent to them from far-off America. These items were also acquired secondhand, having served their old owners well, but leather and denim always improve as they get older. Vitaly Reznikov, for example, deliberately scrubbed his jeans with pumice stone, so that they would look worn. He looked like some incredibly glamorous midnight cowboy in them.

Duke took the belt and put it under his jacket, then walked into the hall with a detached look.

'I promise you,' his mother was saying to someone on the telephone, 'it'll be exactly the same.'

Duke nodded to his mother, and that too could have been interpreted in two ways: 'Hang on, I'll just be a minute' and 'Don't interrupt me. Let me have my own interests. You have yours and I have mine.' He went out on to the stairs and from there out on to the street. And then he went back to Mareyeva's: past the rubbish bins, past apartment block number nine, past the kindergarten, past the school – two whole blocks. Then crossed the road and walked up to the fifth floor (because there was no lift).

'Here!' said Duke, taking off the belt and handing it to Mareyeva. The buckle was rather heavy and looked like burnished silver. It was a bit bulky, but it looked all right. The word 'Wrangler' was embossed on it, anyway, which was the name of a reputable firm. And that incomprehensible word was enough to inspire dreams and awaken hope.

'Wow . . .' gasped Mareyeva, for whom hope had just appeared, indeed perhaps several hopes, not just one. She threaded the belt through the loops on her jeans (which was rather like putting a metal hoop round a barrel), and asked, 'How do I look?'

'Oh, you look completely different now,' said Dukin, although in fact she looked just the same.

Mareyeva went inside and returned with the record, whose surface was no longer black, but grey, having been lacerated a thousand times with a blunt needle.

'Here you are,' she said, holding out the record.

'Look, I don't want to take it right now,' said Duke. 'I've got a favour to ask you. I'm going to come round tomorrow with Kiyashko after school, and I want you to give it to her when she asks for it. And you're not to tell her that I came today, all right?'

'When are you going to give me the belt, then?'

'You can have the belt now. Keep it.'

'Aren't you sorry to give it away?' asked Mareyeva in surprise.

'Well, you have to give away things you like yourself, don't you?' answered Duke evasively. 'Otherwise what is the point of giving a present to someone?'

'I suppose you're right,' Mareyeva agreed, looking intently at Duke all of a sudden.

'What's wrong?' he asked, feeling embarrassed.

'Are you in love with Kiyashko?'

'No.'

'Why did you want to give the belt away, then?'

'It was necessary.'

'For whom? For her or you?'

'For me and her. Separately, though, not together.'

'Interesting . . .' said Mareyeva, shaking her head.

They stood there in the hallway without saying anything. Duke looked at his belt, and he was as sad to say goodbye to it as if he was parting with a close friend, rather than just an object.

'That belt is really for thin people,' he remarked.

'I'll lose weight,' promised Mareyeva. 'You wait. I've just never had the incentive before. And now I do.'

Dukin went out on to the street. He crossed the road slowly and then walked down the two blocks: past the school, past the kindergarten, and past apartment block number nine. A bonfire was burning in front of the building, on which they were probably burning rubbish, and round the fire stood people with thoughtful faces. There is evidently something in the mystery of fire forgotten since ancient times. It attracts people and they gather round it, trying to remember what they have forgotten.

Duke's face started to get warm. He was staring at a flame which he thought looked like a deer, which was leaping about and trying to jump into the sky.

As he walked away from the fire, it got colder and darker. Mareyeva now had a belt and an incentive, he was thinking. Kiyashko had a record and her friendship back. And he had the success of being a talisman. But the success had been bought at the price of giving away the belt, and the belt came at the expense of theft, because the belt didn't just belong to him; he shared it with his mother. And his mother had so few things anyway. Kiyashko and Mareyeva meant nothing to him. He was not even friends with them. But his mother was his mother, no matter whether their interests were shared or separate.

When Duke returned home, his mother was still talking on the telephone. He decided to wait until the end of her conversation to tell her about the belt. She came off the phone quite quickly in fact, but then their neighbour Auntie Zina came round, and they went straight into the kitchen to have a cup of tea. It wasn't right to interrupt when grown ups were talking. And then by the time Auntie Zina left, the fourth part of a detective film he had been watching was just beginning on TV. It was a lot better than the other parts, and he didn't want to spoil things. And then when the film ended he fell asleep. He had fallen asleep even before it had finished in fact. And in the morning they were always in a hurry – his mum had to get to work, he had to get to school – and so it wasn't convenient to start a conversation about the belt then. Duke finally decided he would tell his mother when she brought the subject up. If she asked him, 'Sasha, where's the belt?' then he would reply, 'I gave it to a girl, Mum.' And until she asked, there was no reason to bring the subject up, especially at such an unsuitable time, when they were both going to be late and each second counted.

Duke put his school shoes into a polythene bag and set off for school with a fairly clear conscience.

In their literature class they were studying Chernyshevsky's *What is to be Done?* Today they were discussing Vera Pavlovna's dreams.

Duke had not read the novel. Not because he was too lazy, but because he found it boring. He had asked Honin to tell him what happened in it, but all he could remember was that Rakhmetov slept on a bed of nails, and that Chernyshevsky was friends with Dobrolyubov, and that Dobrolyubov had died very young. And also that a sabre had been broken over Chernyshevsky's head when he went to his mock execution. Or was it a rapier? He didn't know what the difference was between them. A sword was apparently narrower and a sabre was broader. Duke thought that anyone able to break a sword over someone's head must possess exceptional strength, otherwise how could they shatter steel? Then he realized that the sword (or the sabre) was probably filed down first. Executioners cannot afford to take risks in front of a lot of people.

As far as dreams went, he had them too, but not like the ones Vera had. He did not understand how anyone could dream about the reconstruction of society. He knew that dreaming about horses had something to do with lying, and that dreaming about dirt meant money. He sometimes dreamed that he was flying. That meant he was growing. And recently he had a dream about Masha Arkhangelskaya from Upper 5A; they were dancing a slow dance in a red room without touching the floor. He was looking at her lips, not her eyes, and he could remember them very clearly. They were soft and mauve-coloured, like little pink worms. And she had strong teeth, all white and gleaming. The sort the sun has to blink at.

'Dukin, could you tell us about Chernyshevsky please!' asked Nina Georgievna.

Dukin stood up.

'I'm waiting,' reminded Nina Georgievna, since Duke was not hurrying with his answer.

'Chernyshevsky was a social democrat,' began Duke.

'Go on,' demanded Nina Georgievna.

'He was friends with Dobrolyubov. Dobrolyubov was also a social democrat.'

'I wasn't asking you about Dobrolyubov.'

Duke looked down at the floor, trying desperately to remember something he could add.

Nina Georgievna got bored of waiting.

'Sit down. You get a D for that,' she decided. 'If you don't do anything at home, you could at least listen in class. But you go flying off into other worlds when you're in class. I'd love to know where you go to . . .'

Well, you're never going to know, Duke thought, you fat kangaroo. In Duke's imagination a kangaroo was a clumsy and stupid creature which exercised power over others.

Svetlana Kiyashko sat in front of Duke. Her shoulders were sprinkled with dandruff and her school uniform looked as if she had slept in it without getting undressed, on bags of flour what's more. Curiously, she did not seem to remember anything about the record. She must have forgotten about it. Duke focused his eyes on the back of her neck and started hypnotizing her with them by sending out thought waves to her.

Kiyashko shuffled nervously and looked round. She came into contact with Duke's gaze but she still couldn't remember anything. 'What do you want?' she asked, looking round a second time.

'Nothing,' said Duke crossly.

*

The last lesson was PE.

Igor Ivanovich the PE teacher took them all outside and made them run a hundred metres.

Duke squatted down the way you are supposed to do at the start and lifted up his gaunt, rabbit-like backside. Then on the word 'go' he shot upwards into the air like a rocket. He thought he was running very fast, but Igor Ivanovich's stopwatch recorded some extremely pathetic results. Buleyev was faster than all of them – he ran like a god, and Honin was the slowest, because all his energies got channelled to his brain. Duke finished one place ahead of Honin, i.e., second from the bottom, but the exercise, the fresh air, and the excitement all did their stuff. They forced out of him all his feelings of disappointment and left him feeling unexplicably light hearted and cheerful instead. It was in this new frame of mind that he went up to Kiyashko.

'Well?' he asked casually. 'Do you want to go and get your record?'

Kiyashko was let off PE. She was standing at the side of the track in a short coat that she had grown out of a long time ago.

'I can't today,' said Kiyashko, 'because I've got my music lesson. I've got a test.'

'Well, it's up to you . . . You're the one who wanted it back,' answered Duke indifferently.

'Let's go tomorrow,' suggested Kiyashko.

'No. I can't go tomorrow.'

'Oh, all right. Let's go today, then,' Kiyashko agreed obligingly. 'After my test though. Meet you at seven o'clock.'

At seven o'clock that evening she turned up at his apartment block looking so chic and colourful that Duke didn't recognize her straight away. It ought to be explained that Svetlana Kiyashko was actually made up of two different Svetlanas. One was the school Svetlana, who was all grey and dusty, like a mouse living in a windmill; you could almost tread on her without noticing. The other one was the out-of-school Svetlana, and she was as bright and explosive as a firework. School seemed to consume all her personality. Or maybe it did the opposite and revealed her in her true colours – as both a mouse and an imitation sparkler. Most likely she was a mixture of both.

'Hi!' she said condescendingly when Duke appeared. 'Let's go!'

As they walked in silence past the rubbish bins, past the kindergarten, and past apartment block number nine, it seemed to Duke that he been following this route all his life. Somewhere in another world, Masha Arkhangelskaya was dancing a waltz without touching the floor, while he was going back and forth like a yoyo between Mareyeva the barrel and Kiyashko the timid sparkler.

When they arrived at the five-storey building, Duke went over in his mind the scene which had been prepared and rehearsed, and was about to be performed. For some reason he found the thought of it exceedingly unpleasant, so he said, 'I'll wait for you here.'

'Will it work?' asked Kiyashko suspiciously.

'Will what work?' asked Duke, not understanding.

'The talisman. I thought you were supposed to hold it in your hand.'

'You don't have to. It works from a distance too. Up to four kilometres away.'

'Why four kilometres particularly?'

'That's the radius.'

'So how do you do it?' asked Kiyashko with interest.

'You have to be in touch with your bio-rhythms,' explained Duke.

'Your what?'

'You have to feel them. I can't explain it in words,' said Duke, trying to get himself out of a tight corner.

'You could try,' insisted Kiyashko.

'Well . . . I'll be thinking about the same thing you are, you see, and if we both want the same thing, then our wish will increase in intensity, and fix itself to Mareyeva like a lasso. So she won't be able to go anywhere. Then she'll start to want what we want.'

'You're sure she won't just kick me out?'

'Of course not. Now just go,' requested Duke. 'And don't argue with me.'

Kiyashko had begun to annoy him, like people who borrow things and don't give them back. Or like people who were ungrateful. Also, he was in a hurry. The next part of the detective film was going to begin in fifteen minutes and he wanted to be home before it started.

Kiyashko finally left. And then she disappeared altogether. In fact she didn't reappear for the next two hours, and Duke started to turn to ice, like a frozen vegetable in a polythene bag. There was one, or rather there were two particular things about his synthetic fur jacket: in warm weather it was too hot, and in the winter it was unbearably freezing cold.

First he banged his feet together. Then he banged his hands together. Now he was left with the prospect of banging his head on a wall. He could, of course, just leave, but his vanity would not let him. Is there anything people won't put up with for the sake of vanity? Only later does one begin to realize how utterly pointless it all is. But at the age of fifteen, you are ready to sacrifice everything for it: your health and your honour. Even your life.

Kiyashko finally re-appeared with the record tucked under her arm.

'We watched that detective film,' she said. 'Then we had tea.' She was silent for a moment, then added, 'I thought you would have gone home long ago.'

'So you got the record back?' asked Duke, although

Kiyashko was holding the record under her arm and it was impossible not to see it.

'Yes. She gave it to me straight away!' said Kiyashko in amazement. 'I barely had time to open my mouth. Lenka's great, you know . . . I've only just realized how much I missed her being around . . .'

'I sent her four lots of thoughtwaves,' said Duke, reminding her of himself.

The snow was falling in fine, constant flakes. Kiyashko's eyes were looking at him through the snow and they were all yellow and slanted, like a big cat's. Cats generally have very beautiful eyes, and Sasha would have considered Kiyashko's pretty passable if there weren't other more beautiful eyes in the world.

'Hey, Sasha,' said Kiyashko suddenly, and Duke was amazed that she remembered his name. 'Just don't go dishing them out right and left, OK?'

'Handing out what?' said Duke, not understanding.

'Your bio-rhythms. Otherwise people will drain them all out of you, and then you'll die.'

'But you can recharge them. Like a battery.'

'What can you recharge them with?'

'Other bio-rhythms.'

'You mean another person?'

'Yes. Or with nature. The *reasonable* universe.'

'What – you mean there's an unreasonable one?'

'Yes.'

Kiyashko looked at Duke silently with a strange expression on her face. It was as if she was comparing the old Duke with the new one who had been chosen by God. She just could not understand why the Lord had chosen Dukin over everybody else; why He had pointed His holy finger at Duke of all people.

'Why you of all people?' she asked him directly.

How could you answer a question like that? All you could do was gently shrug your shoulders and lift your eyes up to sky, up to where the thread of street lamps faded out, ending with the moon.

Fame and gossip spread with identical speed, because fame is just gossip with a plus sign, while gossip is just fame with a minus sign.

The next day, during break, Vitaly Reznikov from Upper 5B came up to Duke and asked him scornfully, 'So you're this talisman, are you?'

Duke did not answer, but he looked at him straight in the eye, because Vitaly was not just Vitaly; he was also the object of Masha Arkhangelskaya's affections.

Duke had found that out a month ago under the following circumstances.

He was coming home one day from the greengrocer's with a beetroot in his shopping bag that was as large and round as a football. His mum had asked him to go out and buy one for her and then cook it. A beetroot as big as that needed to be cooked for days, like bones for stock. Duke could make stock too. He was a capable and unspoilt boy. But that is to digress. Anyway, Duke had just got into the lift and was about to close the doors, when someone came in through the front entrance and shouted out 'Wait!' Duke could not bear having to share the lift with someone else. He hated being in a confined space with a stranger, and he particularly did not like sharing the lift with the old lady from the eighth floor, who took up three-quarters of the cubicle and reeked of senility. So whenever he got into the lift, he would always try to shut the doors immediately and press the button. But this time they had caught him. He had to wait. A few seconds later Lariska from the fifth floor appeared, accompanied by Masha Arkhangelskaya, who was in floods of tears. The crying had made her eyes all red and her face was covered with nervous red blotches. She looked so unhappy that

Duke started to feel miserable too, and when Lariska pressed the button, the lift seemed to move upwards to the accompaniment of a plaintive organ chorale. Masha did not stop crying when she caught sight of Duke standing there with his beetroot. Evidently she was as bothered by him being there as she would have been by the presence of a cat or a dog. She simply paid no attention to him.

But he stood there shaken to the depths of his being. He was ready to die for Masha if need be, but only on the condition that she knew about it. His fantasy was that she would finally notice him and be with him as he died, her gentle little tears falling on to his face in scalding drops.

When the lift stopped on the fifth floor, all three got out and went in different directions: Masha and Lariska to the left and Duke and the beetroot to the right.

That evening Lariska knocked on Duke's door.

'Sign this,' she demanded, thrusting some kind of list and a ballpoint at him.

Duke cast his eyes over the list. 'Why?' he asked.

'We're moving,' explained Lariska.

'Well, happy moving, then. Why do you need my signature?'

'This is a co-operative building,' Lariska explained. 'And we need the permission of all the shareholders.'

What on earth for? What's the point? thought Duke. What other grown-up rubbish am I going to have to put up with later on?

He signed opposite flat number 89, and, as he returned the pen, asked as casually as he could, 'Why was Masha Arkhangelskaya crying today in the lift?'

'She's fallen in love,' replied Lariska just as casually, before going to knock on the next door.

Their neighbour came out. She was middle-aged and rather ungainly, and looked a bit like a prehistoric dinosaur creature with a long tail, as her body was very large and her head very small. Duke had travelled in the lift with her several times and each time he had almost passed out from the vodka fumes emanating from her. He was always afraid she might fall over on to him and squash him, but she would somehow manage to steer herself successfully out of the lift and then lumber over to her door in a sort of lop-sided fashion, as if she was trying to move some invisible obstacle out of the way with her shoulder. People said she had a lot of money, but it had not brought her any happiness, because she was constantly afraid of it being stolen.

'Could you sign this, please,' asked Lariska.

The dinosaur looked sullenly and distrustfully at the two children, and Duke saw that her face was large and red, and that the skin was stretched tautly, like on a drum. She signed without saying anything and then disappeared back behind her door.

'With whom?' asked Duke.

Lariska had forgotten the beginning of the conversation and the question 'With whom?' by itself made no sense to her.

'Who has Masha fallen in love with?' said Duke to jog her memory.

'Oh . . . With Vitaly Reznikov. She's such an idiot. Utterly and completely.'

Duke could not work out whether she was a complete and utter idiot or whether she was completely and utterly in love. Was she full of love or stupidity?

'Why is she an idiot?' he asked.

'Because Vitaly Reznikov means granted unhappiness,' declared Lariska categorically as she marched up to the next floor.

'You mean guaranteed . . .'

'Oh, really, you're so young,' said Lariska brushing him off crossly from the next floor up.

And now Masha's guaranteed unhappiness in the form of Vitaly Reznikov was standing in front of Duke and asking, 'So you're this talisman, are you?'

Duke looked closely at Vitaly, trying to work out what was so dangerous about him.

The teachers loved Vitaly because he found school-work really easy and always did exceptionally well. He never found it at all difficult – it's just how his brains worked.

Vitaly was loved and adored by both his parents, his two grandmothers, his great-grandmother, and his two grandfathers. And looking over his shoulder all the time was his powerful father, who was carving out a direct road into life for him, rooting out all the stumps, filling in all the pot-holes and covering them over with asphalt. All he had to do was to walk straight ahead, into the sun and the wind.

Girls loved Vitaly because he was good-looking, and because he looked rather noble, like blue-blooded royalty. And he knew it, too. Why shouldn't he?

Everyone loved him in fact. And he was as receptive to love and good times as a bouncy, fun-loving puppy. But there was a certain chemical missing from his biological make-up which in photography they usually call the 'fixing agent'. The trouble was that Vitaly did not fix his feelings, and would switch from one emotional attach-ment to another – probably because he had such a big choice. There were so many dishes on his table of life, it was like being in a Chinese restaurant. It would be silly to fill up on one thing and not try anything else.

It was easier for Duke. Neither the teachers nor the girls liked him. Only his mother did. But he had the capacity to love someone faithfully and constantly. He had a need for love and constancy.

'Suppose I am a talisman,' answered Duke. 'What's it to you?'

'I want to ask Masha Arkhangelskaya to go skating with me.'

'Go ahead and ask her then.'

'I'm afraid she might say no.'

'So what if she does?'

'Oh, nothing. It's just that she seems to hate me,' Vitaly informed him anxiously. 'I don't know what I've done to make her dislike me so much.'

Duke had no doubts about what the results would be, as they had been prepared by events which had already taken place. He knew beforehand that this enterprise would require neither risk nor effort on his part.

'OK, let's go,' he agreed, and they sped off to form Upper 5A at the end of the corridor.

It would have been a shame anyway to miss the chance of getting noticed by an older classmate. And besides, it wasn't just anybody, it was Vitaly Reznikov, who had such an envied reputation, all the more so even for being a bit tarnished. If it worked, his reputation might rub off a bit on Duke and it would make him seem older and more established, like a good pair of jeans.

Masha was just coming out of Upper 5A as they approached.

She was wearing a very pretty reddish-brown dress instead of her school uniform and she looked like a vertical tongue of flame in it. Duke felt his cheeks burning.

Vitaly grabbed Duke by the arm, as if he were clutching a talisman in his hand, and went up to her.

She stopped, her back as stiff as a ramrod, and looked sternly – almost ferociously – at Vitaly, as if she was a headmaster bearing down on a delinquent youngster.

'How about going skating tomorrow?' Vitaly asked nervously.

'Not tomorrow. Let's go today,' Masha said. 'At eight.'

And then she carried on down the corridor with her

back still as stiff as a ramrod, and an expression which was completely impenetrable.

Vitaly let go of Duke and looked first at her and then at Duke, as if he was completely flabbergasted.

'Is she going to come, then?' he asked, finally coming to his senses.

'Yes, today, at eight o'clock,' confirmed Duke.

'Where are we going to meet?'

'You'll have to ring her up and arrange something,' he advised.

'Not bad . . .' said Vitaly, shaking his head and coming slowly back down to the real world, or rather, returning to his usual superior self.

'How did you manage that?'

'I have extra-sensory perception,' explained Duke modestly.

'What?'

'Extra-sensory perception. It means I'm super-sensitive.'

'Oh, so vodka-extra means super-vodka,' guessed Vitaly. That was the only conclusion he could draw for himself. Then he thought for a minute and asked, 'Maybe you could come with me when I take the exam to get into the institute?'

'And maybe I could wash your floors while I'm at it?' asked Duke, feeling extremely offended.

'Wash our floors?' asked Vitaly in surprise. 'Oh, there's no need for that. We have Granny to do that.'

The bell rang.

Duke and Vitaly went off to their respective classes, each with his own thoughts. Vitaly had Masha to think about and Duke had the loss of Masha to think about. True, he had never actually had Masha. But he did have dreams and aspirations, and he had lost that right now – the right to dream, that was, and all for the sake of trying to impress Vitaly and winning some kudos. But Vitaly was never really amazed by anthing. Only things which directly involved him had any importance for him. To him 'extra' meant either vodka or biscuits only because they were things he ate and drank.

They were in the middle of their geography class, and their teacher Lev Semyonovich was talking about climatic conditions. Duke heard on the news every day where it was warm and where it was cold to the accompaniment of music by Tchaikovsky. In Tbilisi, for example, there might be tropical rain, but in Yakutia the fir trees would be groaning under huge amounts of snow. Imagine standing under those trees in his thin little jacket, or in that tropical rain, with his face upturned . . .

'Dukin!' Lev Semyonovich called out.

Duke stood up. He looked at his teacher with a pained honesty, his eyes pleading with Lev Semyonovich to understand him – to pick up his signals like a radio picks up sound waves. But Lev Semyonovich was tuned into another waveband. It certainly wasn't Duke's anyway.

'Kindly leave the classroom!' asked Lev Semyonovich.

'Why?' asked Duke.

'Because your vacant expression is driving me up the wall, that's why.'

Duke went out into the corridor. There were pictures of astronauts and the crests of all the Union republics hanging on the wall. He stood there for a while without moving a muscle. Then he started leaning his back against the wall and sliding down it, until he eventually ended up squatting on his haunches.

Masha Arkhangelskaya came out of the staffroom holding the class register in her hand. She looked radiant, and was walking along as if she was in a dream, with her feet two inches off the ground. She was being borne along by her happiness.

How well she fused with her state of mind. Duke had

seen her looking as if she was the unhappiest person in the world, and now here she was looking quite the opposite. But since Vitaly was guaranteed unhappiness, she would be bound to return to her previous state soon, and then the small tears would once more start running down her face, her eyes would become red and her forehead would be covered with nervous blotches.

She would switch from happiness to sorrow and back again. But perhaps that was what love was like? Perhaps experiencing a bitter sort of happiness was better than a dreary, monotonous life . . .

Masha noticed Duke squatting down there as she went by.

'What's the matter with you?' she asked softly, as if apportioning off to him a tiny piece of the warmth overflowing in her.

'Nothing,' answered Duke.

He had no desire for warmth that was intended for someone else.

'Half a kilo of cheddar cheese, half a kilo of butter, and twenty cartons of sixty per cent milk,' reeled off Duke.

The shop assistant, who was elderly and slow-moving, totted up the bill and said, 'Eight roubles nine kopecks.'

'Can I pay you?' asked Duke, holding out the money.

'No. Go and pay at the till,' the shop assistant told him.

But only one till was working, and there was a queue stretched out all along the shop, which was like a river with lots of bends and curves.

'But it'll be ages if I have to wait in the queue,' said Duke confidentially, carefully establishing eye contact with the shop assistant. The message in his eyes was: you may be as old as a cuttlefish, but you are still very kind, and I expect you are probably very tired and want to go home.

When you look at a person with kindness and talk to them normally, without being too pushy or demanding, you can accomplish everything you want without difficulty, and you don't necessarily have to be a talisman to do it. Just as evil begets evil, good begets good.

The shop assistant looked first at the skinny and rather helpless-looking lad in front of her, and then at the queue at the till, and said, 'All right then. But you'll have to give me the exact amount.'

Duke slapped eight roubles and ten kopecks down on to the counter. The shop assistant swept the money into her hand, and slipped it into a big white pocket sticking out on her overall. Then she transferred her eyes to the next customer: an old woman as withered as a knobbly twig.

'Fifty-seven kopecks. I've got the right change,' said the old woman, putting the money on the counter. 'A carton of cream and some cream cheese.'

By the time Duke left the shop, lugging twenty small triangular pyramids in his bulging shopping bag, trade at the dairy counter was proceeding along a new principle which bypassed the till, and thus also avoided accounts. Duke did not stop to think whether that was good or bad. Probably it was good for some, and bad for others.

Just as he was leaving the shop, he bumped into Lariska's mother, their neighbour Auntie Zina. She was the one whom he would not have wanted to have as a mother.

'Where are you off to with all that milk?' she asked in surprise.

'We make our own home-made cheese from it,' explained Duke. 'Mum can only eat cheese in the mornings.'

'What a good boy,' said Auntie Zina approvingly. 'Helping your mum like that. There aren't enough children like you around. With mine it's just "give me this", "give me that". Now it's a tape-recorder they're after. A Sony. Where I am supposed to get one of those from, eh?'

Duke did not answer. The bottom carton had broken under the weight of all the other nineteen ones on top, and a thin, unending stream of milk was trickling out of it, soaking his right shoe. Duke moved his hand which was holding the bag further away from his jeans, so that the stream would flow at a harmless distance, but holding such a weight at arm's length was not very comfortable.

'Sasha, I've heard that you're a . . . what's it called, I've forgotten the name . . . well, you know, a sort of lucky charm.'

'Who told you?' asked Duke with interest.

He was interested in knowing how he had become famous.

'People are talking about it at school.'

Duke guessed that Vitaly had told Masha. Masha must have told Lariska and Lariska must have told Auntie Zina. And once you had told her, it would go round the whole country. It would get printed as a headline in the evening news.

Duke was flattered that his name was being brought up in circles where the best boys skated to music with the best girls, their arms folded neatly in front of them.

'The thing is, I've got some friends from the Baltics staying,' Auntie Zina informed him, for some reason in a pathetic voice. 'We rent a cottage from them in the summer, you see, and they want to buy some of that Finnish "Tower" furniture. But they can't get hold of it anywhere.'

'English, surely.'

'What do you mean, English?' asked Auntie Zina, perplexed.

'The Tower is an English prison. Queen Elizabeth Stuart was held there.'

'How do you know?'

'Everyone knows that.'

'Well, maybe,' agreed Auntie Zina. 'It has a little wall and some bars anyway.'

'But why would anyone want to buy prison walls to furnish a flat?' Duke asked, trying to dissuade her.

'Will you help them, Sasha, eh? I promised them I would see what I could do. Lariska says you are ever so clever.'

Duke did not know whether he was clever or not. But if Lariska had said so, it meant more.

It was tempting to agree and try to help, but it was risky too. The manager of a furniture shop was hardly going to want to accept a Wrangler belt in exchange, for example, and he didn't have the belt any more anyway. But if he said to Auntie Zina, 'No, I can't,' his radius of fame would immediately be reduced. And fame was the shortest and only real route to Masha Arkhangelskaya's heart. When she realized that Vitaly was guaranteed unhappiness, and that Duke was accomplished and successful, who knows how things might turn out?

'They would have slipped them something,' whispered Auntie Zina confidentially, 'but they say they don't know who to give it to, and how much. They're very decent people, you see, Sasha. They're from the intelligentsia. They let us use their garden, you know. It's got a vegetable patch. We pick blackcurrants from it. And dill.'

The stream from the packet of milk had almost dried up and now just dripped occasionally. Duke returned his hand to its previous position.

'I'll try,' he said, 'but I can't promise anything.'

Operation Tower-Talisman would need some careful advance preparation.

★

The manager's office was situated at the back of the shop, next to the warehouse.

The manager of the furniture shop himself was sitting hunched over his desk with his mouth hanging open, looking like a hedgehog that wanted a drink. His stiff hair was standing up on end like bristles, and all he needed now were some spines on his back. His head made up a good third of his body and seemed to be joined to it without the aid of a neck. His little hands were stubby like paws, and lay on the table pointing at each other.

'Good afternoon,' said Duke as he entered.

The little hedgehog made some feeble muttering sounds. He couldn't be bothered to make the effort to say the words 'good afternoon', especially when they would be addressed to no one in particular. Some little boy who had turned up in his office, who was probably lost and had got separated from his mother.

Duke stood there indecisively, not knowing what to say.

'What do you want?' asked the Hedgehog. He spoke with effort, as if he was being held by the throat and throttled slightly.

'The "Tower" suite,' replied Duke.

'We haven't got any of that in stock at the moment. Who's it for?'

'Friends.'

'Whose friends?' The director was evidently worried that Duke might be an intermediary for some bigwig.

'Auntie Zina's'

'And who is Auntie Zina?'

'Our neighbour.'

'And what is she doing sending you round to buy furniture? Must be completely mad sending a kid round to buy furniture. Really . . . Whatever next?' The manager snorted just like a hedgehog.

'I'm not a kid.'

'What are you then?'

'A talisman.'

'A what?'

'A talisman is a person who brings happiness.'

The manager perked up for the first time in their conversation and looked at Duke like a hedgehog who has just seen something interesting. A mushroom, for example.

'You bring happiness?' he asked again.

'Not by myself, no. But if someone wants something and takes me with them, then they get what they want.'

'You're not lying, are you?' verified the Hedgehog.

'So you really don't have any of that furniture,' said Duke, dodging the question.

'Listen. I'll help you if you help me,' promised the Hedgehog. 'But you'll have to come with me for an hour or two.'

'Where to?' asked Duke.

'A place,' said the Hedgehog evasively. 'What does it matter where?'

'Well, I suppose it doesn't, really,' agreed Duke.

The Hedgehog got up from his desk and stood up on his hind paws, although it did not make him any taller. His head was still on the same level. Duke realized that he had stood up, though, because of the position of his hands. Before they had been placed pointing to each other, and now they faced forwards, like a real person's.

The Hedgehog sat in the front next to the driver in the taxi. He sat with his head drawn into his shoulders and didn't say anything. Except for one time when he turned round suddenly and said, 'If they don't want bribery to exist, they shouldn't create the conditions for it.'

Duke did not understand.

'They're the ones who create the shortages. They're the ones creating the queues,' the Hedgehog continued crossly. 'And what are they hoping to achieve by doing that? Moral correctness? I'll tell them that.'

'Who will you tell?' asked Duke.

The Hedgehog waved his hand dismissively and turned to the taxi driver. 'We're here.'

The taxi driver pulled up near a large, awe-inspiring building. The Hedgehog paid for the cab, then got out and opened the door for Duke.

They took their coats off in the cloakroom, which was cool and lined with marble like a cathedral. Then they went up a spacious staircase, and entered a room lined with oak panelling. There were two gigantic doors with nameplates on them on each side of the room, and a secretary sitting by each of the doors.

'Wait here,' ordered the Hedgehog, as he headed towards the door on the right. But before disappearing behind it, he looked at Duke in desperation, like someone about to toss away the end of a rope before jumping into the crater of a volcano. Or diving into the ocean depths. Or climbing out of a rocket in outer space, when you don't know what might happen to you, or whether you'll be able to get back again. Duke caught the end of the rope with his eyes and nodded.

The Hedgehog vanished behind the door, protected by Duke's thought waves.

Duke stood there without moving a muscle. He was hungry. He hadn't the faintest idea of what was really going on, except that he had worked out that someone was creating the conditions for bribery, and that the Hedgehog, who was not morally very upright, had been raking the bribes into his burrow with his stubby paws. Now the Hedgehog had been summoned and an explanation was being demanded of him, and he was extremely downcast, because it meant he would have to remove from his bristles all the money belonging to other people which had somehow become his.

The secretary on the right hand side of the room was rummaging busily amongst her papers. Then she found what she was looking for and left the room. The other secretary was holding the phone near her ear and from time to time saying exactly the same phrase: 'You're absolutely right.' There would be a pause, then she would say again, 'You're absolutely right.'

Duke started to get bored. He leaned his back against the right door post and started sliding down to the floor. He thought he would squat on his heels for a while just to vary the routine a bit, but he couldn't hold his balance and fell over, his back hitting the door as he did so. This made the door fly open, and Duke naturally went with the door, as a result of which his head and upper body ended up lying inside the office, while his legs stayed in reception. He looked like a corpse that has just tumbled out of a storeroom.

In his recumbent position, Duke could see that there were two people in the room: the Hedgehog and someone who looked like a former athlete who had retired because he had got too old.

'What's going on?' exclaimed the athlete in fright.

'Sorry, he's . . . er . . . with me,' said the Hedgehog in embarrassment.

Duke had meanwhile got up, and the athlete now had the chance to examine him in an upright position – his narrow bones, his round, terrified eyes, and the untidy mop of hair on his head. The athlete looked at the boy longer than might have been customary in such situations, then for some reason he became upset and said to the Hedgehog, 'Look! Just write a letter of resignation and make sure I never see you doing business ever again. I don't want to ever catch you poking your snout back into the trade. Is that clear?'

He was speaking coarsely, but the Hedgehog for some

reason was completely overjoyed by what he was saying, and his eyes even began to sparkle with happiness.

'Thank you!' the Hedgehog mumbled with genuine feeling.

'No need to thank me!' said the athlete. 'I don't feel sorry for you. It's your kids I feel sorry for. I just hope the saying "like father like son" is not going to come true in your case. Now get out!'

The Hedgehog stood there, paralysed with joy. Duke also did not move.

'Come on now, it's time to go,' the athlete suggested gently to Duke. 'And take your pa with you . . .'

They walked down the stairs without looking at each other, and picked up their coats from the cloakroom attendant in complete silence. Then they left the building.

'"Don't let me catch you poking your snout . . ."' mimicked the Hedgehog disgruntledly. 'I wouldn't go near those furniture shops if you paid me. I'd sooner spit on them from a great height! Or even better from a low height, so it would hit them quicker. After you've been working in that business a while, you know, you start to hate people. It's the herd . . . But even herds have certain laws though. Take wolves, for example . . . But what are we standing here for?' said the Hedgehog suddenly collecting himself. 'Let's go and have a drink!'

They crossed the road, enticed by a sign saying 'Grill bar'. There was almost no one in the bar except for a few couples sitting at the tables in their coats. Soft music was playing.

'Hungry?' asked the Hedgehog.

'Not at the moment,' replied Duke.

He had been hungry, then he had stopped feeling hungry, and now he just felt a general ache in his stomach.

The Hedgehog bought a bottle of cognac with a large quantity of stars on the label and a lemon cut into slices.

He poured the cognac into glasses: a full one for himself and half a glass for Duke.

'What's your name?' the Hedgehog asked.

'Sasha,' remembered Duke.

'Well, Sasha,' said the Hedgehog, raising his glass. 'To the success of our enterprise!'

Duke took a large gulp, then nibbled the lemon. He felt the cognac going straight through him. The lemon tasted sour.

The Hedgehog downed his glass, and his face immediately twisted up like a rubber doll. His nose and his mouth were pushed together into one lump. Then they returned to their normal places.

'It's a shame I didn't get put away really,' he said.

'Put away where?' asked Duke blankly.

'In prison,' the Hedgehog answered simply, breaking the lemon ring and making it into a straight line. 'At least I could get away from them all then. It would be a change of scene. You can live decently in prison too, you know. But the main thing – do you know what that is?'

'No.'

'The main thing is to stay a human being. I remember after the war, when German POWs were building houses here. They worked really conscientiously. I asked one of them: "Why are you working so hard?" "I want to return home a German," he said to me. Do you see what I mean?'

Duke listened carefully to the Hedgehog, but the Germans' problems seemed very far removed from his problems.

'You promised me some "Tower" furniture,' Duke said to remind him.

'Sure. Just come and get it,' agreed the Hedgehog promptly.

'But you said you didn't have any,' said Duke, feeling very confused now.

'Not at the shop I don't, but I've got some at the warehouse. There's one suite left. It's a reject, because one of the panes of glass is broken. But it'll be simple to repair. My lads can fix it up.'

The Hedgehog looked at his watch and said, 'Look, I'm not going to go back today, so let's make it tomorrow, OK? Early. Are you going to come yourself, or will you send someone?'

'I'll send somebody,' replied Duke importantly.

'I did promise it to a Georgian, but no . . . I'll give it to you.'

'Thank you,' said Duke.

'No, thank *you*. What you did for me was far more valuable than money. Do you really bring happiness?'

'To everyone except myself,' said the Duke.

'That's understandable,' said the Hedgehog believing him.

'Why?'

'Either you're happy at the expense of others, or they are happy at your expense,' explained the Hedgehog.

'Can't you have both at the same time?'

'Maybe. But I never seem to manage it.'

'So do you make yourself happy at the expense of others?' asked Duke with interest.

'No, I don't make myself happy, that's the whole problem. What do I need anyway?' said the Hedgehog, clasping both paws to his chest. 'I don't need anything. I'm an old man. It's all for them! And if they could only say "Dad, how are you doing?" once in a while I wouldn't mind. It's not much to ask, is it, to take an interest in your own father?'

Duke felt bad for the Hedgehog.

'So how are you doing?' he asked.

'Badly!' The Hedgehog propped up his large, truncated head in his paw and fixed his sad, intelligent gaze into the distance. 'I've lost all excitement for things. I'm bored! Bored! I can't find any meaning in anything. What meaning is there to anything?'

'I don't know,' said Duke.

'I don't know either,' admitted the Hedgehog. 'I thought before, well, the children are growing up. I've got to live for them. But now they are grown up and I can see that they are not my children at all. They're just separate individuals. They live for themselves. And I am a separate individual when you come down to it too. But I am only interesting to them as a source of money. And nothing else.'

Duke remembered his mother.

'It's not very nice of your children to behave like that towards you,' he said.

'I'm afraid it's normal,' objected the Hedgehog sadly. 'If children fulfilled all the hopes their parents placed on them, the world would be an ideal place . . . But it was imperfect during the time of Jesus Christ and it's stayed that way.'

'What is there to be done then?' asked Duke cautiously.

'Nothing can be done. You've just got to live. And always try to be a human being whatever the circumstances. Like those German POWs. We are all prisoners really anyway – prisoners of money, of illness, of our desires, of age, of love, of death. Ah, to hell with it . . .' The Hedgehog waved his hand dismissively. 'Come on, let's go. I'll take you home.'

'Oh, I'll be fine on my own, thanks,' said Duke.

He was as tired of the Hedgehog as if he had been in a lift with him for an infinitely long time. He wanted to be by himself and think about what he wanted, and if there wasn't anything he wanted to think about, not to have to think at all.

★

It took him three hours to get home. He might have been travelling to another city.

He fell asleep while he was in the Underground, and only woke up at Preobrazhenskaya, the last station on the line, because a woman who worked on the Underground was tapping him on the shoulder.

He got out of the carriage then got on another train going in the opposite direction which took him back through the whole city to the next interchange. Duke sat there with his head drooping. For some reason it would not sit still on his neck and was rolling about his chest like a football on a playing field. He felt that he would never get to his destination, and that he would be forever rumbling about in tunnels.

Finally, though, he managed to arrive at his doorstep. But first he called Auntie Zina and told her all the necessary information: where to go and when to go, etc. But he felt as if he was suffering from blood poisoning. Everything, both his own victory and Auntie Zina's reaction was suddenly completely indifferent to him. But her reaction was unexpected all the same.

'What about a carpet?' she asked.

'What carpet?' asked Duke not understanding.

'You know, to go with the furniture,' she declared.

She had evidently decided that Duke really was 'something like a lucky charm' and lucky charms, as everyone knew, could get anything from bathtubs to mansion blocks.

'I don't know about that,' replied Duke drily. 'You'll have to do that without me.'

Everything was making him feel sick, including Auntie Zina.

'Just a minute, then,' promised Auntie Zina, and she spun round on her short squat legs, and carried off into the distance her large bottom, which looked like a television set attached to her back. In an instant she returned, and slipped Duke a ten rouble note, folded in two.

'What's this for?' asked Duke in astonishment.

'Go on, take it, take it . . . Buy yourself something.'

'What can you buy with ten roubles?' replied Duke with genuine surprise. 'You'd be better off buying yourself some . . . toilet paper with it, for example. Then you'd have enough for a whole year. If you were economical . . .'

He put the money back into Auntie Zina's puffy hand and went towards his front door. He got out his keys.

Auntie Zina watched him fumbling with his keys, then said, 'You've become very crude lately, Sasha. And ill-mannered too. You can tell you are growing up without a father. All this fatherlessness, I don't know . . .'

Duke disappeared behind his front door.

His forehead had become cold, and he felt something rising in his throat . . . He went into the lavatory, bent over and expelled from himself the remains of the cognac, the Tower suite, the ten rouble note, and his fatherlessness.

He felt a little better now, but his legs would not carry him. When he transferred to the bathroom to confront his face in the mirror, he discovered it was a bright green colour, like a leaf of young spring lettuce. So he went and lay down on the couch, lettuce-face downwards.

Honin came up to Duke after school the next day and said, 'I've got something I want to talk to you about.'

'No!' snapped Duke.

'Why?' said Honin in surprise. 'It's your mother who has gone away.'

His mother really had gone away – on a trip to Leningrad. The local trade union committee at the computer centre where she worked was very efficient and they always went away somewhere every year. But what did his mother have to do with this?

'What is it you wanted?' asked Duke.

'To get together for a party,' suggested Honin. 'Svetka's tape recorder, Seriozha's cassettes, your place.'

'Oh, I see. No, that would be fine,' Duke replied happily.

They had never included him in any of their parties before. First of all he always got Cs and Ds, so he wasn't prestigious enough for them. And secondly he was small, which didn't look good. It lowered the general tone.

'We could get together at Svetka's dacha. But it takes two hours just to get there.'

'Oh, no, really,' confirmed Duke readily. 'Come over to my place . . .'

When he returned home from school and went into his flat, Duke tried to survey his home with an outsider's critical eye. Lariska's eye, for example.

At Lariska's there was lots of crystal and china like in the antique shops on the Arbat. Duke had just gawped the first time he saw it all. On the sideboard there was an entire scene made of porcelain. A gentleman in a green waistcoat, with his hair in a pigtail, was leading a lady in a wig and countless skirts by the hand. This was all taking place in a leafy glade, where there were porcelain flowers in bloom and a dog barking. The dog had a pink tongue and on the flowers you could count the number of petals, even the stamens.

There was nothing like that in Duke's flat. All they had was a couch with a broken leg which he had bandaged himself with insulating tape. The couch's disability was not all that noticeable, but you couldn't plonk down on it with all your weight. And they had little rugs on the chairs to hide their threadbare upholstery and general poverty.

But they were not all that poor. His mum worked as a computer operator. She fed punched cards into a computer and got results; and a wage. And alimony on a level with her pay. To judge from the alimony, his father was doing rather well somewhere. He and his mother lived no worse than other people in fact. It was just that his mother was not disposed to living comfortably. She almost did not care what her surroundings were like. The most important things to her were the things inside her: her thoughts and feelings. That suited Duke, because it meant you didn't have to take care of everything the whole time and make people take off their shoes in the hall, like at Lariska's.

Duke was wondering whether he should go over to her place now while Auntie Zina was out and ask to borrow the china figurines. But it was horrible having to ask, and actually rather pointless. Ornaments don't count for anything when there's a party going on. The lights would get turned off and then you wouldn't be able to see anything anyway.

Duke looked round the room once again, this time more condescendingly. There was a watercolour of Chekhov in Yalta hanging over the couch; tall, thin, stooping Chekhov, wearing a tight-fitting coat and a hat. Chekhov's fame lived separately from him – his loneliness and his tuberculosis were what lived with him.

Duke was often saddened by the fact that Chekhov had died long before he was born. He was sorry that he could not go to visit him in Yalta and tell him all the things he wanted to get off his chest, which Chekhov might have wanted to hear about. Duke felt that it was a great pity that there were no direct links between ancestors and their descendants. He had piled up quite a number of ancestors with whom he wanted to receive advice on various matters, and their recommendations would have been decisive for him.

He sighed. Then he picked up from the radiator the sleeve from his old pyjamas which served as a rag (and which in actual fact was a rag), and started wiping the dust off all the polished surfaces. Then he turned on the vacuum cleaner and started pushing it back and forth across the carpet. As he did so, the carpet grew brighter and the room became fresher.

Then he went into the kitchen. He washed up all the dishes that had piled up over the last three days, then peered into the fridge. He realized he would have to dash over to the shops.

He spent three roubles buying twenty cream cakes in the delicatessen, then he went over to the wines and spirits section. He got into a long queue of seedy-looking, unkempt men who all looked as if they had been knocked down by the streetcar named Desire, and with the remaining money bought three bottles of dry Bulgarian wine.

This was the first party on his territory and he had to rise to the occasion.

The guests arrived in two shifts. First to arrive were the lads: Honin, Buleyev, and Seriozha Kiskachi.

Seriozha was the noisiest person in the whole class. He transmitted his exuberance and restlessness to everyone like a rabid dog. You had the impression that if you were to be bitten by him you would be bound to become infected with his manic high spirits, and that no amount of injections would help you. Seriozha was planning to study at a school for performing arts to become a compere.

Buleyev was the athlete, dressed from head to toe in denim. He ran ten kilometres every day round the area where they lived, driving out all the poisonous toxins from his body together with his sweat. Afterwards he would get under the shower, rinse the toxins off, and enter the world free and easy again. His healthy body housed a healthy spirit, which was impervious to all kinds of nonsense like vanity and the search to find oneself. Why search for yourself when you are already there?

The girls – Kiyashko, Mareyeva, and Eliseyeva – arrived half an hour later.

Kiyashko turned up in a dress with straps that was so elegant that everyone was completely knocked out.

'Hey, Svetka, that's really cool . . .' said Seriozha Kiskachi.

Mareyeva had slimmed down to approximately half her previous size. Cheekbones and eyes had appeared in her face and the serenity of intense suffering was evident in her eyes.

'Have you been ill or something?' asked Duke in amazement.

'No. I've lost weight. I'm down to the fifth notch.'

Mareyeva showed him the Wrangler belt on which there was one notch still to go.

'Hey, you look really cool . . .' said Kiskachi, shaking his head. All his emotions – admiration, surprise, annoyance – were expressed by the one phrase: 'Hey, that's cool . . .' It might be enough for a compere. But it was obviously going to be insufficient for an audience.

Olya Eliseyeva looked the same as always. She was like a porcelain doll with a pretty, rosy-pink face. She laughed when there was reason to and also when there wasn't, and she was easy-going and fun to be with. One was always struck by the contrasts in Olya Eliseyeva: by her apparent health and her actual serious illnesses, and by her pretence at stupidity and her exceptional capabilities. She got As in all her subjects.

With Duke on the other hand, everything was harmonious; he was the same inside as he was outside.

There were seven people present including him. Four boys and three girls. So they were one girl short. Or one boy too many.

At first they all congregated in the kitchen. Seriozha Kiskachi rubbed his hands, exclaiming delightedly: 'Great! Free tea!'

Each person got three cakes and two glasses of wine.

When they were on to the second glass, Svetlana Kiyashko asked, 'Sasha, are there any of your bio-rhythms left?'

'What bio-rhythms?' asked Mareyeva in surprise.

As she was at a different school, she didn't know about Duke being a talisman. Svetlana Kiyashko had not said anything to her as she did not want to waste Duke on other people. In her dislike of waste, she was behaving like a true woman. Mareyeva was also behaving like a true woman in not letting on about the swap, because she wanted to seem more magnanimous. Magnanimity is just as important a factor in friendship as it is in love.

'Why?' asked Duke cautiously.

'Buleyev is going in for the junior championships in a week's time. How about going with him?'

'You had better ask me first whether I want him to!' suggested Buleyev, not sharply, but none the less firmly.

'Buleyev,' said Kiyashko theatrically, 'do you want Alexander Dukin to go with you to the race?'

'No, I don't want him to,' Buleyev replied calmly.

'Why not?' asked Honin in surprise.

'I'll win by myself. Or I'll lose by myself. And I'll do it honestly.'

'I'll do it honestly!' exclaimed Seriozha, repeating his words. 'Here are you going to be honest, when you know they will have got a list of winners ready beforehand.'

'That's their business,' answered Buleyev. 'But I answer for myself.'

'Quite right too,' said Olya Eliseyeva with her mouth full. 'It's not interesting otherwise.'

'If you win by yourself, great. But what if Duke were to protect you? Would there by anything bad about that?' said the crafty Honin, putting forward his suggestion. 'It never does any harm to be protected.'

'It's not interesting to me if there's no risk,' explained Buleyev. 'I just can't run if there's no risk.'

'You may feel that way now,' remarked Svetlana Kiyashko, 'but as they say, steep hills wear out horses.'

'If they do, they do,' Buleyev concluded. 'But that's not the right attitude.'

'I agree!' exclaimed Duke.

He was doubly glad, both because Buleyev was taking such a principled position on things, and also for his own sake. Otherwise he would have had to have gone to see the adjudicator and prepared Buleyev's victory in some way. And who knows what sort of person the adjudicator might turn out to be? Or what he might demand from Duke? Maybe he would ask for his young soul, like Mephistopheles. Although what use would that be?

'Well, it's your decision,' said Svetlana, feeling slightly hurt. 'I was only thinking of you.'

'What has Duke got to do?' asked Mareyeva.

'Nothing!' replied Kiyashko.

Mareyeva shrugged her shoulders. She did not understand what this was all about, but this was partly because all her mental energies and all her willpower were directed at not eating a cake, so that she would be able to reduce her physical size one further notch.

Duke had noticed that it often happened that there were situations when everyone except for one person knew about something. And that was apparently perfectly normal. Auntie Zina's husband, for example, who was

Lariska's father, was seeing a younger woman. Everyone in the building knew about it, but Auntie Zina didn't.

'Let's dance!' suggested the clumsy Olya Eliseyeva, jumping up first from her chair.

They all moved back to the main room, turned on Kiyashko's tape recorder and started grinding the carpet into the floor with their feet.

Everybody danced together and Duke felt he was joining in extremely well. He moved his legs as if he was stamping out endless cigarette ends with the balls of his feet. He was enjoying himself and feeling very daring.

Kiyashko was telling Olya Eliseyeva something funny. She was laughing so much she couldn't keep her balance and she suddenly collapsed on to the couch with all her many kilograms. The leg gave a crack and the couch listed over, which made everyone start laughing. Duke squatted down to examine the leg. It had now broken completely and there was no way it could be mended. Neither was it clear what should be done.

He went to get a a pile of magazines from his room and shoved them under the corner of the couch where the leg should have been. The poverty which had been concealed was now painfully obvious.

The cassette player continued to blare out music from the group Genghis Khan. The clumsy Honin went a bit mad at this point and hit his head on a pendant from the candelabra hanging from the ceiling. The pendant fell straight into the wine glass Seriozha was holding in his hand, which also made everyone laugh. Duke noticed that what made things funny was when the principle of 'the way things ought to be' was overturned. The pendant should have been on the chandelier, for example, and not in the wine glass. And there should have been wine in the wine glass, not a pendant. Everyone was laughing because the principle of 'the way things ought to be' had been turned on its head, and also because the wine had put everyone in a good mood and given them the sensation of feeling out of control. That was almost freedom itself, and the broken couch was one of the manifestations of that freedom.

The wine glass gave a crack, emitting a farewell crystal groan. Duke took it from Seriozha's hands and carried it into the kitchen to see if the crack could be mended. But there was no way it could be repaired; the traces of the crime could only be covered up. The glass had been given to his mother as a wedding present sixteen years ago. Since then, out of twelve glasses, only two remained. Now there was only one.

Duke went out on to the stairs and threw the glass into the rubbish chute, but when he came back into the room, he saw that the lights had been turned off and everyone had split up into couples.

Honin was with Mareyeva, since they were both intellectuals with a leaning towards mathematics. Kiskachi, meanwhile, was with Eliseyeva, since he made her laugh, and nothing brings people closer together than shared laughter. And Buleyev was with Kiyashko, on the principle that if two people are more good looking than everyone else around them, they are bound to be attracted to each other.

Duke tried to dance between the couples by himself, like a soloist amongst the *corps de ballet*, but no one paid any attention to him. They were all wrapped up in each other.

He went into his bedroom, without knowing why. Eliseyeva and Kiskachi followed him in there.

'You don't believe me, do you?' exclaimed Seriozha in despair.

'But you say that to everyone,' replied Eliseyeva.

'Do you want me to swear on it?'

'You swear on it to everyone else too.'

'That's only what people say!' objected Seriozha hotly.

'It's just that people don't like me. Only I don't understand why no one likes me. I feel so lonely . . .'

He bowed his scruffy, bespectacled head. He really did look unhappy and lonely all of a sudden.

Duke felt that Eliseyeva was about to clasp Seriozha to her bosom, so that she might ease his loneliness with her tender body. He started to feel embarrassed and decided to go back to the dancers.

Only Buleyev and Kiyashko were dancing still, and the room was heavy with sexual tension. Duke did not feel like hanging around with them and so he went into the kitchen.

Honin and Mareyeva were sitting at the kitchen table, and looked as if they were solving some complex problem. Honin was turning something round on a piece of paper and Mareyeva was leaning her now slimmer body over the table, resting her knees on a stool. They both looked at Duke with a blank expression, then plunged back into what they were doing.

Duke stood around for a while and then went out into the hall, but there was absolutely nothing to do there. So he took his jacket off the hook and went outside, pulling the door shut behind him and locking it.

It was drizzling outside, and the snow underfoot was saturated with rain. That meant spring was on the way.

An old man with a pram was keeping watch by the front door of the building, and the hood of the pram had been pulled up.

Duke suddenly missed his mother so much that he felt that he might start crying. He missed their mutual dependency. Tears even sprang to his eyes. It was at that moment that he caught sight of his mother, but for some reason she had slimmed down to half her size. Like Mareyeva.

When she came up to him, he realized that it was not

his mother at all, but another woman, who was like both his mother and Masha Arkhangelskaya. If his mother and Masha were to be mixed up in a cauldron and a new person was made out of them, then you would get this woman with a face blue with cold. She looked like Aelita, Alexei Tolstoy's Martian heroine. She had glasses with large, clear lenses, through which peeped her large, grey, clear eyes.

'Excuse me, you don't know where flat number eighty-nine is, do you?' asked Aelita.

Duke did know, because that was his flat.

'Who are you looking for?' he asked.

'I don't know the name. I'm looking for that shaman boy.'

'You mean the Talisman,' corrected Duke. 'That's me.'

'You?' asked Aelita in surprise. She even took off her glasses to have a closer look at him.

She could not see anything special about him, so she returned her glasses to their previous position.

'It's lucky that I ran into you straight away. That's a good sign,' she concluded.

'It's just a coincidence,' said Duke philosophically.

If there had been four girls at the party, and not three, then he would have been at home right now, and he would not have opened the door to anyone except his mother. Aelita would have stood there, and then would have finally gone away.

'There is no such thing as chance,' objected Aelita. 'There's a reason for everything.'

That was something Duke thought about often. What was fate? Was it just an accumulation of coincidences? Or did everything happen for a reason? And if everything did happen for a reason, what was the reason? Why, for example, was this strange Martian woman smelling of air and water (rain to be precise) standing in front of him?

She was someone he had never seen before in his life, yet he felt he had known her for a long time.

Duke looked at Aelita and pondered what to do. Should he invite her up to the flat or not? He could, of course, go back to the flat and turn the lights on, suggest loudly to his guests, 'Be so kind as to leave!' as Lev Semyonovich so often did. And that would have been perfectly fair on Duke's part. But the last thing his guests wanted to do right now was to leave, to have to go out into the dank, cold, and gloom. They wanted to be where they were.

'Do you mind if I don't come up?' asked Aelita. 'It's just that I'm a bit shy of meeting your parents. They'll think I'm weird.'

'Oh, no, not at all,' Duke agreed happily.

'Let's go into the hallway,' suggested Aelita. 'There'll be a radiator there.'

They went in through the front doorway and went up one flight of stairs.

Aelita put her large checked bag on the windowsill and took off her mittens. She put her hands on the radiator and warmed them for quite a long time. Then she asked, 'How old do you think I am? Tell me honestly . . .'

Duke looked with exaggerated honesty at Aelita and said, 'Twenty-five.' He had added his mother's and Masha Arkhangelskaya's ages, which was 34 + 16, then divided it by two. That came out as twenty-five.

'I'm forty,' said Aelita in a low voice.

Duke looked at her more closely and did not believe her.

'You can't be,' he said.

'I don't believe it either,' agreed Aelita. 'When I wake up in the mornings and remember that I'm forty, I feel as if I've just had an operation. You know, when you are coming round from the anaesthetic and you realize that they have chopped your leg off . . . It's awful . . . It's as if it wasn't happening to me. Then I remember that I was born before the war, and that I've been alive a long time. And then I realize it really is happening to me . . .'

Aelita fell silent and gazed into the darkness.

'So what? Forty isn't all that much,' said Duke artfully, since that age seemed so hopelessly far away from where he was; way past the station called Love, anyway. At that age it seemed ridiculous to him that anyone could want to engage in love affairs. But then he had no idea what people were supposed to do at forty.

'No, it's not much,' agreed Aelita. 'But not much is left either. All that remain are the treasured moments of youth. And youth is more necessary to me now than ever before. It never used to be . . .'

A tear trickled out from behind her glasses. She wiped it away with a finger, but another tear, identical to the first one, was already running down the same path.

'Don't cry,' said Duke. 'You're in the same boat as everyone else in the long run. If it was just you who had to get old, while everyone else stayed young, that would be something to get annoyed about. But that isn't the case, so why are you worrying?'

'Everyone is everyone. But I am me,' said Aelita, refusing to agree. She sniffed stubbornly.

'You want me to make you younger, is that it?' guessed Duke.

'Just a little bit,' Aelita implored gently. 'Just ten years younger. I'm not asking for anything else . . .'

'But that's not within my capabilities. You would have to be a magician to do that, and I'm only a talisman.'

'Don't say no!' shrieked Aelita in a whisper. 'It's not for me that I'm asking this. I don't really care. When it comes down to it, I would be happy with myself the way I am. I'm doing it for him.'

'For whom?'

'I'm getting married.' Aelita took off her glasses and

her face became short-sighted and helpless. If she were to start walking, one felt she would hold her arms in front of her like a blind person, testing the air with her hands and the ground with her feet. 'And he's ten years younger than me. When he was born, I was already in secondary school . . .'

'So what? If he loves you, why should he care?' asked Duke, sounding more and more offhand. 'Really, it's only ten years . . .'

'It's psychological,' said Aelita raising a finger. 'He mustn't know about it.'

Duke looked at her finger and mentally agreed with her. Knowledge certainly does change things. When he discovered that Aelita was forty, and not twenty-five – or rather, at the precise moment he found out – she had grown older before his very eyes. She had somehow grown dimmer, as if shrouded by time, like a layer of dust.

'Just don't tell him how old you are. He'll never find out,' Duke said.

'Just don't tell him how old you are,' said Aelita sarcastically. 'You mean I've come a thousand kilometres just to hear that.'

Duke was confused.

'Claudia Ivanovna put me on to you. She's got friends who live on the Baltic. They said you were a friend of their friends.'

Duke realized that rumours about him must have spread all over Russia, gathering momentum along the way like a snowball.

'Well, you've come for nothing,' said Duke fiercely, feeling his cheeks burn. 'I'm not a talisman.'

'Oh, yes you are,' objected Aelita calmly.

'Well, I should know,' smiled Duke painfully.

'You can't know.'

'What do you mean?' said Duke in confusion.

'Because your – your power is like a talent. And you cannot feel a talent. It's a part of you. Like the colour of your eyes. Can you feel the colour of your eyes?'

'No.'

'Well, there you are then. You can only feel an illness. But your talent is something normal. For you at any rate. That's why you can't feel it . . .'

Aelita put on her glasses and looked at Duke with such conviction that he was completely dumbfounded. Maybe she was right? Maybe he suddenly really was a talisman, and now he didn't need to find himself, because he already was someone . . .

'Do you really think so?' asked Duke.

'Why would I have flown a thousand kilometres otherwise?'

Duke was silent. He was experiencing a number of feelings, amongst which were ones like responsibility. When people believe in you, you have to act accordingly.

'What have I got to do?' asked Duke, feeling a readiness to do everything within and also beyond his powers.

'My passport needs to be changed. I've got 1940 down as my date of birth and I need it to be 1950.'

'Where can it be done?'

'At a police station. You've got to go to the police station with me.'

'Is that all?' asked Duke in amazement.

He had been thinking that he would have to put out three cauldrons in the yard like in the fairy tale: 'one freezing cold, the other boiling hot, and the third with bubbling warm milk': Then Aelita would have to be lowered into them and he would have to make sure she didn't get cooked. But it turned out that all he had to do was get on a bus and travel three stops to the local police station.

'Yes, that's all,' confirmed Aelita. 'If I have 1950 in my passport, he will think I am thirty. And I'll start thinking that too. I will deceive time. I will be younger for him.'

'Just like that,' said Duke.

'I've waited all my life for him, you know. Since I was seventeen. I've waited every single day. Even when I got married, I still kept on waiting. I had a child and still waited. And then I lost heart because I was about to become old. And then I saw him! Do you know where? At the museum. I was walking through all the galleries, feeling sad and forlorn, looking at all the portraits. I was wondering what all those people in them would look like if one were to dress them up in jeans. They still would not seem modern, you know, because their faces are different. And it was then I saw *him*. He seemed to have come down off the wall. His eyes were just the same – they weren't modern. It was as if he knew something quite different about life than other people.

'I knew it was him straight away, so I followed after him. First from gallery to gallery, then from the museum on to the street. He said later that he was following me! That he had been struck by my face. He said he had waited for me since he was seventeen and that we were bound to meet some day . . . I don't have any rights to him. But I won't give him up either. I am going to fight.'

The look which Aelita gave Duke was full of the determination to fight like a soldier at the front, until victory was won.

'So will you go with me to the police station?' she asked.

'Yes,' said Duke, like soldier to soldier.

'Tomorrow then,' ordered Aelita.

'Three o'clock,' fixed Duke. 'Let's meet here.'

Aelita drew Duke to her and kissed him on the cheek. She smelt of rain on a jasmine branch. Duke's heart rose slightly in his throat and his breathing stopped for a moment. His cheeks were burning as he suddenly realized, or rather made the discovery, that people who were forty could fall in love. That there were all kinds of trains which stopped at the station called Love. He waited for his heart to get back to normal, then asked, 'Give me your passport.'

'Why?' asked Aelita with interest.

'I need to exercise powers over it.'

She got her passport out of her bag and held it out to Duke. He tucked it away in the top pocket of his jacket and did up the zip.

'Couldn't you have gone to the police station near where you live?' he asked.

'Why do you think I have flown all the way here?' said Aelita in mock sarcasm. 'Why do you think I would have gone on unpaid leave and spent all that money on a ticket? I don't regret it though, because even if nothing happens with you and me, I've seen something that is far more valuable than money. Do you know what it was?'

'No,' replied Duke. How could he know?

'I saw the sun rise from the aeroplane window. I always thought the sun sort of came up gradually. But in fact it just pops up all of a sudden. One, two three . . . and up!'

Aelita was looking at Duke, but was actually seeing the globe of the sun shooting up over the Earth instead of him. And she was seeing herself between the two globes, flying to meet her own youth.

'Do you have somewhere to stay the night?' asked Duke. 'Otherwise you could stay at my place.'

'Oh, no,' said Aelita, brushing him aside. 'That would be too much. I don't want to turn into crystal.'

'What do you mean?' Duke asked, mystified.

'I'd be a burden to you,' explained Aelita simply. 'When a person is around too much, they turn into crystal. Like when there is too great a saturation of salt in a saline solution. The laws of chemistry extend to human relations too, you know. I am telling you that as a chemist.'

Aelita once again drew Duke towards her. She kissed him again, enveloping him with wafts of jasmine, then got up and left.

Duke stood up, gathering himself together, like Prince Vladimir trying to unite the broken parts of Russia. If it was Vladimir, and not some other prince. Duke wasn't very good at history either. But he failed, and so had to trudge on up to the fifth floor with his soul all in pieces.

He knocked on his front door, and it was not opened for a long time. Duke actually started to worry whether maybe his guests had gone home and locked the door, leaving the keys inside the house. If that was the case, he would either have to break the door down or kip the whole night on the stairs. But suddenly he heard a scraping sound and Honin opened up. Duke did not immediately recognize him. He must have been kissing to distraction, or at least to the point of losing all his human features, because his face was all red hot and stretched in various directions: his mouth reached to his ears and his eyes reached to the top of his head.

'It's you!' said Honin in surprise. 'Where are we then? I thought we were at your place.'

Duke realized that Honin's brains had transferred from his head to a place that was unusual for them.

Just then, Olya Eliseyeva poked her head round into the hall, and her slender face filled with delight. 'Hey! Duke's come back!' she said, smiling merrily.

They all came out into the hall and expressed their pleasure in the best way they could: Buleyev in a gruff condescending way, Kiyashko in a soft, feminine way, and Mareyeva in a contemplative sort of way.

Duke felt like crying. He thought that his heart would not bear the weight of his gratitude. Let them break everything in his house, as long as there was some sort of mutual dependency.

Seriozha Kiskachi shook his head and said, 'Hey, this has been really cool . . .'

That could have meant surprise. But more likely he was expressing his gratitude that Duke hadn't bored his guests while they were at his home, and so hadn't turned into crystal. He had been around just enough.

Duke did not go to school the next day. Instead he set off first thing for the local police station.

The passport section was closed, so Duke started poking his head round doors until he found a policeman in one of the offices. This policeman was a fairly young person in early middle age, but looking at him, it was impossible to imagine that he had ever been really young. It seemed that he had always looked the way he did now.

'Can I help you?' the policeman said.

Duke tried to establish eye contact with him, but failed. It was like a goldfish trying to establish eye contact with a bull.

There are two states of being, the state of being alive and the state of being dead. But actually there is a third state: that of being a zombie, when someone dies long before their natural death. Zombies dwell amongst people as if they were alive too, but nothing human ever penetrates through to them.

The policeman had a completely motionless face, and Duke did not like the look of it. But he could not choose the people he had to talk to. He had to deal with the people who were there.

'Can I help you?' repeated the Zombie.

Duke got out Aelita's passport from the top pocket of his jacket. Confused and rather thrown by the absence of human contact, he started to explain why he had come.

He talked about love and the thousand kilometres. About thirty and forty, which in time would merge into forty or fifty, and about the psychological barrier. Duke noticed himself raising a finger like Aelita had done when he pronouncd the word 'psychological'.

The Zombie looked at the raised finger and said, 'Let me see your documents.'

'I don't have any. I'm under age. What do you need them for anyway?'

'For identification purposes.'

'Whose? Mine?'

'Yes. And that of your comrade who wishes to falsify her passport.'

'Not falsify it. Just correct it,' said Duke.

'Same thing. Do you know how the correcting of documents is regarded?'

Duke was silent.

'As an act of criminal responsibility according to point 3 of article 241/17. Why does this citizen wish to falsify her passport?'

'So she can get married.'

'Let me see.' The Zombie stretched out his hand.

Duke realized that if the Zombie got hold of Aelita's passport, he would arrest her and put her in prison according to article 241/17.

'If it's not possible, then never mind,' said Duke hurriedly. 'I only wanted to get some advice. I thought it wouldn't matter. What difference does it make whether a person is forty or thirty?'

'What do you think passports are for?'

'I don't know.' Duke really did not know why the passport system existed.

'There are two thousand Ivanovs in Moscow alone,' said the Zombie indignantly, as if the Ivanovs themselves were guilty of there being two thousand of them. 'How can we tell them apart? By their first names. By their patronymics. By the year in which they were born. Where they were born. By their passports. Get it?'

'Got it,' said Duke, nodding his head enthusiastically.

'And if everyone started using their own judgement, what do you think would happen?'

Duke looked the Zombie obediently in the eye.

'Chaos! Confusion! Complete bedlam! Who would we register? Who would we bury? Whom would we pay pensions to?'

'But she wants to be younger. She'd get her pension ten years later, so it would save the government some money.'

'The government doesn't save money on hooligans,' snarled the Zombie, snapping the fingers on his outstretched hand. 'Show me your documents,' he said again.

Duke had no option but to put the passport on the desk. The policeman opened it and started looking at the photo of Aelita. If an artist had been looking at it, he would have looked for extraterrestrial beauty in her features. A doctor would have looked for symptoms of hidden ailments. But a policemen looks for criminal intent, trying to gauge a person's potential as a lawbreaker.

'Why hasn't the citizen come herself?' said the Zombie squinting suspiciously at Duke. 'Why is she acting through a third party? Through a middle man?'

Duke wanted to explain that he was a talisman, not a middle man. But then the Zombie would have suspected him of forging his own identity, and to some extent that would have been true.

The telephone rang.

'Khrenyuk speaking,' said the Zombie.

Duke was now convinced that passports really couldn't be altered, otherwise the Zombie would have definitely given himself a more romantic name. Something linked to nature, for example, like Roshchin, which sounded like grove, or Ozerov, which suggested a lake, or Kostrov which was reminiscent of bonfires. But Khren-yuk just sounded like horseradish, as well as something worse . . .

'I'll be back in just a minute,' promised Duke. He swiped Aelita's passport off the desk and left the office without looking round.

He went out into the corridor. The walls were painted beige and the chairs and benches were brown. As he sped along the corridor, a beige-brown stripe flashed past his eyes on both sides. He raced out on to the street and looked around on all sides before heading off across a tram line. Then he dived into an underpass, and surfaced again on the other side of the road, in front of the recreational goods shop.

He walked into the shop with his hands deliberately sunk into his pockets in a casual way, whistling a tune. He thought that was the most natural way to behave. He glanced over to the windows, expecting to see policemen chasing after him with whistles, but no one was chasing after him or blowing on a whistle. There were just people walking along the pavement occupied with their own problems, all of which were very far removed from Duke's problems, and cars moving carefully along the road, stopping at the traffic lights.

Duke thought that he ought to be buying something if he really wanted to look natural. That's why people went into shops after all.

'Could you show me a pen, please?' he asked.

The young shop assistant, who was made up as if she was about to go on stage, and was a head taller than Duke, put three sorts of pens on the counter and then went off to the music section without waiting to see which he would choose. She started chatting to the shop assistant in the music section, who also happened to be young and heavily made-up. They both looked as if someone was about to come to the shop who they were afraid of missing.

The pens were expensive and weren't any good for Duke because he always wrote with biros that cost thirty kopecks. But he nevertheless dipped one in some blue ink and wrote 'Masha' on a piece on paper. It had a hard nib. All a pen like that was good for was for filling out certificates of merit in italic, which had happened to be something he had done once or twice before in his life. Or for forging documents, which did not happen to be something he had done before in his life.

Duke imagined Aelita turning up at three o'clock. She would look at him with her crystal eyes and say, 'And to think I believed you.' He opened the rescued passport and looked at Aelita's Martian face with its fine, rather luminous oval shape. Then he turned the page and saw the year of her birth. 1940 it said, but the last zero was slightly unfinished. So Duke picked up one of the other pens, on which there were no traces of blue ink, and dipped it into the black inkstand, which was also standing right there. He held his hand over the page, then lowered it to put an accurate black curve on to the bottom of the zero. Now it was a nine. It looked a bit pregnant in comparison with the other nine, but it still looked more like a nine than anything else. Now the date of birth read 1949.

The shop assistant came back to Duke. 'Are you going to take one?' she asked.

'Yes, I'll take this one, please,' said Duke, pointing to it.

'That's seven fifty, then,' said the assistant, putting the pen into a plastic case.

'Excuse me, but I can't see very well. Could you tell me what date of birth it says here?' asked Duke, showing the assistant the open passport.

'1949,' said the shop assistant indifferently, staring at the door. Nothing aroused any doubts in her at least.

Duke tucked the passport back into his pocket, paid for the pen with his last ten-rouble note and went outside. He was not far from home, and so he set off on foot.

He walked along calmly with his hands in his pockets, not regretting a thing. He knew that Aelita would now be happy for the rest of her life. And so little was needed to bring it about. Just a thin black curve under a zero.

There was still an hour to go before three o'clock.

It would be boring to hang around in the doorway of his building. And he did not want to go into the empty flat. So he went and sat in the little garden at the front of his building. He spread his arms out along the bench and lifted his face up to the sky. He loved open spaces and he loved to sit like this, with his arms outstretched and his face upturned, as if he wanted to embrace the whole world, including all those who had temporarily come into it and all those who had left for ever. Where had they gone to?

He did not notice Aelita coming up to him, and so her face with the large glasses loomed up all of a sudden.

'I came early,' said Aelita.

'I came early too,' answered Duke.

Aelita sat down on the edge of the bench, but did not take her worried eyes off Duke once.

'I couldn't manage ten years, I'm afraid,' apologized Duke. 'Only nine.'

He held the passport out to her.

Aelita opened it and glued her eyes to the page. Then she turned to look at Duke, and he saw the sun popping up in her eyes.

'You'll be one year older,' said Duke. 'But that's all right.'

'At last . . .' sighed Aelita. 'I'm young! I'm thirty-one!'

She got up from the bench and became younger right in front of Duke's eyes. He saw her straightening up, shaking the dust off herself – or rather the dustiness of time – and beginning to sparkle, like a newly polished piano with its cover taken off.

'I knew it would work,' said Aelita, screwing up her eyes in anticipation of all the possibilities that were now opening up for her.

'How did you know?'

'It had to. How could it have been any different?'

Duke shrugged his shoulders. He knew how it could have been and also how it actually was.

'I hope you'll be happy, Mr Talisman!' said Aelita. 'Don't forget to take care of yourself.'

'No,' promised Duke. 'I won't.'

She smiled through her tears. Happiness was obviously a burden and a torment to her. She walked out of the garden still beaming. She had a long, happy life ahead of her and was steaming full speed ahead into that new life. But Duke was staying behind in the old one. On the bench.

When he turned round, Aelita was no longer there. He had not even found out what her name was. Where had she come from? What sort of person was she? Did she really exist?

But a new pen with traces of dried black ink on its hard nib lay in his pocket.

She was real, then . . .

His mother returned home from Leningrad that evening.

She saw the broken couch, and said, 'Well, thank God! Now we can change the furniture. We've been living like refugees long enough. It's more like a camping ground here than a home.'

She had brought Duke a stamp album as a present, although he had not been collecting stamps for more than a year now. His mother, it turned out, had not noticed. She had generally not been very attentive recently, and

Duke wondered whether she had maybe got involved in a romance with some unmodern person ten years younger than she was, or even someone of the same age. If that was the case, most of his mother's love would now go to this new person and he would have to put up with whatever was left over. He already hated this person in advance and his mother with him.

He started stalking round the flat looking despondent and suspicious, like a bison in the jungle, but his mother did not notice anything, because she was submerged under a heap of household chores. She was doing the laundry, putting dinner into production and walking back and forth between the bathroom, the kitchen and the telephone, which summoned her from time to time with a triumphant ring from the outside world. She would hurry to the phone whenever it started ringing, wiping her hands on the way and her shoes clacking. Each time the phone rang, Duke suspected that this was the lover ringing up and that the process of theft had already begun, or was about to begin any minute.

Finally his mother noticed his moodiness. 'What's up with you?' she asked.

'Nothing,' Duke answered, or rather didn't answer. 'I just didn't sleep well, that's all.'

He went to bed at half-past nine, but he could not get to sleep because he had suddenly realized that he was doomed. They would catch Aelita pretty soon, he worked out, perhaps even at the registry office, because she would have to present her fake passport. They would ask her a few questions, which she would of course answer, and Duke would get sent to prison according to article 241/17. Khrenyuk would come down to his cell and say, 'I warned you. You knew what would happen. You deliberately forged a document, thus undermining the passport system, which is a part of the system as a whole. You're a state criminal.'

They would not break a sword over him, of course, as they had done with Chernyshevsky, but simply pack him off to prison along with all the thieves and bribe-takers. True, he could remain a human being in prison, but since he was a nonentity anyway, he wouldn't manage to gain any authority, and would get lumbered with all the heaviest and most degrading work. Like peeling a whole barrel of potatoes in freezing cold water, for example.

Duke heard someone howl, then suddenly realized that it was his own howl. A spiralling wave of fear threw him out of bed, then propelled him out of his room and on to his mother, who was just about to fall asleep. He took refuge with her under the blankets, howling more quietly now as he sobbed into her hair.

'What's the matter, my little talisman?' said his mother, pushing his hair back firmly but softly, and kissing his warm forehead. 'I thought you were grown up, but it turns out you're still quite little . . .'

He really was quite little in her eyes. He still got frightened and cried just like he used to. He still ate the same way, pursing his lips with an expression of slight distaste. He also still smelt of hay and steamed milk, just like a little lamb.

'Come on, what's the matter with you? What is it?' asked his mother, melting with tenderness.

Duke realized now that there would never be any lover. His mother would never get married again and he would never get married either. They would live together for the rest of their lives, and wouldn't give even an ounce of their love to anyone else. His mother warmed his face with her lips, as her love flowed into him, and he felt as protected as a little animal in a burrow, close to its mother's warm belly.

'Well?' insisted his mother.

'Promise you won't tell anyone?'

'I promise.'

'Do you swear?'

'I swear.'

'On what?'

'I don't know – what do people normally swear on?'

'Swear on my health,' suggested Duke.

'No, I'll swear on anything but that . . .' objected his mother.

'Then I won't tell you anything.'

'Don't then,' agreed his mother, and that was the most insulting thing she could have said. He had not expected his mother to behave like this.

The need to talk was tearing at his insides, and he felt that he might explode if he did not talk soon. He lay there for a few more seconds, then started to tell his mother everything: from the very beginning when they were in form time at school, to the very end, when he committed a state crime. But his mother for some reason didn't seem to be at all worried.

'What an idiot,' she said pensively.

'Who is?' asked Duke, not understanding.

'Your Nina Georgievna, of course, who else? What does she think she is doing trying to educate people by humiliating them? Do you want me to tell her?'

'Tell her what?' asked Duke in fright.

'That she's an idiot!'

'Whatever for? I'm going to have a bad enough grade as it is on my leaving certificate. I won't get in anywhere with it.'

'Shall I get you transferred to another school?'

'Mum! Please! If you're going to interfere like this, I won't tell you anything,' said Duke in distress.

'All right,' promised his mother. 'I won't interfere any more.'

Duke lay in the warm, comfortable darkness and realized that a new school would mean new friends. And new enemies. But he wanted his friends and enemies to stay the same. He was used to them. He fitted in really. He had made Masha Arkhangelskaya happy. He had made Mareyeva thin. He had made his protest to Auntie Zina. He had provided Lariska with summer holidays on the Baltic, with a garden and a vegetable patch.

'Do you know what your mistake is?' asked his mother. 'You're not living your own life. You aren't a talisman, after all.'

'You don't know that,' objected Duke feebly.

'Yes, I do,' said his mother, kissing him as if to smooth over the revelation with a show of affection. 'You're not a talisman. But you are living as if you were one. That means you aren't living your own life. That's why you have been stealing things, telling fibs, puking up all over the place, howling . . .'

Duke listened carefully. He even tried to breathe more quietly.

'Do you know why I divorced your father? He wanted me to live his life. And I couldn't. And nor can you.'

'Is that good or bad?' asked Duke, not understanding.

'In the Bible it says that you should never let your son, your wife, your brother, or your friend rule over you so long as you live and breathe. It says that you should never allow yourself to pretend you are someone else . . . You have to be who you are, you see. The most important thing in life is finding yourself and being true to yourself.'

'But how can I find myself if I'm not there to find?'

'Who said that?'

'Nina Georgievna did. She said that I had no initiative, and that I was just like a sheep.'

'Well, so what? Even if that is so, not everyone can be a leader . . . There are leaders, and then there are those who are led. Joan of Arc, for example, led an army to save Orleans, and soldiers had to march behind her. They had to fight and lose their lives when it became necessary.

It is not a question of who is doing the leading, but who is being led. It is a question of where those people are going and what their aim is. Do you see?'

'Not really,' confessed Duke.

'Just be a decent person. Be a man. That's all I ask from you.'

'Why?' asked Duke, not understanding.

'Because you already are the fulfilment of all my dreams.'

'And that's all?'

'No,' said the mother, 'that's not all.'

'How did you find yourself?'

'Through love.'

'For whom?' asked Duke cautiously.

'For everything. I even love that chair I always sit on. And the cat next door. I don't despise anyone, or think anyone is worse than me.'

Duke transferred his eyes to the chair. In the darkness it looked different than in the daytime. It had somehow acquired a secret other meaning.

'And you are happier without my father?' asked Duke, penetrating into his mother's life. This was the first time they had talked in this way about all of that. Duke had always thought that his mother was his mother, and that was all there was to it. But it turned out that she was also a woman and a separate individual with a need to develop her own identity.

'He wanted me to embody everything he stood for.'

'But maybe that's not such a bad thing,' suggested Duke. 'I mean I wouldn't mind embodying everything Chekhov stood for . . .'

'No,' said his mother firmly. 'Each person is unique. That is why you must be yourself and no one else. Give me your word and you will stop being a talisman.'

'I give you my word,' promised Duke.

'This talisman business will just turn out to be a

vicious circle. Everyone you have done a good turn will come back tomorrow and stand in the queue again. And if you refuse them, they will start to hate you, and will only remember what you haven't done for them, not what you have done for them. Gratitude is an amorphous feeling.'

Duke imagined them all coming back. Aelita coming back for a child for her new family, Auntie Zina coming for a carpet, Vitaly Reznikov for a place at university, Masha coming for Vitaly. Kiyashko would want everything that she had ever given away returned to her.

'I give you my word,' swore Duke.

'And now go back to bed and go to sleep. And don't be scared. Nothing will happen to you.'

'But what about Aelita?'

'Nothing will happen to her either. She just won't live her real age. Until she gets bored of being young, anyway. And that's all that will happen. Now go on, be off with you, or I won't get any sleep.'

Duke ran quickly back to his room, before the cold could catch up with him, and crawled in under the blankets. He put his head on the pillow and immediately started going up some mysterious staircase. Then he took a flying leap and sprang into flight. He knew that if he strained with all his might, he could fly higher and higher. But he would not let himself, because he was scared. Dogs probably feel the same way when they are playing with their owners. They will nip their owner's hand playfully, while their teeth are just itching to bite more strongly. But Duke couldn't restrain himself any longer. He felt as impatient as a dog. He couldn't hold himself back, and was thrusting upwards so hard that he was shaking all over. He was flying up into the sky; up towards the rosy clouds. Happiness! Here it was! Then suddenly he grew frightened: how would he get back again?

And at that moment the phone rang.

He tore his head from the pillow, and looked dumbfoundedly at the phone, experiencing both his dream and reality at the same time, as well as a sensation of alarm that was connected to the phone ringing.

He picked up the receiver and spoke hoarsely into it.

'Hello . . .'

There was silence at the other end. But a person could be felt behind the silence, not emptiness. Who was it? Aelita? The Zombie? Masha Arkhangelskaya? Who needed him now?

'Hello,' Duke demanded in a firmer voice.

'Sasha, is that you? I'm sorry to wake you . . .'

To his great surprise, Duke recognized the voice of his teacher Nina Georgievna. He imagined her face with her frequently blinking, nervous eyes.

'They've just rung me from the hospital and told me that my mother is feeling very poorly. And that I should come. I'm awfully scared.'

Duke was silent.

'You see, that's how they prepare relatives when a patient is dying. They can't just come out and say it. It would be cruel . . .'

Nina Georgievna's agitation spread to Duke like a forest fire.

'Come with me to the hospital, will you? Please?'

'What, now?' asked Duke.

'Yes, now. I know you should be sleeping. But . . .'

'Which hospital is it?' asked Duke.

'Number sixty-two. It's not far.'

'And what is your mother called?'

'Anna Mikhailovna Sidorova. Why?'

'Ring me back in fifteen minues,' Duke requested.

'All right,' agreed Nina Georgievna in a crushed voice.

Duke put the phone down and dialled directory enquiries. They answered immediately and the line was very clear since it was not very busy at that time. Duke was given the number of hospital number sixty-two straight away, and at the hospital they answered straight away. You could feel that the hospital was not far away because the voice that answered sounded very near.

'We're not taking enquiries now. Ring back at nine tomorrow morning,' said the voice.

'I can't ring tomorrow!' shrieked Duke. 'I need to find out now! Please . . .'

'Who are you?' asked the voice. 'Are you a boy or a girl?'

'A boy.'

'What's the name?' asked the voice.

'Whose? Mine?'

'No. What have you got to do with it? The name of the patient, of course. The one you want to ask about.'

'Anna Mikhailovna Sidorova.'

The voice disappeared somewhere. Duke even thought that he had been cut off.

'Hello?' he shouted.

'Don't shout!' asked the voice. 'I'm still looking.'

'Are you a man or a woman? asked Duke with curiosity, since the voice was low and could have belonged to a representative of either sex.

'I'm an old lady,' said the voice, before disappearing again.

Finally it reappeared and asked, 'What relation is she to you? Grandmother?'

'No. Not mine anyway,' replied Duke evasively.

'She's passed away,' the voice said, not immediately.

Duke was stunned by the words 'passed away'. That meant she had been there, but had passed away.

'Thank you . . .' he whispered.

The person sighed and hung up.

The sigh seemed to linger in the room. Duke looked towards the blackened window in horror, as if a dead face might suddenly appear in it. He sat there without a single concrete thought, as if perching on the top of the sigh.

Then thoughts began running through his head, one after the other.

The first thought was that Nina Georgievna was about to ring up, so he would have to think up a reason for not going. Because to go to the hospital with her would mean an admission of failure. It would destroy the whole elaborate edifice of his being a talisman, which he had worked so hard to create. Nina Georgievna would see that Duke was worse than a nonentity. Being a nonentity was not all that bad, because at least then you are neutral and you don't get in anyone's way. But Nina Georgievna would see that he was a nonentity with a minus sign. He was also a liar and an imposter who had criminal tendencies. And if he was like that at fifteen, what would he become later? The next form time would probably be devoted to discussing precisely that.

The second thought, which followed the first and resulted from it, was that if he didn't go with Nina Georgievna, she would have to go alone because there would be no one to accompany her. She lived with her old mother and a young daughter. He imagined her plodding off into the night, as blind as a bat, in glasses as thick as binoculars. Then getting that news alone. And coming back alone. How would she get home?

The phone rang. Duke picked it up and said, 'I'm just leaving. Meet me at the bus stop.'

'Why?' asked Nina Georgievna in surprise. 'The buses don't run at this hour . . .'

'Just for orientation,' explained Duke.

He put the phone down and started to get dressed.

Of course it was a shame to fail after so much work. And how could he be of help to her? He could only be by her side . . . But he was a man after all. That was what he was supposed to be. That was nature's intention.

The buses started running at six, and it was now half past one.

Duke and Nina Georgievna set off on foot but kept turning round the whole time to see if a taxi with a bright green light might appear. A taxi did actually show up, but by that time they were almost at the hospital. There was no point in getting into a car when they had already got there. Duke always got the things he wanted eventually, but they always came too late – when he no longer needed them. It had been like that with his bicycle. And it would probably be like that with Masha Arkhangelskaya.

The hospital was all white like a hospital coat. Its whiteness glowed even in the darkness, and seemed to make everything near it glow too. While somewhere behind those walls, perhaps down in the basement, there lay a dead body.

'I'll wait for you here,' said Duke.

Nina Georgievna nodded and walked towards the wide glass doors at the entrance to the establishment. She turned round before she went in and asked, 'You won't leave, will you?'

'Of course not,' said Duke bashfully, amazed at how helpless and childlike an adult could be.

'I never understood her, you know,' said Nina Georgievna suddenly. 'I didn't want to understand . . .'

It was as if she was shifting some of her despair on to Duke. He accepted it, bowing his head.

'Right then, I'd better go,' said Nina Georgievna. She walked away, lolloping clumsily like a kangaroo. She really did look like a kangaroo with her small head and more developed lower body.

Duke stayed there waiting for her.

A little island of forest had survived in front of the hospital on the other side of the road. Some smart brick houses clung to its edge, surrounded by lots of cars. It seemed as if the people who lived in those houses never got ill, never died, and never cried. They did not have to equip themselves with a talisman to get hold of furniture or records. They just went and bought them. But Duke was not envious of the people who lived there, because he shared a character trait with his mother. He loved only that which was his, like his hat with the tassel. His country. His life. Even the night belonged to him.

A new wing was being built behind the hospital, and the building site was unpleasantly dark and full of rubble. It seemed that rats might come scrabbling out of it at any minute. Duke had a mystical fear of those creatures with their low bodies and naked, shameless tails. He was convinced that rats have neither a sense of shame nor a conscience. But they did have a brain, so that meant they were consciously shameless and unprincipled. A rat would realize that Duke was standing all alone there in middle of the night. It would scrabble up to him and bite off a chunk of his face.

Duke started to feel chilly and wanted to start shouting out to Nina Georgievna. But just at that moment the glass doors opened and she came running out, as clumsily and as excitedly as a kangaroo running in a race. Duke noticed that was also something which often happened to him. He just had to think about a person, summon them up mentally, and hey presto, they would appear. He would bump into them on the street or they would ring on the phone.

Nina Georgievna flung her outstretched arms round Duke in a great burst of happiness, and even lifted him up on her marsupial stomach. Then she put him down and told him, breathless with emotion, 'I can bring her home on Monday . . .'

'In what condition?' asked Duke in confusion.

'Satisfactory,' answered Nina Georgievna.

She started walking down the hospital path, and Duke moved off after her, wondering what had happened.

Perhaps they had given her the wrong information, not wanting to upset her? Or maybe they had got things muddled up and had said the right thing to him on the telephone? Or maybe they were having a joke? Although it was hardly likely that anyone would want to joke about that sort of thing. Or perhaps what they had said was actually correct? If there were two thousand Ivanovs in Moscow and about three hundred Sidorovs, why shouldn't there be two Sidorovs in hospital number sixty-two?'

'Why did they ring you, then?' Duke asked.

'Oh, my mother insisted. She forced the nurse on duty to call me,' said Nina Georgievna peevishly. 'She's so selfish. She never could think about anyone else. She's still a spoilt little child even in her old age.'

Now that Death had passed by, Life had stepped out once again on to the stage with all its everyday cares and worries.

The way back seemed three times shorter. Firstly because they did not turn round any more, but just walked straight ahead into the arms of their great success. And secondly because Nina Georgievna was going home still a daughter, not an orphan. Duke had played the part of the talisman for the last time with true brilliance, but it was better to retire unbeaten, like in sport. Win for the last time and then retire gracefully.

They reached the bus stop where they had begun their journey, so full of trepidation.

'Thank you, Sasha,' said Nina Georgievna, looking into Duke's eyes, not as a teacher looking at her pupil, but as an equal looking at an equal.

'Don't mention it,' said Duke modestly.

'No, I must mention it,' objected Nina Georgievna seriously. 'Doing schoolwork, taking part in out-of-school activities and being a troublemaker is something everyone can do. But being a talisman and making people happy is a rare gift. I'm going to give you an A for literature, and I will have a talk with Lev Semyonovich. I'm on good terms with him. He will give you an A too. And then I will talk to Inessa Danilovna. We can't give you top marks for everything, but we could stretch to an A- as your overall average. That's pretty good. With a A- you could get a place to study wherever you want. Even at Moscow University.'

'You don't need to do that,' said Duke in embarrassment. 'Really.'

'Oh, yes, I do,' said Nina Georgievna with conviction. 'People need to be taken care of. And you are a person.'

Duke did not try to substantiate that new opinion. Or argue against it. He suddenly felt like going to sleep, and that desire proved stronger than any other desire. His head was being pulled downwards, as if someone had placed a heavy hand on the back of his neck.

'Well, see you tomorrow, then,' said Nina Georgievna. 'Although it's tomorrow already. If you end up oversleeping, you can come at the beginning of third lesson if you like.'

She set off from the bus stop to go to her home. And Duke set off to go to his home. He didn't have far to go. Just across the little garden.

The garden looked quite different at night. It looked like a distant relative of a real forest. And the bench looked more independent. Not so reliant on people.

Duke sat down on the bench in his usual position, with his face upturned. The dark sky with all its little gold perforations was like one of those punched cards his mother used. Or maybe this was the eternal punched card and people from generation to generation had been trying to decode it. It would be good to feed it into a computer and learn one's destiny.

Duke gazed at the astral code, trying to read his fate. But nothing could be known in advance of course. That is our salvation. How terrifying it would be if a person were to know everything about his life in advance: whom he would love, when he would die . . . Knowledge extinguishes hope.

But if you cannot know these things, it seems you will never die. You think you will live for ever. And in that case there really is a point to searching for yourself and trying to establish your own identity. Fulfilling yourself as a person. Finding yourself. Digging holes in the ground until you hit the source and can let people around you drink: please, go ahead, drink. And wanting nothing in return except for 'Thank you, Duke,' or 'Thank you, Sasha.' Or even just 'Thank you.'

Gratitude was not an amorphous feeling, as his mother had said. It was just as real as petrol. With gratitude you can fill up your soul and travel further along life's path, soaring as high as you want, even to the very stars and the eternal punched card in the sky.

His mother was sleeping. Duke got undressed silently and stole into his room.

His unmade bed lured him, but for some reason he went and switched on his table lamp instead, and sat down at his desk. He opened *What is to be Done?* He remembered that his mother from time to time would organize a slimming campaign for herself, when she would start a diet and eat nothing but unsalted rice for three days in a row. And to make herself eat it, she would say to herself, 'What's wrong with eating this? It tastes quite nice. It's very palatable in fact.' Duke was choking on Vera Pavlovna's dreams and saying to himself, 'Hey! This is very interesting . . .' But he did not find it interesting. He was as bored as ever. He couldn't permit himself to get an A for nothing, though, or even for free as Seriozha might say.

He could only get Ds for nothing.